THE BOY AND THE LAKE

Also by Adam Pelzman

Troika
The Papaya King

THE BOY AND THE LAKE

ADAM PELZMAN

JACKSON HEIGHTS PRESS
NEW YORK

ISBN 978-1-7332585-2-4 (paper)
ISBN 978-1-7332585-0-0 (e-book)

Library of Congress Control Number: 2020911912

 Cover design by Andrea Ho

In Memory of the Extraordinary Sherman Sisters

PROSPECTS

We have set out from here for the sublime
Pastures of summer shade and mountain stream;
I have no doubt we shall arrive on time.

Is all the green of that enamelled prime
A snapshot recollection or a dream?
We have set out from here for the sublime

Without provisions, without one thin dime,
And yet, for all our clumsiness, I deem
It certain that we shall arrive on time.

No guidebook tells you if you'll have to climb
Or swim. However foolish we may seem,
We have set out from here for the sublime

And must get past the scene of an old crime
Before we falter and run out of steam,
Riddled by doubt that we'll arrive on time.

Yet even in winter a pale paradigm
Of birdsong utters its obsessive theme.
We have set out from here for the sublime;
I have no doubt we shall arrive on time.

                              —Anthony Hecht

Chapter 1

~~~~~~~

June 1967

I can recall with near perfect clarity the moment I saw Helen Lowenthal's bloated body slide up through a carpet of emerald water lilies and bob on the water's surface like a ghostly musk turtle. In the seconds before her lifeless ascent, a constellation of fireflies—tiny flickering furnaces—danced and glowed in the early summer dusk; a white egret, all legs and neck, landed atop Split Rock and stood regal guard over the lake; a long-eared bat carved wicked arcs through the sky before devouring a plump imperial moth.

From the direction of Second Beach, Nathan Gold's pontoon boat—the *Ark*—puttered along the shoreline with four prosperous couples reveling in their evening cocktails. A symphony of big bands, laughter, and giddy howls poured off the boat and tumbled across the lake's still water. Nathan and his wife, Bea—a gregarious, stocky woman—called out to me as they passed, and I waved back with delight, wondering how two people could be so festive, so happy, so often.

Bonnie Schwartz, my mother's friend, was also on the boat. She was considered by many to be the prettiest woman on the lake, as was her mother before her. I waved to her with the hope of some reciprocity—maybe a nod or a simple smile in my direction—but this auburn beauty, distracted by her empty martini glass, did not notice me—an omission that punished my fragile sixteen-year-old heart.

I sat on the edge of the dock, my feet immersed in the water of our beloved New Jersey lake. As the *Ark* turned north toward the clubhouse, the boat's wake caused the pungent, algal water to lap against my calves. I held a wooden fishing pole that Papa, my grandfather, had given me when I was six. The hook baited with a throbbing night crawler, I watched as the red-and-white bobber teased me with a quick downward thrust, only to rise to the surface and drift with rippled ease. *Clever fish*, I thought.

A few seconds before the swollen body emerged, I turned back to look at my grandparents' summerhouse. I could see Nana flitting about the screened-in porch, setting the table for yet another dinner party, while Papa probed the lawn for moles, angling empty glass bottles into their holes with the open ends facing downward. "Makes a howling noise, Ben," he once told me as he guided a beer bottle into the earth. "Drives them crazy, like psychological warfare."

What I noticed first in the water before me was not a body, but a flutter in the lilies that I mistook for a jumping frog. It was only when the attenuated rays of the descending summer sun flashed off Helen's gold and diamond watch that I realized something terrible had occurred. I gasped and leapt to my feet. "God," I mumbled and raised my right foot as if to take a step forward, toward the body. "Papa!" I yelled, dropping the rod to the dock. "Papa, come down!"

Despite his old age, my grandfather was a lithe and energetic man who, after numerous injuries and surgeries, had somehow managed to retain much of the athleticism of his youth. He was alarmed by the distress in my voice, for he threw a bottle to the ground and dashed down the slate path to the water's edge. I glanced up to my grandmother, who stood frozen on the porch, right hand on chest, her mouth open.

"There!" I shouted to Papa and pointed to the blue-white body of his next-door neighbor. Helen Lowenthal, whose rare kindness had evoked in me the greatest loyalty, was dressed in a pink tennis skirt and matching top. Barefoot, she floated on her back, her face dappled with lake slime, her dyed blonde hair draped over a mat of lilies, her pale arms elevated above her head as if she were a surrendering soldier. I took another step closer, toward the water. I found myself drawn to her body, to its deadness, to its serene, haunted passage, as one is drawn to the very things—once beautiful, now rotten—that intrigue us, that repulse us with their incomprehensible transformation.

Papa reached the dock and grabbed my arm. He stared at the body in silence, then, as if looking for a clue, scanned the shoreline and the lake's expanse. A hundred feet from the dock, in a pool of quiet water, an elderly couple fished from an anchored motorboat; the *Ark* continued its journey toward the clubhouse, a familiar Ella

Fitzgerald melody drifting off the stern; a small sailboat floated in the windless dusk; and the white egret elevated from Split Rock, relinquishing its perch in search of food.

"Go inside and call the police," Papa cried. "It's Helen, you know." He wiped the sweat from his face then, panting, bent over at the waist. "Helen ... Lowenthal," he said through heavy breaths, before stepping down, fully clothed, into the shallow water.

I watched as he struggled to traverse the muddy lake floor, the water rising from his knees, to his waist, to his chest. When he reached Helen, he touched a small bruise on her forehead. He then grasped her left hand and guided her—belly-up—toward the shore, her body slicing through the water with ease and purpose. As I watched this scene unfold, I was immobilized by my first close contact with death. I stared at her corpse with a vast fear, with a revulsion that shamed me, and, I would later acknowledge, with something approximating wonderment.

With great care, Papa placed his palm on the side of Helen's head—a tender movement that protected her from hitting a protruding rock. Now just feet from the shore, the water knee-deep, he turned to me. "Go, Ben," he demanded. "Go *now!*"

Unable to divert my eyes from the scene before me, I moved slowly up the dock. I watched as Papa stepped up onto the shore, his legs heavy from the weight of his sodden pants. I watched as he lifted Helen, as he groaned in exertion, and then gently laid her down on the spongy moss. I took one last look at the woman. She wore the fancy watch her husband had given her for their twentieth anniversary, and on her left hand was an engagement ring, the one with a diamond so large that some of the women from the bridge club had started a rumor that the stone was fake. I glanced at her toenails, painted cherry red, and at her slime-lacquered face.

"Go!" Papa screamed, now with fury in his eyes. And then I ran to the house and into my grandmother's fleshy, perfumed embrace. I ran to a safe place.

Chapter 2

~~~~~~~~

Two days after Papa and I found Helen floating among the water lilies, several hundred people attended her funeral at the local synagogue, with many of Red Meadow Lake's luminaries delivering beautiful eulogies. Helen's husband, Sid, was a prominent orthopedic surgeon, on staff at Mount Sinai and a respected mentor to young residents. Handsome, tan, and impeccably tailored, he spoke about Helen's extraordinary beauty—her appearance and her character—her generosity, her social ease, the proficiency with which she raised their two children and managed their home, her powerful topspin forehand. "It looked like she never broke a sweat, but the truth is she worked hard to keep things running smoothly. *Very* hard," he said with an admiration, an awe that suggested some concern about how he would function without her.

Throughout the loving eulogy, Sid somehow maintained his composure while his two college-age daughters sat in the front row and cried. Later that night at shiva—the Jewish mourning period—I heard several people marvel at his equanimity. "He's a surgeon," one mourner remarked with a chill that suggested disdain. "That's how they're wired, you know, cold as ice. If you cut flesh for a living, you've got to control your emotions."

Nathan Gold, captain of the *Ark* and president of the property owners association, praised Helen's commitment to the community—how she donated money to rebuild the concession stand at First Beach and how she led the fundraising effort to construct the Circus, the day camp for the younger children. "She gave ... and she gave quietly," he said in a solemn tone that was in stark contrast to his otherwise boyish temperament. "She did it the right way, without fanfare." He announced that a plaque in Helen's honor would soon be installed in front of the town courts. "Everyone knows how Helen loved tennis." Like a medium using a prop to communicate with the dead, he raised a tennis ball in his hand—a dramatic and incongruous gesture that made me wince.

Nathan's reference to Helen's tennis prowess triggered thoughts of the many times I'd seen her play. Helen's game was a model of consistency. She was not inclined to creativity on the court—no angled drop shots or maddening topspin lobs from her. But what she lacked in flair, she made up for in steadiness. A rarity, her forehand and her backhand were of equal effectiveness. She moved well from side to side, hitting crosscourt shots low over the center of the net and elevating down the line to avoid the net's peak. Regardless of the speed or depth of her opponent's shot, she scampered into perfect position, assumed a classic, knees-bent stance, and made the cleanest possible contact with the ball. On the rare occasion when her stroke resulted in a mishit, there was usually a good reason: a bad bounce, sweat in her eyes, the sun slipping out from behind a cloud's sharp edge.

When matched against an inferior opponent, Helen was thoughtful, but not so thoughtful that her play could be perceived as condescending. Rather than move the ball from side to side, she would keep it in the center of the court—nothing crosscourt or down the line. Her serves, normally hit with a biting spin that kicked up to her opponent's shoulders, were delivered straight and flat. She rarely went for winners, preferring instead to keep the rally going until the other player made an unforced error. Both players knew exactly what was happening, but Helen would win in a way that allowed her opponent to leave the court with pride intact.

Helen would sometimes play the better men at the lake, and she often beat them. When she was on the court with Irv Solomon or Nathan Gold or even the surprisingly talented Rabbi Rabinowitz (our next-door neighbor, who had a vicious backhand and a confounding slice serve), her otherwise steady demeanor changed. She might bark at herself when hitting an easy shot into the net or smash her racket after double-faulting; she would argue questionable calls and make distracting grunting sounds when she made impact.

Once, when she thought the rabbi cheated her on a baseline call, she drew him to the net with a drop shot and then smashed the ball at his face. After the ball hit him on the forehead and he dropped to the ground—his kippah dislodged and rolling like tumbleweed in the wind— she walked to the net and, with a sly smirk, apologized half-heartedly. Something about these men brought out a fierce streak in her.

On one late summer day Helen gave me a free tennis lesson, feeding me ground strokes, volleys, and overheads for over an hour. Bernice, my little sister, was nine years old at the time—a year younger than I. She sat on a bench with our mother and watched Helen run me through a series of demanding drills. Under a blazing August sun, my mother, Lillian, rested her hand on Bernice's right thigh—on her withered leg. I can recall my sister's twisted body, her emaciated arms, her thin neck barely supporting her head, which was disproportionately large relative to her frail body. Dear Bernice watched us move and hit, and I saw in her face a familiar awe, one reserved for those whose bodies worked in ways that hers did not— and I also saw in her face a weighty sadness that arose often, when her limitations were announced by the easy movements of those she most loved. In her body—in the way she strained to straighten her spine—I saw the extent to which she was tortured by her condition. I understood that Bernice would do anything to be on that court, to be part of the group—to be like the rest of us.

I tried to ignore her pain and instead focus on the form of my backhand, but I could not stop myself from glancing in Bernice's direction. On several occasions I hit the ball into the net on purpose—an attempt to manufacture a physical equality between us, but which I conceded was preposterous and had no such effect. And when my sister dropped her head after another mishit ball, I feared that she had experienced my generosity as condescension, that I had insulted her.

At the end of our lesson, Helen walked over to Bernice and extended a racket. "Come, sweetie," she said, nodding in the direction of the court with an earnestness that contrasted so sharply with my netted balls.

My sister gasped and looked over to our mother, who paused for a moment. I believe that Lillian feared her daughter would suffer another disappointment, an embarrassment of her physical limitations—but she smiled and nodded sweetly to Bernice. Helen spent the next half hour teaching my sister how to bounce a ball, how to grip the racket, how to get into the ready position. At all times, Helen kept a guiding and supportive hand on Bernice's hip, and was patient and unwavering in her encouragement. After many misses, my sister somehow made perfect contact with the ball, and we watched it arc majestically over the net and land on the other side of the court. We howled at her accomplishment, which prompted Bernice to attempt the most awkward and proud curtsy. As my sister waved a triumphant hand above her head, Lillian sat on the courtside bench and cried with a mixture of exhilaration, astonishment, and profound sadness. That is one of the final images I have of my sister, for she would die a few months later, her damaged body unable to keep up with her fierce will.

As I looked around the synagogue at the hundreds of mourners, this memory evoked in me feelings of immense affection for Helen, for the tenderness that she extended to my sister—and I mourned the death of this special lady.

Nathan Gold finished his eulogy and, tennis ball in hand, returned to his seat. I turned to my grandfather. "That's really strange, holding a tennis ball at a funeral," I said, a bit too loudly, which prompted my mother to twist my ear in reproach.

Next up to the bimah—the podium—was Rabbi

Rabinowitz, who tapped the microphone and spoke about the will of God, how one cannot comprehend his plan at the moment of death, how it may take many years to understand what good has come from the deepest loss. I thought about my sister's death, and how I still saw nothing good in her loss. The rabbi discussed how death may appear to us as evidence of the nonexistence of God, when in fact it is the opposite—for to march on with grace following the death of one we love, to work, to laugh, to comfort in the face of loss, these are the gifts of a divine power. He talked about the permanence of the soul, how every ripple in the water, every warm summer breeze, every sunset was evidence of Helen's enduring spirit. I wondered if there was any truth to his words.

Papa sat to my immediate left, and as I listened to the people speak about Helen, I felt as if we had our own special link to her. We, after all, had been her caretakers for a few important minutes; we were the ones who found her floating in the lake and shielded her from further harm, delivering her with dignity to her family and, he assured me, to God himself. "It's a blessing, what we got to do," he told me on more than one occasion—reassuring himself or me, I did not know.

As we filed out of the temple after the service, I turned to Papa and whispered in his ear. "How did she die? Do they know?"

He looked at me, his expression grim. "They don't know. Probably tripped off the dock and hit her head. A terrible accident."

I recalled the image of Helen in the water, her dyed blonde hair floating on the water's surface, her arms above her head. I pictured the green patina on her face as Papa guided her to the shore and laid her down on the moss. And as I looked over to the idling hearse and imagined Helen in the coffin, I pictured the bruise on her forehead when we found her. I pictured her impeccable balance on the tennis court, her athleticism—and I wondered if it was indeed a simple fall that had killed her.

After the service, as hundreds of somber mourners milled about the parking lot, we prepared to get into our big Ford and join the procession to the cemetery, which was located far away, behind the Tick Tock Diner in Clifton. Before we reached the car, I noticed Missy Dopkin walking with her parents. Missy was my age, and I had known her since my first days at the lake. She possessed the rarest intelligence, an unusual mind distinguished by both an intellectual hunger that bordered on insatiable and the nimbleness required to excel in every topic: math, science, history, English, French. She was an ebullient, sprightly girl, wiry and knobby-kneed, who found amusement in the oddness of life and in the eccentricities of others. "I like 'em weird," she once told me as she held down a sunny's spines with one hand and extracted a hook from the fish's eye with the other. "The weirder, the better."

Unlike me, Missy lived at the lake year-round. Her relationship to Red Meadow was thus different from mine, and we often talked about how peculiar it was that two people could experience the same place in such dissimilar ways. For me, the lake was a wonderland, a sanctuary, a respite from the congestion and noise of Newark and from the competitiveness of my school; it was a vacation, a holiday, a destination, and a gathering place for my extended family. For me, the lake was a magical place.

For Missy, the lake was not a destination but rather her home. It was a state of existence, one in which there were ebbs and flows of energy that moved with the seasons. In the winter, when the vacationers were in their primary homes, the community turned quiet. Houses were shuttered and unoccupied, the clubhouse was sparsely attended, few people walked the winding streets—and other than the occasional skater, the frozen lake was desolate. During the summers, though, the lake came alive. People and light, music, cocktails, food, and laughter filled the homes. There were costume parties at the clubhouse, tiki torches on the beach, barbecues, swimming races, regattas, fishing tournaments, motorboats hopping sociably from dock to dock like playful water bugs, and cocktails on the *Ark*.

My friendship with Missy was thus defined by the seasons. From Memorial Day to Labor Day, we spent much of our time together—at day camp, drawing worms from the earth with dried mustard, fishing for sunnies and largemouth bass, walking down to Tom & Mary's for comic books and candy (I was partial to the bubble gum in the shape of a cigar, while Missy loved the wax lips), going to the Denville Shack for the most delicious fried shrimp dinners, and catching crayfish in the little creek that ran down from Hope Pond and that, according to local lore, supplied all of the lake's water.

At the end of the summer, Missy and I would say goodbye and assure each other that we'd talk on the phone and visit during the off-season. But our calls and visits were instead infrequent, leaving us with huge gaps in our friendship, gaps during which our physical appearances changed, our experiences accumulated, our emotional complexities evolved. Such was the velocity of our growth during those nine-month spans that the start of each summer brought with it an awkward period of re-acquaintance in which we both feared that our connection was forever lost.

Outside the temple, the hearse driver turned on the headlights, indicating that the procession would soon start its journey to the distant cemetery where Red Meadow Lake Temple had purchased dozens of plots. As Missy stepped into her parents' car, she looked at me. Her brown hair hung unrestrained, a seemingly endless series of curves and counter-curves. She smiled and waved. "Weirdo," she mouthed with the impish glee of one who ridicules the person she adores. I reached for my sore ear, the one my mother had pinched. My palms moistened, my heart rate ticked up, my confidence teetered—and I feared, as I always would, that I would never be smart enough for her.

Chapter 3

~~~~~~~~

My maternal grandparents came to this northern New
Jersey lake in 1949. Louie and Harriet Fox were among
the first settlers to purchase a lot in what was then one of
the few communities that permitted Jews. "We couldn't
go to Mountain Lakes," Nana often said. "It's restricted ...
gentiles only. And besides, it's too expensive." Nana
and Papa had at that time lived for decades in the same
small house in a section of Newark called Weequahic—
pronounced *weak way* by us locals. Their side of the
family had arrived from Germany in the late 1800s, so
they had the good fortune to avoid the scars of the world
wars. Like many German Jews whose families came
here in the nineteenth century, they possessed a sense
of superiority over the more recent immigrants. They
would never admit it, but when my grandparents were
introduced to the more recent arrivals—with their strong
accents and funny customs—a wrinkle in the brow and
an expression of disproportionate compassion suggested

that my grandparents somehow believed that they'd come over on the *Mayflower*.

Papa was an accountant and Nana a travel agent who together had managed to save $300 for a lovely double lot on West Lake Shore with a hundred feet of waterfront. On the wooded property, thick with white birches and sugar maples, they had planned to build a simple cottage: a two-bedroom, one-bath Worcester model, which in the brochure had fine lattice work, mullioned windows, and decorative shutters, but in reality was simple, plain, modest. When my mother was fifteen years old, though, when my grandparents were just months away from laying the home's foundation, Papa was betrayed in a way that would wound him deeply and that, I would later come to believe, helped mold my mother's complicated relationship with both money and social status.

Papa's accounting partner, a childhood friend whom he'd trusted like mishpochah—like family—had stolen money from their clients. When my grandfather learned of this treachery, he demanded that his partner return the funds. What followed became part of our family's oral folklore, and on several occasions my grandparents had, in my presence, reenacted the debate that followed the theft.

"Get the money back," Nana had implored Papa.

"There's no money to get. He's already squandered it all. Gambling, some crazy oil scheme, even ponies. So there's nothing for me to do but go to the cops... report him."

"You can't do that," Nana had replied. "You can't tell on a fellow Jew."

"What do you mean I can't tell on a Jew? He stole the money! I don't care if he's a Jew or an Italian or an Arab."

When it came to religion, to the teachings of our people, Nana was the most knowledgeable in our family. She was raised in a strict Orthodox home, and although she embraced a more relaxed religious life as an adult, she had roots in Talmudic law that guided her and allowed her to resolve the most complex conflicts. Nana's words thus carried the force of a decree.

"You know the rules, Louie," she said with judicial bearing. "You know how things work. Mesira. The community can punish the moser, the informer, even if he's reporting someone who's guilty of doing bad things, illegal things. There's exceptions, of course. If a person physically harms someone, if he's a threat to the community, to *our* community. But for something like this, a money issue, we stay quiet. We stay together ... and not just us." She would spread her hands, palms up, to indicate our immediate family. "But *all* of us." And then she'd raise her arms and spread them wide to indicate all Jews. "And beyond the interests of our people, it's better for your business if you just keep your darn mouth shut."

Nana's judgment prevailed: Papa fired his partner but never said a word to the authorities. He swept every personal bank account that he had, sold off the family jewelry and silverware, and paid the clients every penny that had been stolen. The financial loss set my grandparents back almost a decade, and for years they could only visit their undeveloped lakeside lot, have a picnic in a clearing, maybe a drink at the clubhouse, and return to Newark at dusk while their friends remained in their lovely lakeside homes. It took years of hard work for Nana and Papa to make enough money to build their dream house—and when they did, they felt the pride not only of having achieved their middle-class dream but also of having overcome an unexpected and painful obstacle on the way.

Nana and Papa would come out to their new home on the weekends, driving their old Dodge along what was then called Route 6, stopping in Denville on Friday night for the weekend's food and liquor. During the summer, when the lake was at its social peak, Nana would move out on Memorial Day weekend and stay until Labor Day. Like most of the lake men, Papa would come in from the city every Friday night—often on the train to Dover—and get up early on Monday morning to make it back to the office for the start of the workweek. Each summer, without exception for twenty-two years, he took off the last three weeks in August and spent them at the lake. "Better than the French Riviera," he would say, as he sipped a gin and tonic from his Adirondack chair and watched a middle-class version of paradise unfold before him. I once asked him if he'd ever been to the South of France. He shook his head and smiled. "Don't need to. I got the Cap d'Antibes right here," he said.

Soon after my grandparents bought the lot on West Lake Shore, other families followed. There was my grandmother's twin sister, Jennie, and her husband, Phil. At the time, they were the wealthiest members of our family, and they purchased a four-bedroom waterfront house with a wet bar, a bocce court, and a hundred feet of lake frontage. The Frankels, childhood friends of my grandfather's, were the only religious people we knew, the only devout ones; they moved into a ranch that was within walking distance of the temple. Herb and Ann Coleman, who owned two kosher butcher shops in Essex County that

carried the very finest capons, bought a house with spectacular water views. ("Must be solid gold in the corned
beef," Papa would remark every time Herb drove up in
a new car.)

Within a couple of years, the lake was filled with families named Adler and Aaronson; Brinker, Bloch, Berg, and
Baum (our family name); Ehrlich, Eichler, and Einhorn;
Frank, Fried, Friedman, and Fox (my mother's family
name); Karnett, Klein, and Kleinmann; Lerner, Lipsky,
Lowenthal, and Levitan; Rosen, Rosenbaum, and Rosen-
berg; Stein, Stern, and Sternlight; Wein, Weinberg, and
Weinstock. There was even a family named O'Brian, but
somehow they too were Jewish.

My parents were one of the last arrivals to the lake,
and the reason often given by my mother—but never by
my father—was my sister, Bernice. She had a rare disease
called progeria, which caused her body to age, at least in
appearance, at a frightening rate. The doctors said that
her condition was one in several million; they'd never
seen a case like hers, and it took a famous geneticist in
Manhattan to make the diagnosis.

Bernice's appearance was unusual: her head was large
relative to the size of her tiny body, she had protruding
eyes and ears, a pointy nose, and long teeth that slipped
out over her lower lip. So uncommon was her condition
that people on the street often looked at her with a com-
bination of shock and horror—and, after a few seconds
of reflection, with compassion. With the most sickening
shame, I can now admit that there were times when the
sight of my lovely sister stunned me, even frightened me.
But despite the audible gasps and the cruel ogling she
endured from strangers, despite the fact that she knew

she wouldn't live to her bat mitzvah, Bernice was kind, upbeat, even hopeful. She reveled in being close to the people she loved and to those who loved her, soaking up our affection and protectiveness with a desperate thirst. My sister was courageous, intrepid, determined.

Bernice also had moments of all-consuming fear—understandable moments when she could not ignore her appearance, her condition, and the imminence of her death. "You're going to go on without me... every one of you... and I'm going to miss all the fun," she once cried. We did our best to console her, to encourage her, but during those moments of terror there was very little we could do to relieve her suffering.

On top of the emotional pain that my sister's illness inflicted on her and our family, there was also a tremendous financial toll. While the doctors extended my father every possible professional courtesy, refusing to charge a fellow physician for Bernice's care, the hospitals and the labs could do no such thing: every hospital admittance, every blood test and X-ray, every emergency room visit was costly, draining my parents' accounts. So, while our friends were moving up and out to Short Hills and West Orange, spending weekends at the lake, and taking vacations in Miami Beach, the Catskills, and sometimes Europe, we stayed in our modest house in Newark.

To bring in some additional cash, to help pay for Bernice's medical bills, my mother started selling housecoats, used clothing, shoes, and costume jewelry out of the garage. Although her motives were noble, Lillian was still embarrassed by her cottage business. "Wife of a doctor, daughter of an accountant, and look what I have to do," she once lamented to the beautiful Bonnie Schwartz over a martini. She then quickly recognized the pettiness of her words. "But of course I'm happy to do it for Bernice. It's a privilege." My mother appeared to have conflicting feelings about Bernice's condition: she loved my sister, but hated the devastation that the disease, at so many levels, had caused our family.

With my father's salary as an inner-city doctor, my mother's extra money from selling schmattas, and some financial support from my grandparents, we clung tenuously to the middle-class life that was so important to my mother. For a Jew at this particular time and place to slip backward, to lag the lifestyle of the prior generation, would have been a humiliation—and while my sister was alive, we barely held on. For many years, Bernice's illness left us so stretched financially that we could not join our friends and family at the lake—that beautiful body of water that had become the symbol of everything our community strived so hard to achieve. We visited friends and family on weekends, and my grandparents' home was always open to us, but it was not until several years after Bernice's death that my parents could at last save enough money to buy a waterfront home at Red Meadow— directly across the lake from my grandparents' house.

I recall that day when we drove down the driveway of our new home for the first time, and the expanse of glistening water that framed our new four-bedroom, three-bath ranch.

"Here we are," my mother said, twirling the keys to the front door victoriously. "We're finally where we're supposed to be. *Finally.*"

As Lillian fiddled with the lock, my father and I watched her with a certain detachment. I thought about

Bernice—and I concluded that, without my sister, we were nowhere near where we were supposed to be.

Chapter 4

~~~~~~~~

A week after Helen's funeral, a wicked storm took out power on the lake. Heavy rain strafed the side of the house, spackling the windows with an abrasive mixture of dirt and leaves; the wind roared through a cluster of towering oaks; bending boughs groaned like funeral mourners; and in the rough water, the dock banged against the stone retaining wall.

That evening, my father and I built a fire in the living room hearth using dry pine and kindling stored in the basement, and we lit candles throughout the dark house. Rather than being frightened by the storm and the blackout, I felt secure, for I was home with my family, snug and protected, cut off from the outside world—the flames' cozy glow dancing off the walls, the mirrors, the slick grass outside. That for a few hours we were transported to a simpler world brought me comfort. I felt as though my development were being frozen for the duration of the storm, encapsulated, my childhood somehow prolonged:

I felt as if I had *stolen time.*

I lay in my bed and tried to sleep, but the lake blared and cried around me: the lashing rain, a chorus of mad crows, the creaking branches, the thump of the dock against the wall, incessant and ominous, the house bending, resisting, lowering its achy shoulder into the wind. The noises unsettled me, and my thoughts turned to Helen. I looked out of my bedroom window—across the water—and there, in the patch of black before my grandparents' house, I noticed what appeared to be the distant flame of Papa's kerosene lantern.

My grandfather and I had developed a secret form of communication that involved two lanterns and a rudimentary version of Morse code. One flash meant *come over, it's dinner time,* two meant *come over, the fish are biting,* and three meant *good night.* The phones worked fine, of course, but Papa and I found something pleasurable in our lantern signals, something primitive, coded, and secret.

That stormy night, I glanced at the windup clock beside my bed and saw that it was a few minutes before midnight—and I was puzzled by the possibility that Papa could be up at this hour, outside during a storm. I pressed my nose against the window to get a better look, to confirm that I had not been mistaken. Again, I saw the lantern. One light, two lights. *Come over, the fish are biting. It can't be two,* I thought. Maybe it was three for *good night*? Maybe I hadn't counted correctly, for my grandfather would never be out in this weather, at this hour, when the fish were quiet. Papa typically flashed two lights as dusk approached, during feeding time, and I could not recall another instance when he had asked me to go fishing so late at night.

The distant lantern suddenly darkened, and all I could see was the radiant house of Herb Coleman—the rich butcher—who had installed a gas-driven generator that would now be the envy of the entire powerless lake. I kept my eyes trained on the patch of black that enveloped my grandparents' house and waited for the next lantern flash. A few moments passed and the lights—misty white halos in the moist air—started again. I concentrated on each flash, counting with the tap of my foot. *One, two. One, two. Yes, that's fishing*, I thought.

This strange communication from Papa, coupled with the mysteries that a storm can conjure in one's mind, agitated and intrigued me. So I hopped off the bed and put on a pair of jeans, a nylon jacket, and my ankle-high rubber boots, grabbing my Coleman lantern before I left. Out in the hallway, I eyed the sliver of space below my parents' door. With no sign of the candlelight that had earlier seeped out of their room, I walked down the hallway, my bare feet slipping in the rubber boots, the soles squeaking.

I stood alone in the messy night, unprepared for the weather conditions, which had worsened significantly since I was last outside. The wind was no longer gusty but now steady and continuous; the rain, moving almost parallel to the ground, mixed with leaves and dirt and stung my face; the branches of the old oaks twisted and growled, while the sagging arms of a rotten willow tickled the wet grass. As I walked to the shore, my feet sank into the sodden ground and water slid over the edges of my boots, which had become swollen, leaden, earthbound.

I raised the lantern above my shoulder and flipped the switch. *One, two, three. Good night*, I signaled. I waited, but my grandfather did not respond. Again, I signaled three times to Papa—but still there was no response. Then, through the screeching wind, I heard a noise that sounded like a door swinging on its rusted joints, then a frightful crack above me—the crack of rotten wood, an oak branch breaking from the stress of the wind and shooting like a spear into the ground before me, its jagged tip piercing the earth only feet away. I gasped and took a step back, away from the point of impact. I looked up to the canopy of oak branches and watched as branches swayed in the wind. Terrified, I took several more steps back toward the house, then raised the lantern. *One, two, three*, I announced again. *Good night.* I awaited a response from Papa, but to my disappointment, there was nothing but darkness and, at the far end of the lake, the rich butcher's house lit up like a carnival midway.

I had trouble sleeping that night, as my mind was astir with thoughts of falling branches, of spears thrown and disasters averted, imaginary lanterns and headless horsemen, Papa and Nana too. I had a nightmare about Helen waving to me from her shiny coffin.

I awoke in the morning to discover that the storm had passed and power was restored. I stepped outside and marveled at the clarity and resolution of the world around me. Every impurity seemed to have been purged from the sky, the water, the trees, and the wind; the swallows, as if reborn, sang with remarkable range and perfect pitch; a woodpecker launched a ferocious, rapid attack on a sweet birch. The lake, bathed and scrubbed clean, had been restored to its pristine state.

When I returned to the house, my parents were in the kitchen preparing breakfast, and I could see that my mother was in one of her moods. Lillian was for the most part a pleasant and loving woman, but during times of stress or disappointment or loss she could turn irritable, condescending, even cruel. Despite the infrequency of these dark moods, I kept vigilant watch for signs of her transformation and adjusted my behavior in an attempt to avoid her wrath. And on the rare occasion when I complained about her to my father, he would remind me to be patient with her, to channel some deep empathy for her loss—for the loss that we had all suffered when my sister died.

Lillian and Abe stood before the refrigerator, and I watched as my father sniffed the open bottle of milk.

"How is it?" she asked, testy and curt. Helen's death had darkened her mood, and the storm and the power outage had made it worse.

My father poked his nose into the opening of the bottle. "I think it's okay but I can't tell." He sniffed with a desperation that conveyed his fear of my mother's temper. "The power was only off for a few hours, so it should be fine."

"Get your nose out of there," Lillian barked, then slapped at him with an oily dishrag. "And give me that." She grabbed the bottle and passed the opening under her flared nostrils. "It's turned," she said, prompting my father to sigh. "The fridge is hot as an oven. If we had a generator ... the Colemans have one, you know ... if you got a generator like I asked you, we wouldn't have to worry about spoiled milk." She pulled a package of cream cheese from the refrigerator and examined it. "Now *would* we?"

Abe turned and saw me standing in the doorway. He winked at me, and I winked back—my attempt at showing solidarity with him. "No … no, we wouldn't," he replied to Lillian in an inevitable concession. "Ben and I, we'll run down to Shop-Rite and pick up some things for breakfast."

Eager to escape my mother's irritation, I tugged at Abe's elbow and led him out of the house, toward the car. "You know how much those generators cost?" he asked. "The one the Colemans have?"

As we drove downhill, I looked out the car window and spotted Missy delivering papers on her bicycle, a heavy sack over her shoulder. *She's had a late start*, I thought. I waved, but she didn't see me. "I don't know, Dad. How much?"

My father drove in silence for some time, perhaps a minute. "I don't know either," he said. "Expensive, though."

When we arrived at Shop-Rite, my father directed me to get dessert while he searched for milk, juice, eggs, lox, whitefish, and second-rate bagels. I pushed the cart in search of aisle five, which, because it was packed with every type of sweet, was my favorite aisle at the supermarket. Upon my arrival at this corridor of confection, I gazed at the many treats: pies of all sorts, candies, babkas, hamantaschen, cake mix, chocolate syrup, and more. I took in this sugary paradise, one filled with fantastical collages of colors and smells, sweets and snacks. After scanning the shelves, I grabbed an Entenmann's coffee cake, a cherry pie, and a bag of mixed chocolates, then turned to see my father standing at the end of the aisle with a full cart.

"Ready?" he called out.

I held up my booty. "Ready."

"Excellent." He beamed.

When we arrived back at the house, Abe entered the

kitchen with the pride of a hunter who'd just bagged a fourteen-point buck.

"See," he said, dropping the bags on the table, "fit for a king." My mother scowled at him. "Or a queen," he corrected.

Moments later, the jingle of the chimes on the front door announced my grandparents' arrival, and I ran to greet them. I had been eager to see Papa, for I wanted to understand the mystery of the prior evening: the flashing lantern during the storm. I hugged my grandmother, inhaling her soothing rose perfume, and then turned to my grandfather.

"Papa, were you out last night? With the lantern?"

He appeared confused. "Last night?"

"Yes, you said you wanted to go fishing. Two lights, I counted. You did it twice, and it was after eleven thirty."

Papa tousled my hair. "You must be mistaken, sport. Only a crazy person would go out in that weather. It was storming like I haven't seen in years. And fishing no less!"

He guided me to the dining room, where we all sat down for breakfast. Papa's denial had left me confused, and as I took a sip of orange juice, I considered the possible explanations for his response. Was he playing a joke on me? Or did he really not remember? Had he, perhaps, been sleepwalking? Tipsy? Was it possible that I had mistaken the flashing lights of a car for Papa's lantern? Or, in the darkness, had I looked in the wrong direction?

"You sure?" I asked, apprehensive and skeptical. As I recalled the branch that almost brained me, my thoughts turned dark. Since Helen had died, my mind was filled with scary notions, paranoia, and conspiracy theories. My closeness to death, to the corpse of a woman I had adored in life, tortured me with irrational fears and nightmares.

He smiled and then shook his head. "Sure, Ben. You must've been imagining. All that stress from what's happened here over the past few days. Or maybe Dr. Lowenthal was out doing something on his dock next door. He's been acting crazy since Helen died, you know. Poor guy."

"Okay, Papa," I replied, unconvinced. I wondered if Papa was right, if Helen's death had influenced my mental state, made me suspicious, confused—crazy like the surgeon.

My mother glided in from the kitchen and placed a basket of hot bagels on the table, next to a spread of cream cheese, red onions, sliced tomatoes, kugel, egg salad, lox, and smoked whitefish. A smile on Lillian's face signified that her foul mood had passed. Now surrounded by delicious food and the people she loved, she had returned to her usual state of contentment—a transformation, sudden and extreme, that brought me both relief and apprehension.

As a frenzy of hands grabbed at the food, I imagined another possibility about the prior evening and the lantern lights: that this memory might have been nothing more than a dream, one that was inspired, magnified, and given life by the stormy night. But then I glanced over to the foyer and saw that my boots were right where I'd left them the evening before—untouched and surrounded by blades of grass and clumps of mud. I looked across the table to Papa as he draped a strip of lox on a sesame bagel. When he bit into it, a dollop of scallion cream cheese stuck to the tip of his nose.

He smiled at me—and I assured myself that it was not a dream.

Chapter 5

~~~~~~~~~

My great-uncle Max was a full-time salesman and a part-time comedian who worked the second-tier Catskills resorts. On the rare occasion he played one of the top places like the Concord or Grossinger's, he was never the lead act but rather the tummler, the master of ceremonies, the one who got the crowd warmed up and kept the show moving. Some of the emcees were so funny, their talent so obvious, that they were promoted to the top bill—but like the career minor league baseball player, talented but never quite good enough to make the majors, Max was not so fortunate. The closest he got was one night in 1959 when Milton Berle was playing the Nevele and got stuck in traffic on Route 17—"the Derma Road," named after the traditional Jewish sausage filled with matzo meal, chicken fat, and vegetables—and the story went that if the legendary comic had not gotten a ride from a motorcycle cop, my uncle would have been bumped up to the lead act. All he needed, my aunt Muriel often said, was just another five minutes and he'd have been famous.

Max had a comedian's build, of which there seemed to be only two types: stocky, chubby, and barrel-chested, or thin, gangly, and wiry. My uncle was of the latter ilk, a lanky man with a bald scalp—freckled and shiny—a droopy, pendulous nose, and an exaggerated, loping gate that made him look like he was in a rush to get somewhere—which he most certainly was not. A cheerful, garrulous man whose happiness was tainted by periodic bouts of insecurity and depression that coincided with his professional adversity, he was adored by the great majority of those he encountered—except for the grudge-carrying butcher, Herb Coleman, who was furious that Max once returned a brisket with the claim that it was "tougher than a frozen pig tuchus."

Despite his likability, there were baffling things about Max. One was that he was evasive about what he sold, and we never knew what he was peddling. Pots and pans, said one aunt; life insurance, claimed another; vacuum cleaners, according to my father; oh, *you know*, his wife, Muriel, said defensively. Another mystery was that we couldn't tell how much of his act was original and how much he'd stolen from other comics. He asserted that he wrote every joke, but my mother once insisted that she saw another comedian deliver an identical shtick at Kutsher's. ("That ganef stole my act," Max claimed when confronted with this accusation, calling the comedian a thief.) Either way, whether his material was original or plagiarized, he kept us entertained.

As a young boy, I would sit on his lap and wait for his routine to start. He'd ask me about my day ("good"), whether I had a girlfriend (I'd roll my eyes), what sports

I liked ("baseball"), which team I favored ("the Red Sox," I'd joke)—and then he'd bounce his legs with vigor, causing me to elevate off his lap.

"Benjamin, if you can't sit still, then you'll have to go to the couch."

"But Uncle Max," I would squeal, "I didn't do *anything!*"

He'd settle down, I would stay on his lap, and we'd resume our conversation, with each of us anticipating the next round of bouncing. Soon, his knees would again launch me into the air, and I'd howl and deny any misbehavior on my part.

"Benjamin! Stop bouncing. Stay still or you're off."

And this routine would go on until one of us tired.

The first time I realized that I had an impulsive and nervous disposition—one that would cause me considerable pain—was when Max entertained us a few weeks after Helen died. My parents had invited a group of people that evening—the lake's first festive gathering since the funeral. Sid Lowenthal was there, looking sad, weary, and withdrawn. At the end of the meal, when the adults were intoxicated, smoking Pall Malls and devouring chocolate babka, my uncle announced that he wanted to perform his new routine.

Even I, still a few months short of my seventeenth birthday, could anticipate that the material would be old, corny, and likely stolen. By this point in Max's life, his late sixties, he had been repeating the same stale jokes for years, but somehow delivering each one as if it were the first time. I would watch the adults fidget when he would set up a joke, glance at each other with unease, then force a laugh and a thigh slap after the predictable punch line. Although they were tiring of their own pretense, they loved Max and didn't want to embarrass him.

That night, my uncle started with one of his oldest routines: the roll dance. With this particular routine, Max made no claim of newness or originality; he'd learned it from his idol, Charlie Chaplin, who had performed a similar shtick in *The Gold Rush*. The routine involved stabbing two dinner rolls with a couple of forks and draping a napkin over them. The rolls were to be the high-heeled shoes, the forks were the legs, and the napkin the skirt. Next came Max's goofy, humming soundtrack, the rolls tap-dancing across the table, and then the grand finale— an up-and-down flicking of the forks meant to resemble the Rockettes' extraordinary leg kicks. And even though Max had performed the roll dance for us dozens of times, we always laughed, and we did so earnestly. For him and for us, it was a sacred, post-meal tradition.

At the end of the routine, Max ate one of the rolls. For me, that was always the highlight of the roll dance— for what could be funnier than eating a joke? Perhaps, I thought, having it end up in the toilet. That night after the roll dance, my uncle took a sip of gin and launched into his stand-up routine. There was a bawdy joke about a rabbi's randy wife and a disobedient puppy named Leviticus. I didn't understand it; the adults looked appalled, but laughed. There was a joke I'd never heard before about a kosher cannibal who starved to death while stranded on a remote island—something to do with cheesecake and gentiles.

When he had exhausted his inventory of new material, he returned to his old library. He stood up and bent forward at the waist, a pained expression on his face, then reached for his lower back.

"Oy," Max moaned, "oy I have a weak back." I watched as the adults shifted in their seats (this was, after all, not only one of the jokes that he was rumored to have stolen but one that he repeated frequently). After limping for a few steps, he turned to us and asked, "You know when I got it?" I watched my father place his fingertips to his lips. Lillian stuffed a huge piece of cinnamon rugelach into her mouth, while Aunt Muriel, looking on adoringly, released an anticipatory giggle. My uncle paused for a few seconds to create a dramatic buildup to the punch line—one that we'd heard so many times that even the tiniest speck of drama was impossible—and shrugged in an exaggerated manner. "You know when I got it?" he repeated coyly.

Out of affection for Max, the adults remained silent. My uncle paused, but before he could finish the joke, I blurted out the punch line. "We know, we *all* know," I yelled, "you got it about a *week back*! Weak back, week back."

My regret was instantaneous, and when I looked around the room I saw signs of our family's distress: Aunt Muriel looked downward, flattening a cloth napkin over her lap, my father dropped his face into his palms, and my mother stuffed two pieces of apricot rugelach into her mouth. Lillian then took a swig of bourbon and glared at me; she mouthed something I could not understand, but which was nonetheless ominous and caused me to twitch in fear.

The most distressed of all, though, was Max. His lower lip quivered thin and quick, his cheeks flushed a soft pink, his eyes moistened. "That's right," he whispered, an attempt to reclaim ownership of the joke. "A week back, I got it about a week back." He rubbed his lower back, then grimaced and limped back to his seat, this time without even a hint of his customary playfulness.

As the adults giggled nervously, my uncle looked at me. He smiled with obvious weariness. It was a smile that revealed some painful acknowledgment—an existential defeat, maybe, or a submission to the passage of time, to an inevitable generational shift. My interjection forced him, I would later imagine, to concede that the tiny aperture in which his humor once glistened had forever closed, and that his obsolescence had not only been sealed—but sealed by *me*. Years later, I would read the memoir of a famous comedian who wrote that "if you steal a man's punch line, you steal his soul."

So, when Max sat down next to Muriel and dropped his head, when Muriel rubbed his back and pushed a plate of babka in front of him, when Max pushed the plate back in her direction—a declaration that he had lost his appetite—I understood that I had in some way contributed to the decline of a man. I had humiliated my uncle in such a way that he could not recover—and other than a few half-hearted roll dances in the coming months, Max retired from comedy that night.

So distraught was I by my impulsivity, by my lack of sensitivity to my cherished uncle, and by the critical judgment of my mother, that I suffered an array of troubling symptoms that would afflict me well into my adult life: my hands shook; my heart raced; sweat covered my palms in a slick film. I hunched over, reducing the size of my body to conform to my sense of smallness. I switched from self-confident to self-loathing, a binary state that permitted nothing between the two extremes. I had my first anxiety attack.

I wiped my wet palms on my pants and stood to take my dirty plate into the kitchen. "Excuse me," I said. As I placed the plate in the sink, I noticed a bottle of red concord wine on the counter. I turned to look through the doorway and saw that the adults were sitting at the table, absorbed in a vigorous debate about whether the lake's five-horsepower limit on motorboat engines was too low or too high. My mother glanced over and saw me spying on the adults. She scowled, which caused me to retreat deeper into the kitchen. I again eyed the bottle of wine. I picked at the paper label and wondered about the transformation that this wine might offer me. I screwed off the top and sniffed its sweet, syrupy aroma. I gazed out the kitchen window, across the water to the Lowenthals' house—to *Helen's* house.

I placed the cap on the mouth of the bottle and prepared to seal it, but the cap slipped in my wet palm, dropped to the linoleum floor, and, as if it were a runaway tire, rolled under the refrigerator. *Klutz,* I thought and got down on my knees. After poking around and scraping my knuckles, I was able to extract the dust-covered cap. I washed it off in the sink and again placed it on top of the bottle. A crack of laughter from the dining room caused me to think of Max and his kindness, and the years of humor he had provided us—and how I'd stolen his punch line. My self-loathing intensified, and I gripped the bottle.

Other than a few sips from the kiddush cup at my bar mitzvah, I had never touched alcohol. But as I stood in the kitchen and considered my nervous state, I pulled the bottle to my mouth and gulped. I felt a warmth in my chest, a sticky-sweet grape candy coating of the throat, and, within seconds, a sense of ease, a Manischewitz high, a physiological tranquility that was foreign to me: my palms stopped sweating, my heart rate moderated, my confidence was restored. I no longer hated myself. I felt *different*. And it was at this moment that I discovered an elixir for my fear, for my psychic condition—and for some battle that I could not yet comprehend.

Chapter 6

~~~~~~~~

One month after Helen's funeral, I witnessed a rarity in my family: a conflict of some sort between my father and Papa. The cause was at first hard to imagine, as their in-law relationship had always been so close, so supportive. But that Sunday afternoon at the lake, I looked outside my bedroom window to see Abe and Papa on the side lawn, engaged in a heated discussion. My father was pointing furiously toward the garage, where my mother was sorting through several boxes of housecoats.

Dressed in one of her bright floral numbers, which flapped in the breeze like a sheet on a clothesline, Lillian emerged from the garage, marched down the driveway, and approached the two men. She stood between them and placed one hand on my father's back and the other on her own father's back, then spoke to them with what appeared to be a maternal authority, at first prompting angry shakes of their heads and then a retreat from her grasp. Soon, though, the men drew closer and nodded as if they might be open to whatever compromise she was offering. Finally, they laughed, heads down, cheeks flushed, and all three walked into the house. When I went to greet them—to discern the nature of the conflict—I found them in the highest spirits, as if there had been no conflict at all.

After giving me a warm hug, Papa checked his watch and realized that he was late for golf with the butcher. He made his way down to the dock and his waiting boat, and I joined him.

"Everything okay?" I asked nervously. "With you and Dad? Mom too?"

Papa smiled in a manner that suggested I had just asked the most absurd question. "Everything's fine." He reached down to release the rope on the boat's bow. "You get that one," he said, nodding in the direction of the stern. After I untied the rope and tossed it onto the deck, Papa gave a few tugs on the Evinrude's cord and brought the engine to life. He was off within moments—a gleeful wave and a playful swerve of the boat indicating that all was well.

Back in the house, my parents were engaged in a tense conversation. "It's time to get out," my mother implored as I listened behind the kitchen door. "The city's going to blow ... only a matter of time. And, Abe, it seems you're the only one who doesn't have a clue. You're blind, naive as always."

I suspected that this was the cause of the conflict on the side lawn: the growing racial problems in Newark and the resulting exodus of Jews from our neighborhood. Tensions in the city had been building for years, with a worsening conflict between the black community, which made up much of the city, and the dwindling number of white people, who maintained a tight grip on the government and the police force. Crime had grown worse in both frequency and severity, and our insular enclave of Weequahic had seen a spike in burglaries and vandalism, even muggings. Just weeks earlier, Lillian noted for emphasis, someone had torched the Feins' miniature Swiss chalet mailbox.

"The city's not going to blow," Abe countered, as if correcting an excitable child. "It's a phase. All they have to do is put some black cops on the force, show a bit of respect, and things'll settle down. I've got faith in them … good people who just need a break for once."

I stepped into the kitchen, and my presence caused them to pause briefly before returning to their quarrel.

"You're being naive," my mother said. "As always. A few black cops won't do a damn thing. They're out of control, these people … like wild animals in the streets, robbing, fighting. There's just nothing to do about these schv—"

My father smacked the table with his palm—a rare display of authority directed at my mother. "No, no … not that word," he cautioned. "Especially in front of *die kinder*." He nodded in my direction, and I found myself soothed by my father's capacity for empathy, his compassion for those who lacked our good fortune.

Lillian sneered at me. "He's not a kid anymore," she said.

"Kid or not, no one needs to hear that word." My father paused, allowing himself time to calm down. "What I think is that it's going to be worse for black people if we leave. I feel like we've got an obligation to them, to the city … to stay and make it work, be helpful to them. And all I can say is that I'd be angry too if I was black."

"You're angry enough being white," Lillian snapped, then cleared her throat in a show of displeasure. She poured herself an afternoon chablis. She had always been a sporadic drinker, one who might go months with little or no alcohol, but then, when her mood soured, she might drink excessively—or perhaps, I would later think, it was the booze that caused her change in mood.

"I'm not angry," he said angrily. "Naive or not, we're not leaving. We'll stay and see if we can't help them. And if it gets worse, well, we can always leave ... but no reason to cut bait now."

Just then the doorbell rang, announcing Missy Dopkin's arrival. As she had been traveling to look at colleges, I had seen her only once since Helen's funeral—for a brief moment at First Beach—and we had made plans to take a drive to New York City that evening.

I opened the door and greeted her with clammy hands and a damp brow—metabolic manifestations of my anxiety. We hugged with an awkward tension befitting an undefined adolescent relationship and then withdrew to examine each other, trying to interpolate data into the gap that had separated us. There was a tiny freckle on the bridge of her nose that I did not recall seeing before, a crinkle in her otherwise fine hair, another half inch in height, a fullness in her chest that caused me to look away with some shame, and her percolating exuberance—always present—that was now so intense I feared she might crack wide open. She was still the skinny, knobby-kneed girl I had known for years, but for the first time since I had met her I could see a path forward, anticipating her physical and intellectual growth; rather than merely filling in the historical blanks, I could now *extrapolate*. I could see that Missy was destined to do great things, and I feared that I would always find myself a few steps behind, trailing her with maddening futility.

With her familiar playfulness, she pulled on the sleeve of my shirt. "You look exactly the same," she said, no doubt intending it as a compliment—but it was a remark that nonetheless wounded me.

Before taking her into the house to see my parents, I walked her over to the garage bay and revealed my mother's collection of dusters and housecoats—rows and rows of garish polyester things that Lillian planned to sell to the neighborhood women. Her cottage business, which had once caused her shame, had become a meaningful source of income for our family and helped us reclaim the comfortable middle class life that my mother had so desired.

Missy was awestruck. "My God!" she shrieked. She skipped over to the racks, which were arranged according to size. She settled in front of the extra smalls and ran her hands across dozens of housecoats in every color and pattern. When she reached a royal blue one with huge yellow sunflowers, she stopped. "This one is divine," she said and turned to me. "I must have it. Do you think your mother would sell it to me?"

I knew that my mother wouldn't accept a penny from Missy and that she'd take pleasure in giving the housecoat to my friend as a gift—especially since this unappealing smock had hung from the rack for several months without any interest. "I'll buy it for you," I said with false generosity, aware it would cost me nothing. "A birthday gift."

I had no idea when Missy's birthday was, and she

knew it. She rolled her eyes and removed the housecoat from the rack, holding the hanger up to her shoulders. Giggling, she twirled around—once, twice. "You like?"

The duster covered her like a tent. So ugly was it that I shielded my eyes. "I like."

Missy gave me a hug and tossed the dress into the back seat of her car. With money that she'd saved from her paper route (and from babysitting, tutoring, and helping the rabbi and his wife tend to their prize-winning roses bushes), she'd purchased a dented 1957 Dodge Coronet—salmon pink and white with sharp tail fins—from a used car lot at the bottom of the hill, around the corner from the Howard Johnson's that sold the most delicious milk chocolate lollipops.

From a young age, Missy had learned, by necessity, to be entrepreneurial and self-reliant. Her father was a brilliant engineer, but he was temperamental in a mad scientist sort of way. The result was a series of blowups with supervisors who, after tiring of his outbursts, placed greater value on a stable workplace than the contributions of his genius. His mercurial nature had put their family in a state of chronic financial distress, and on several occasions the bank was mere days from foreclosing on their home.

Missy's self-financed Dodge brought her—and me—freedom. Between bikes, boats, and our feet, we could get everywhere we needed around the lake, but to get away from the lake we had long been dependent on the cooperation of adults. Her car allowed us to explore the world beyond our little community.

Missy had already made the hour-long drive into the city several times with Becca Gold, the *Ark* captain's daughter, so that evening she drove downtown with an expert's confidence. We found a parking spot on the street and walked around the Village. "There's a record store I love on MacDougal," she said as we stood under the arch in Washington Square Park. "And a café on West Fourth. Oh, and there's an old bookstore...first editions, art books, that sort of thing...on Grove." Her brain was firing so rapidly that her mouth could barely keep up with her thoughts. "And a costume store on Christopher, they sell the craziest stuff, really scary. And a gallery on... on...I think somewhere off Sixth...Sixth Avenue, not Sixth Street...really avant-garde, I can't understand half the art they have there. And a comedy club back on Mac-Dougal—they say Lenny Bruce once did a routine there."

Missy's energy threatened to overwhelm me, and I placed my hand on her shoulder. "Why don't we start with just one?" I said, an attempt to calm her down. "How about some food?"

She exhaled and allowed her shoulders to drop. "Aaaaahhh," she moaned, pointing to her head. "Too much going on in here sometimes."

We started at the café on West Fourth. She loved it because Dylan Thomas was rumored to have had a seizure there. "They say he fell off a barstool and hit his head right there on that step," she said. "It's possible, right? I mean he's the type of guy who probably fell off a lot of stools."

I knew that Dylan Thomas was a poet and a drunk, but that was the extent of my familiarity with him; Missy, however, had been reading his work for two years. As I sat across the table from her and scanned the menu, an unsettling thought occurred to me. When we ate together at the lake—at the Denville Shack, a bag lunch at camp, a sandwich on the dock—I felt like we were nothing more than two friends sharing a meal. But something about this setting—a cozy Village café, the jukebox playing Dave Brubeck's "Take Five"—jolted me. I looked around the room, at the couples laughing and holding hands, at the couples engaged in serious conversations. And as I watched Missy run her finger down the right side of the menu, I was able to identify the cause of my burgeoning anxiety: I felt like we were on a date.

I searched the restaurant for some diversion, for something that would distract me and relieve my stress. Above the bar were dozens of autographed photographs of famous people, including Marlon Brando, Bob Dylan, and Billie Jean King. The photograph of the tennis champion—knees bent, eyes trained on the ball—reminded me of Helen Lowenthal. "Horrible about Helen," I said. "Still can't get over it."

Missy eyed me. I had once told her of Helen's kindness to my sister, and she well understood my deep affection for this woman and my pain over her death. "It's terrible, just terrible," she said, searching for the waiter in a discreet manner designed, I believed, to honor the gravity of the topic. At last she flagged the waiter, an aloof man with the countenance of an aristocrat; rather than approach us, he raised his index finger imperiously and continued his stroll toward the kitchen. Somewhat exasperated, Missy turned back to me. "I heard the police were over at the Lowenthal place again…just yesterday," she said.

I was startled. In the weeks since Helen's death, Sid had revealed to close friends the results of the autopsy: a bruise on her forehead and water in her lungs led the medical examiner to indicate drowning as the cause of death. The toxicology report revealed that she had only a minimal amount of alcohol in her system—a glass of wine at most. After receiving the ME's report, the police chief speculated that Helen had slipped on the dock, fallen into the water, and hit her head on a rock. "An unfortunate accident," he'd said to Sid. "One in a million."

Nonetheless, the police conducted a thorough investigation to see if anything criminal had occurred. They spoke with Sid, who was performing a knee operation in Morristown when his wife died. No one knew of any tension between Helen and her husband; they were, according to their children and all who knew them, a happy couple. The chief also spoke to the neighbors on West Lake Shore, my grandparents included, and no one had seen anything suspicious that day or the days preceding. The police searched the area where Helen had died—the water, the dock, her house—but found nothing unusual. As a community, we accepted the inconclusiveness of the inquest, the uncertainty of her death. But every time I recalled Helen's perfect balance on the tennis court, her ability to glide across the red clay with the most fluid grace and dance along the baseline without even the slightest misstep, I wondered how she could have slipped on the dock. Unlike the rest of the lake, I wasn't convinced that her death was an accident.

"What were they doing there?" I asked, intrigued by the news.

"I heard they were talking to Sid ... and walking the property again."

"Why's that? I thought it was settled. A fall, head injury, accidental drowning."

"I'm not sure. My father heard from Nathan Gold

who heard from the butcher that the police might still be taking a look. But that's just gossip, and you know how the lake is. It's hard to tell what's true and what's not out there. They thought it was closed, but who knows with the Rockaway cops, right? They're not Scotland Yard or anything."

I thought about the time that the befuddled Captain Nethercott parked his car in neutral near the clubhouse willows, and how I watched in delight as the police cruiser rolled into the lake. "Definitely not."

We sat in silence for a few moments, taking in the restaurant's buzz. "This is fun, isn't it?" she said. "You and me in the city? Together..."

Her sweetness—her use of the word *together*—banished my thoughts of Helen. "It is."

Missy again waved at the waiter, who at last strolled over to our table. We ordered burgers and a plate of fries with thick brown gravy. She ordered a club soda. I was about to do the same when I looked to my right and saw a couple sharing a bottle of red wine. I recalled the night I had humiliated my uncle Max, when I took a gulp of sweet concord wine and, in an instant, changed my body chemistry.

Missy smiled at me—and I wondered if she, too, felt like this was a date. Either possibility—that she did or did not—was equally terrifying, and triggered the onset of another panic attack: the sweats, a subtle shake of the hands, a struggle to swallow. I craved a glass of wine, a *bottle* of wine. I craved relief—but instead ordered a club soda.

Chapter 7

~~~~~~~

In July 1967, six weeks after Helen's death, Newark blew up. After years of poverty, abuse, and disenfranchisement, the black community vented its righteous fury at the city's levers of power, at the Italian mayor and the Italian cops. They were fed up with the crime and unemployment, with the graft, the racism, the police brutality, the dismal housing and the run-down schools, fed up with being under-represented in every corrupt institution in the city. So they burned it, looted it, tried to destroy their city—the very thing that had once offered them the possibility of advancement, but that now represented only an unyielding force dedicated to their submission.

We happened to be in town when the riots broke out, there for a few days for the funeral of some distant relative whom I'd met only a few times in my life. At the ceremony, Uncle Max was so distraught, so bereft and confused, that he reverted to his days as a cheerful tummler, stepping up to the synagogue's bimah to introduce each eulogist with a showman's gusto: "And our next speaker comes all the way from the proud state of Maryland!"

I leaned over and whispered in my mother's ear, and the sour scent of her face powder caused a slight convulsion in my throat. "It seems like he's doing a show ... like he's on stage."

Lillian smiled and whispered back, "That's where he's most comfortable."

The riots broke out on the last day of shiva, and we left for the lake the following evening, the thirteenth of July. As we drove west on Lyons Avenue, I sat in the back seat of the car and peered out the window, looking north toward the violence, toward what I imagined was a Hobbesian nightmare of club-wielding mobs, torched buildings, cars overturned, banks robbed, windows smashed, street curs eating garbage, and abandoned children weeping in the streets. Even at a young age, I was a master of apocalyptic thinking. In this case, I wasn't far off.

I rolled down the car window and inhaled the sweet summer air, a soothing bath of honeysuckle tainted now by the acrid smell of burning tires. I heard an unintelligible bullhorned voice emanate from some vague point in the murky darkness and watched a forest of flames dance over Clinton Avenue—and I knew that we would never return. The Jewish exodus had been going on for years, but the riots were the official end of our community in Newark.

On the morning after we left the city, as a low, yearning sun glanced off the lake, my father announced that we were leaving Newark for good—that we had *already* left.

"Where are we living?" I asked. "West Orange, near Papa?"

My father looked out to the lake and pointed toward the water. "We're living here, right here."

"We're living *here*?" I asked. "At the lake?" I turned to my mother, who offered me a wink that suggested some satisfying validation of her cynical views on race relations. "Dad!" I pleaded. "I'm going to school *here*?"

Abe folded the newspaper before him. "The schools here are fine ... just fine."

"But not like Weequahic," I replied with a protest borne of the rupture that had just occurred in my life. I was, without any warning or preparation, leaving my friends, my school, the streets on which I'd played countless hours of stickball, the local shops, and the energy of our city.

He looked at my mother and with the blink of his right eye deflected her glare, one that conveyed her breezy righteousness. "Not quite as good, but more than satisfactory," he said. "You'll get a fine education here." I could sense in his face, in the mournful tone of his words, that he believed he had fallen short—that he had failed his poor patients from Newark, that he had abandoned them in their moment of utmost need.

My father lifted a coffee mug to his lips and took several indelicate gulps. He was a genteel man, except when it came to drinking coffee. "We have to go, Ben. We're leaving because our city doesn't have a chance ... and the reason the city doesn't have a chance is because, sadly, the black people here don't have a chance." He reached for the sugar and dropped a heaping teaspoon into his coffee. "And here's why black people don't have a chance. It's not because they're not capable ... they're plenty capable ... but because they're screwed the second they come out of the womb. We don't give them a chance, and by the time they're five, the schools are so bad ... the crap they have to live with every day ... by the time they're five ... three, even ... they're so far behind they can't catch up. The game's over before it even starts. And it keeps going, generation after generation." He took another crude sip of coffee. "It's just terrible ... unfair. *Wrong.*"

Lillian squirmed, and I could tell she didn't agree. "I don't think that's it at all," she said. "I just think they've gone nuts. They just don't have the discipline." My mother had moments when she lacked compassion, when empathy was elusive, when she ignored her own father's financial struggles—when she ignored the adversity we ourselves faced when Bernice was sick and the periodic support we received from her parents. It was as if only by rejecting any possibility of predetermination, could she take pride in her family's ascent from lower to middle class.

On matters of race, I deferred to my father. For years he'd worked at a poor, inner-city hospital and run a private practice that cared for the neediest residents of the city. Many of his patients were black or Hispanic, most relied on government assistance to survive, and few could afford to pay him much. The result was that he made less money than those of his peers who refused to treat the indigent, and even though he was smarter and harder-working than most, that intelligence and work ethic failed to translate into our middle-class version of wealth.

"Missy Dopkin, for instance," he said, continuing his defense of the impact of environment on a child's development—a reference that caused my heart to race. "You could take Missy Dopkin, no less the smartest girl at Morris Hills High School, and put her in the slums of East Harlem and there's no way she has the same success ... no way. She'd have a better chance than anyone else, no doubt, but she'd still struggle. And you wouldn't see Stanford or Princeton in her future."

I wondered if this was true, if it was possible for Missy's intelligence to be restrained by environmental forces. I was determined to believe that even if she were raised in the most challenged, impoverished community, she would nonetheless achieve greatness. My thoughts now on Missy, I considered how she would react to the news that I'd be living at the lake year-round. Would she be excited? Indifferent? Would our relationship grow closer? Would it, despite our daily involvement, still retain the thrill of intermittence? Or might our friendship devolve into the quotidian, crushing whatever excitement our long separations had fostered?

I called Missy that afternoon, and we agreed to meet at Tom & Mary's—a ten-minute walk for each of us. One of only a few stores at the lake, it was a small place that offered an eclectic hodgepodge of food, snacks, candies, comic books, baseball cards, beer, pool toys, and newspapers. There were nooks and crevices in which were hidden strange and mysterious goods, and we walked the aisles looking for new arrivals. Behind a bucket of pink Spaldeen balls, Missy discovered an electric bug zapper in the shape of a small tennis racket. She pretended to turn it on and then waved it near my face—and by vibrating her lips she made a ridiculous buzzing sound that made me laugh.

Mary looked up from the cash register and called out to us: "Don't waste your money, it doesn't work. It couldn't kill a gnat."

Tom put down a roast beef sandwich that he was preparing. "It works just fine," he countered, sounding irritated.

I picked two Yoo-hoos out of the refrigerator, one for each of us, and walked to the counter. There, I bought a Wacky Pack—the silly trading cards that satirized popular brands. I tore it open and found that I'd gotten some of the more entertaining ones: *Ratz Crackers, Jolly Mean Giant, Grave Train.* Missy looked over my shoulder as I flipped through the deck. "Oooh! Oooh! Can I have that one?" she asked. I handed her the card: *Crust Tooth Paste.*

As we walked away from the store, Sid Lowenthal pulled up in his Lincoln. He appeared happy to see us and shook our hands with confidence and strength, as if we were his peers. I watched him stride toward the store, and I thought about the breezy confidence of this man— for he did not look to me like a man who, just six weeks since the death of his wife, was grieving. I recalled how, the morning after the storm, Papa said that the surgeon had been acting crazy.

I turned to Missy. "You hear any more news about Helen's death?"

She looked into the store and eyed Sid. "It's been quiet since the police were there again," she whispered. "But Nathan Gold said something about the toxicology report. He's got a friend on the force. There's some con- fusion about the lab results, apparently ... whether or not there was lots of booze in her system. Again, it's just more lake gossip. I think she tripped and fell, hit her head on a rock. Simple as that."

I admired Sid's polished Continental. I watched him

through the store window as he laughed with Mary. "I'm not so sure," I said. "Sometimes I wonder if it was something worse."

"Don't be silly," Missy replied impatiently, then gave me a playful punch on the arm to counteract her annoyance. "Everyone loved Helen. She didn't have a single enemy in the world, let alone the lake. And no one ever saw her drunk. *Ever.*"

Just then, Sid stepped out of the store holding a bag full of groceries and the electric bug zapper. "I heard the big news," he said to me. "Good move, good move." I marveled at the speed with which personal information whipped around our small lake like a summer storm. He skipped over a puddle and glided toward his car.

She took a sip of Yoo-hoo. "What big news?" she asked.

"I was going to tell you. Right now, actually. We're moving here full-time ... year round at the lake."

Missy grabbed my elbow. The first expression on her face was one of elation. "Hell yeah!" she yelled, then composed herself and said that she was thrilled to have another friend at school, a companion during those cold and boring winter months. But what soon followed was a look of compassion for me, for while she understood that I was leaving Newark and my school friends, I think she anticipated another painful loss: the inevitable end of my romance with Red Meadow Lake.

She released my elbow, and we continued to walk toward our homes. At the intersection of Hibernia and Lake Shore, a shimmering bronze Seville approached, going too fast and wide around the bend. We jumped to the curb to avoid getting hit, and when we looked into the car's window, all we could see behind the wheel was Pearl

Lipsky's shock of salmon-colored hair and a gold-draped hand waving to us.

We paused and watched our elderly neighbor's Cadillac speed toward the clubhouse. After a few moments, we turned back and observed the split road before us. Missy would take Hibernia to the left, and I would take Lake Shore to the right. She gave me another playful punch in the arm—innocent contact that nonetheless caused a tingling of my skin. "Don't worry," she said. "Being a townie ain't so bad."

Chapter 8

~~~~~~~~

That summer, after the riots, my father reluctantly gave
up his practice in Newark. He arranged for privileges at
Saint Clare's in Denville and opened up a small office in
town. With patients who were mostly white and insured,
Abe's suburban practice could not have been more different from the one he'd left, and although he made a bit
more money at the lake, he returned home dispirited at
the end of each workday, bereft of his lively Newarkian
stories. ("You wouldn't believe who came in today," he
once howled after a day at his bustling clinic in the Central
Ward. "Ace Richards! You remember him ... the Tuskegee
pilot with the glass eye? I could've sworn he was dead a
hundred times over, but turns out the rascal's still alive ...
alive and *kicking*.") After practicing in the suburbs for
only a few weeks, my father described his workday with
all the curtness of a surly teenager: "It was fine."

My mother moved her entire inventory of housecoats
and dusters out to the lake and continued to operate her

cottage business. As she had in Newark, she hosted a weekly bridge game at home, and every Thursday, as she had done for a decade, she met her high school friends for lunch and gossip at Eppes Essen—a Jewish deli that, like the people who ate there, had over the years migrated westward, from Newark to Orange to Livingston. For Lillian, life continued in similar form and substance, and she adapted to our new life easier than the rest of us did.

In the middle of August, before the formal end of one relationship with the lake and the beginning of another, my grandmother threw one of her famous dinner parties: fifty guests, racks of chicken and brisket, pierogi, knishes, an endless supply of booze, and, always, a theme. Past themes included a Hawaiian luau, cowboys and Indians, flappers, even Victorian England.

I had driven our motorboat to the party that night. Now that I'd reached an age where my parents trusted me with the boat, they let me take it out to visit friends and family. My newfound freedom, the ability to transport myself from point A to point B without supervision, was one of my first tastes of adult independence—and I volunteered for any errand that might involve the boat. If my mother ran out of cooking sherry, I was in the boat and on the way to Nana's house for a bottle; if my father needed a lure for largemouth bass, I revved up the Evinrude and dashed across the lake to Nathan Gold's boathouse.

That evening, I cut the engine a few feet from my grandparents' dock and glided in with such controlled speed that the boat gently kissed the bumper and came to a rocking stop just inches from the dock's edge. I stepped up, tied the lines, and began my walk up to the lawn, where cocktail hour had begun. Until I caught sight of the butcher and his wife, I was not aware of this party's particular theme.

Herb Coleman, the butcher, was a corpulent man with a round belly that hung low over his belt. He wore his obesity not with shame but with pride, as if his swollen gut were proof of his prosperity; to be thin, he implied with his distended paunch, was to be poor. The butcher was also afflicted with an enormous hernia that he refused to have surgically corrected. ("I don't trust doctors ... they're butchers, every one of them," he once said to my father without irony.) The massive hernial bulge below his belt was the size of a grapefruit, and it merged with his belly to create an odd, lumpy mass that ran from his solar plexus to the top of his thighs. "Like Moe Berg," Papa once said, referring to the Newark legend, Jewish baseball player, and spy who also had an enormous hernia. Unlike her husband, Herb's wife, Ann, was trim and fit. An attractive woman in her mid-forties, she was an avid golfer and tennis player who, she often bragged, rarely ate sweets.

As I stepped out from behind a towering oak, I saw the butcher and his wife. Herb was dressed in a shiny, light blue suit with flat epaulets and a wide-collared shirt, the first four buttons of which were open. His belly button, by virtue of the mass beneath it, protruded like an engorged nipple. He wore white patent leather loafers and around his neck some sort of gold medallion. Ann wore a short skirt made of shimmering silver cloth and cut several inches above the knee; her tan legs were set in white knee-high boots; her considerable breasts were harnessed in a sheer, skintight blouse. She cracked a wad of bubble gum, her jaw in near constant motion.

I looked around the lawn at the other guests, all of whom were dressed in similar attire. My grandfather wore a tan suit with an open shirt and a ridiculous feathered fedora; Nana was wrapped in a tight scarlet dress, and in her hair was a peacock feather that matched the one in Papa's hat. To my horror, my mother wore fishnet stockings and a garter belt. Missy was sipping a soda alone near the water's edge, and I walked down the gentle slope of grass to join her. I was relieved to see that she was wearing jeans, a tee shirt, and sneakers.

"What the hell is this?" I asked. "What are they dressed as?"

She looked at her own oddly dressed parents and winced. "Pimps and prostitutes," she said, rolling her eyes.

I turned and watched as the butcher's wife stuffed a dollar into her cleavage. "Pimps and prostitutes?" I asked, incredulous.

"Yup."

"Have they gone mad?"

She nodded in the direction of Sid Lowenthal, who was wearing a shiny, teal-blue suit, his shirt unbuttoned to reveal his tan chest. "He certainly has. Just a couple of months since Helen died, and he's dressed like that. Not much of a mourning period."

I looked at Sid and thought about what normal behavior might be on such a day: a celebration so soon after his wife's death. Should he stay home and grieve Helen's loss? Should he perpetuate his loneliness? Or should he be among friends, enjoy a glass or two of wine, dress up in a ridiculous outfit, and have a few laughs? I thought that I, too, might choose the latter. But there was another issue. Was it appropriate for my grandmother to throw a party of this magnitude so soon after Helen's death? And for all these guests to join in the festivities, continuing to live and laugh in the face of this terrible loss? Maybe, I thought, this was Red Meadow's special way of honoring the dead—our version of a New Orleans jazz funeral.

"I thought you liked weird," I said.

"I do, but this is beyond."

I walked around the party and, when the adults weren't looking, snatched half-empty glasses of wine, vodka, Scotch—anything. I drank more than I did the night I humiliated Uncle Max, and I got sloshed to the point that Missy glared at me as I took a gulp of diluted, lukewarm gin. "For Chrissakes, it's got ashes in it," she fumed, and grabbed the glass from my hand. I felt sloppy, inarticulate, clumsy. I felt *high*. And in those intoxicated moments, I was mercifully distracted. I wasn't thinking about friends lost or starting at a new school. I wasn't thinking about how the lake might change for me. I wasn't thinking about Helen's dead body. I was just enjoying the buzz.

"You really should watch yourself, you know," Missy said.

I recalled our meal in Greenwich Village. "I thought you had a thing for drunks. For Dylan Thomas ..."

"I like to read him, but I wouldn't want to be his friend," she said, wounding me.

Later in the evening, there was an altercation between Sid Lowenthal and the Colemans. The butcher's feisty wife, Ann, had downed a half pitcher of sangria and had become progressively more annoyed with the fact that the surgeon was dressed as a pimp so soon after Helen's death.

"I'm going to say something," she said to her husband. "It's sickening and someone needs to set him straight."

"You're not going to say *anything*," Herb commanded, as he pushed her toward the buffet, which was filled with his finest chicken, steak, and ribs.

Defiant, Ann wriggled free and darted over to Sid, and before her husband could intervene she was lecturing the surgeon. "You're sick," she slurred. "Twisted sick. Dressed up like this … like a … like a pimp, of all things." Herb tried to pull his wife away, but she again shook free. "Makes me wonder," she said.

Sid stiffened. He flattened his enormous lapels. "Makes you wonder what?"

The butcher's wife took an aggressive step toward Sid and waved a finger in his face. "Makes me wonder if you're indifferent. Or maybe it's worse than indifferent. Maybe it wasn't an accident after all." She adjusted her bra, and a dollar bill floated to the grass. She took a sip of sangria and tossed the empty glass over her shoulder. "Makes me wonder if you had something to do with it."

"That's enough!" the butcher cried. He wrapped his arms around her waist, lifted her so that her flailing feet couldn't touch the ground, and carried her toward the car. With his wife kicking the air furiously, Herb turned back to Sid. "Sorry," he said to the stunned doctor. "I'm really sorry."

I watched as Sid examined his own outfit, as he buttoned up his shirt so that his tan chest was no longer exposed—as he removed the gaudy gold chain from his neck and slipped it into his trouser pocket. I watched as he shook his head and appeared to experience a moment of recognition. So uncomfortable was this moment that the party came to an abrupt end. Some streamed down to the dock and got in their boats, others returned to their Cadillacs and Lincolns, and a few said their goodbyes and walked back to their nearby homes. The Dopkins offered Sid some reassurance, but the others didn't know what to say and slipped out with only a thankful word to my grandmother and a polite yet uncomfortable nod to Sid. As I watched the crowd disperse, I was struck that Ann Coleman would make such an accusation. Was it simply because Sid was dressed as a pimp? Because he was laughing and drinking? Because he didn't appear to be mourning Helen's loss?

Or was there something that the butcher's wife knew that the rest of us did not?

Chapter 9

~~~~~~~~

After we'd moved to the lake, my mother expanded her business beyond housecoats. She had a friend in Montclair who had retired and was closing her theatrical wardrobe company, so Lillian bought the lady's jewelry, dresses, blouses, wigs, skirts, and shoes at a cut rate, and started selling them from our basement. For the women of the lake and the surrounding communities like Dover, Hopatcong, Parsippany, and Mountain Lakes, our basement became an underground market of sorts. Even a few men came by to purchase things for their wives. My mother carried vintage gowns by Chanel, Dior, and Gucci, as well as more modern dresses by Bob Mackie and Halston. She also sold the gaudiest costume jewelry imaginable: fake pearls, garish gold-plated brooches, plastic cameos, rings with chunks of blue glass masquerading as sapphires.

As the inventory flew off the racks, Lillian accumulated stacks of cash, which she kept in an attic safe. So good was business that after a year of bustling trade she purchased a new car: a canary-yellow Fiat Spider that made my modest father blush with discomfort. ("Too flashy," he said, although he seemed to drive the convertible with the same thrill that I drove the motorboat.) Even though Abe had begun to make enough money to support us comfortably, my mother continued to work and spend with a fervor that bordered on obsessive. Since my sister's death, Lillian's expenditures had increased, and I suspected that her spending was a diversion from her grief, an understandable coping mechanism to deal with the loss of her child. And I often wondered if her own experience as a teen—when Papa's partner stole client funds—had caused Lillian to strive for financial comforts as an adult. Either way, she built a thriving, successful business.

That September, I started my senior year at Morris Hills High. I can recall the first day of school, when I picked up the yellow bus around the corner and found that Missy was already sitting in the back row. The seat next to her was open, and she waved for me to join her.

"Townie lesson number one," she said as I sat down, "always sit in the back row."

I looked around the bus: the five rows before us were all empty. "And why's that?"

She exhaled dramatically, suggesting some exasperation with me. "Shtick, silly. Back here, we've got the best view of what's going on."

"Huh?"

"We get to observe," she said, pointing to a pair of identical twins whose sharply different styles made them appear to be unrelated: Scott was longhaired and wore a Jefferson Airplane tee shirt and engineer boots, while Gary had a crew cut and wore a button-down oxford with penny loafers. "There's not much out here but material, you know... especially when the summer ends."

"Material for what?" I asked.

Missy shook her head. "How would I know? That's up to you."

Just then, a car blew through a stop sign at the corner of Hibernia and Seneca, causing the bus driver to hit the brakes. The sudden deceleration hurled us forward into the backs of the high, padded seats before us. I scuffed my forehead, and Missy got a scrape on her nose.

"Fucker!" she yelled, pointing to the car.

I peered out the window and saw Sid Lowenthal's Lincoln—the model with the suicide doors. The surgeon was behind the wheel, and an unfamiliar woman sat by his side in the passenger seat. He waved an apology—sincere or not, I couldn't tell—and then sped off. Still tormented by suspicions that Helen's death was no accident, I bristled at the thought that he had already moved on from Helen, to another woman.

"Fucker," I said, rubbing my forehead. "Is that the type of material you were talking about?"

Missy rubbed the bridge of her nose. "Not really. I was talking about school stuff."

After only a few classes at Morris Hills, the differences between my old and new schools were clear. At Weequahic the manifestations of achievement and resulting stress were apparent everywhere. In the cafeteria, an entire table of kids spent lunchtime discussing famous Jewish politicians (Feldman, our valedictorian, spoke incessantly of Disraeli and Léon Blum). There was another table dedicated to the mysteries of mathematics and the scientific achievements of the twentieth century. But not everyone at Weequahic was focused on grades and college. There was a group of boys, well-known to all of us, who were the sons and nephews of Jewish gangsters—notorious, violent criminals who evoked both fear and pride in our community. Although my friends and I aspired to be doctors, lawyers, and engineers, we basked in the potent glow of men like Longie Zwillman, Dutch Schultz, and Meyer Lansky. The gangsters were proof to us that Jews were not weak, that we could inspire terror and respect among even the most evil people; these criminals, Jews just like us from the same places, made us feel powerful.

Out in the suburbs, the energy was different. There were plenty of smart kids at Morris Hills, but they lacked the all-consuming intensity of my old classmates. There were no lunchtime discussions of Fermat's theorem or Zeno's paradox—just normal teenage stuff. Cars, sports, crushes, cliques. My new classmates didn't confuse achievement with survival. There was nothing existential about good grades; they wouldn't die if they got a B. After the pressure cooker of Weequahic, my new school was a pleasant change.

During the first week of my senior year, I met with the guidance counselor to go over my transcript and extracurricular activities. My grades at Weequahic were good, but not perfect: mostly As, with just a few Bs. I was on the baseball team, although with my weak arm and slow feet I wasn't good enough to attract the attention of college coaches; I played Ito in *Auntie Mame* but showed little talent as an actor.

"You're going to need some more extracurriculars if you want to get into NYU," said the guidance counselor, a dour woman who had been placing kids in college for so long that she approached her craft with a rote indifference.

"More extracurriculars? Like what?" My trip to the Village with Missy had magnified my desire to attend my father's alma mater.

She examined me as if trying to determine which activity might best suit me. "Audiovisual?" she offered. "The Fuse Busters?"

The Fuse Busters were the ones who managed the sound systems, lights, and recordings at school plays, concerts, lectures, and the like. They were without exception the most nebbishy kids in school, and I was insulted by the guidance counselor's suggestion. "What else is there?"

She reviewed a list of activities. "Debate team?"

Missy was captain of the debate team and had led Morris Hills to the state championship the prior year, which I had attended in support of her. The topic at the championship round against Cherry Hill was: "The State of Israel: Does it have a right to exist?" Missy's team was selected to make the con argument, which violated her most deeply held belief in the importance of a Jewish state. Her personal view at that moment was not complicated by nuance, but years later she would become an expert in world politics and would come to understand that things—Israel included—were much more complex than she had originally thought.

I watched from the audience as Missy stood at the lectern and took several deep breaths. I saw her overcome her emotions and focus on the task at hand, arguing with conviction and strength for the rights of the Palestinian people—that Israel and the entire Middle East was nothing more than an artificial construct of postwar European powers, that the guilt of the Holocaust was no justification for displacing an entire people who had nothing to do with that catastrophe, that Palestinians, too, had a deep, historical right to the land. When Missy came off the stage after closing arguments, she fell into her father's arms—victorious, yet drained.

"I'll take debate," I said.

Later that day, I met the coach, who handed me a list of topics and a tape recorder. "Take this home," he said. He tapped the case of the clunky machine. "Record your voice ... record your arguments ... and I think you'll be surprised how you sound. Half of this is how good your argument is and the other half's how you come across." He paused to look at me. "I thought you were joining Fuse Busters."

"Nope, not me," I fumed.

During those first weeks of September, my connection to the lake retained its strength and familiarity. I still fished for sunfish and took the boat to Split Rock; I traded baseball cards on the steps of Tom & Mary's; and, while looking out for my favorite sports cars on Route 46, devoured the tastiest fried chicken. My parents were there, as were my grandparents on the weekends, and I had Missy too. The air remained hot, humid, thick—and the lake still felt summery to me. Where others saw withered blossoms and hints of amber in the green leaves, I saw only the verdant lushness of summer, and where the wiser ones smelled the imminence of leaf burns and chimney smoke, I could detect only the pleasing scents of tanning oil and my mother's watermelon-mint salad. As long as it felt like summer, the sadness of my displacement from Newark remained hidden deep within.

On the seventeenth of October, though, as the lake was shedding its last layers of flaky summer skin and slithering into the browning autumnal brush, there was a snap of cold so sudden and severe that I could not help but feel as if some permanent, fundamental break had occurred. I went to sleep the night before in what felt like the summer's midst and awoke the next morning in the grip of an early winter. Overnight, green leaves had mutated into a patchwork of gold, apricot, scarlet, and rust; the gnats, mosquitos, lightning bugs, and dragonflies that once hovered over the water had disappeared; the lush yards—filled for months with badminton, bocce, and volleyball, parties and fire pits—were now empty, fallow fields, the bleakest mats of yellow and brown. And it was at that moment, when I stepped out into the cold air and watched the most enormous egret elevate and glide south, that my romance with the lake ended.

Chapter 10

~~~~~~~~~

That autumn, Nana and Papa hosted Thanksgiving dinner. Two dozen friends and family, many displaced from Newark and redomiciled around northern New Jersey, drove out to Red Meadow for the holiday and gathered at my grandparents' house. Included on the guest list that evening was Sid Lowenthal. Papa was the surgeon's accountant, and the two men counted each other as good friends. Still, while my parents had always maintained a courteous relationship with Sid and Helen, the two couples were never particularly close. Over the years, they had attended many of the same parties, played mixed doubles against each other, and once sat on the same clubhouse fundraising committee—yet they seemed to maintain a certain social distance.

Five months had passed since Helen's death, and I had not seen Sid since he blew through the stop sign with a strange woman in the passenger seat. It was that image of Sid in the car—waving glibly, a woman by his side—that had infuriated me and had, in part, inspired me to search for the truth, accident or not, behind Helen's death. I had pleaded with Missy to help me, and after some resistance, she had agreed—not because she believed the death was anything but an accident, but because she understood that finding Helen's body had triggered in me some deep pain, and that this quest, despite its folly, was an undertaking required for my own healing.

So, during that autumn, Missy and I would meet and plot our investigation. When Sid was away from the lake, we would surreptitiously walk his property, pretending to retrieve a stray ball or a folding chair that had blown over from my grandparents' place. We would walk the short dock and peer down to the boulder shaped like a lion's head. "That rock looks like it's too far away for her to hit her head on ... if she just fell off the dock," I offered.

Missy pulled a tape measure from her pocket and ran it out until it reached the rock's edge. "Just under five feet," she said. "It's possible."

"Five feet sounds like too much. You'd have to dive to get that far."

"It's possible," she countered. "You trip and fall forward, headfirst ... go right out to the rock. And it's not like Helen was tiny. A lady of her size, what was she? Five seven? Five eight? A lady her size could easily reach it. *Geometry. Physics.*" With a bit of flair designed to prove the logic of her argument, she snapped the button on the tape measure, causing the metal snake to furl wickedly into its encasement.

"I guess," I said, disappointed by the force of her logic.

Missy and I were vigilant when it came to eavesdropping. We listened for any lake gossip, any conversation, any reference to Sid or Helen that might reveal what had happened.

"Sid's a wreck," Nana once whispered when she thought I was asleep on the couch. "Been arguing with people right and left, which isn't his nature."

"Never gets out of the house, other than work," my father observed when he'd heard that Sid had taken a short sabbatical from his successful medical practice.

"So depressed that he doesn't even wear his nice suits anymore," noted Muriel after she saw him at Green Brook Country Club in violation of the club's dress code.

Several months after the funeral, Missy overheard her father and Sid talking about a new surgical device that they were working on together. Hours later, Missy listened from the next room as her father complained about Sid: "He's being a real prick," he said to Missy's mother. "Doc wants 80 percent of the profits and he's only doing 20 percent of the work. You'd think he'd be a little more generous in light of what happened."

Missy relayed the conversation to me the next day. "What do you think it means?" I asked, hungry for clues.

"I don't think it means anything. Just two men with totally different views of their own worth ... which seems to be the cause of all the conflict in the world: an inflated sense of self, or a deflated one. But my dad thinks this might be his big break ... our big break ... and the way I can go to college without loans, to graduate school ... maybe even a nice wedding one day." I imagined Missy in a bridal gown—and me standing beside her on the bimah, a gold ring in my sweaty palm.

Uncle Max and Aunt Muriel were the first to arrive for Thanksgiving dinner, and my uncle's appearance shocked me. His posture, once long and straight, had slackened. His shoulders, pinned back high, were now sloped forward and rounded toward the center of his chest. The tan, freckled skin for which he was known appeared blanched, dry, and droopy. Most alarming, the sheen in his wet eyes—which long glistened under the stage lights—had wasted into a dull matte finish. Max looked like a broken man, diffident and insecure, and I feared that my shaming had in some small way contributed to his decline. I reclaimed my regret from that sad evening, and I suddenly craved a glass of syrupy concord wine.

Sid arrived a few minutes after Max and Muriel with his comportment restored: he was again energetic, charismatic, confident. His daughters, home from college for the holiday, were there too. And to everyone's surprise, joining him that evening was the woman I'd seen in the car, when Sid's reckless driving caused our bus driver to hit the brakes. Bottle-blonde with the plastered smile of a C-list starlet, Cammy stuck so close to Sid's side that she resembled a trepid child clinging to her father's hip. She was about a decade younger than Sid—forty, perhaps—and possessed only a fraction of Helen's social grace. Martini glass in hand, she spent the night listening attentively to whatever conversation Sid was engaged in, smiling when smiling was appropriate, interjecting an observation or quip only when it was entirely safe to do so and the chance of social embarrassment was minimal. She spoke and moved in a way—restrained, cautious—that suggested she was observing carefully constructed boundaries of either her own or Sid's making.

As Cammy reached for a cracker, I noticed her watch: gold with pavé diamonds. She turned to her left, toward

Sid, and the chandelier's light reflected off the watch's radiant face. This quick flash triggered a recollection of Helen in the water—her slime-lacquered face, her painted toenails, her glistening watch. I looked again at the woman's watch and, imagining Helen's, compared the two. The watches were so similar, perhaps identical, that I wondered if Cammy was wearing *Helen's watch*. My interest must have been unsubtle; she turned to me, followed my eyes to her wrist and pulled the sleeve of her sweater down, covering the gold band.

After a few minutes of nodding and smiling by Sid's side, she excused herself and went out to the deck for a smoke, glancing back at me as she opened the glass door. Sid soon followed, and I watched as they stood next to the grill, as she shook her head and gazed down at her wrist. He responded with a pleading motion—palms up—then put his arm around her shoulders and tried to soothe her.

Cammy's watch disturbed me—and I recalled the pimp and prostitute party when Ann Coleman accused Sid of insensitivity and perhaps even some involvement in Helen's death. My thoughts turned to that day when Helen gave Bernice a tennis lesson, how my beautiful sister giggled with delight, and how our mother was so moved, and something else as well: how Lillian had cried, her sorrow arising from her unwarranted belief that she had somehow failed Bernice, that she had failed to produce a healthy child, that she was somehow responsible for her daughter's pain. I recalled my sister's smile, a smile of the most inviolable goodness. I recalled the time when she was so weak that she could barely stand, and how my father modified a brace from the hospital so she could move around, sit up, watch television, and eat with us.

My grief was so vast that I craved immediate relief—and that immediate relief took the form of alcohol. By this time, my parents had permitted me to have a glass of either wine or beer on special occasions, with the understanding that I would not exceed the one-drink limit. I had, however, become an expert at acquiring and drinking booze without being noticed by the adults. One way was by volunteering to keep the tables clean. I would identify an abandoned glass—lipstick on the side and two fingers of gin at the bottom—take it to the kitchen, drink the remaining liquor, then wash the glass and return it to the bar. I did the same with small plates that held crumpled napkins and smudges of dried mustard; although the plates gained me no alcohol, they provided me with cover, the credibility of being an attentive host and a great help to Nana. I got alcohol and I got credit for being a mensch—a good guy.

I had no trouble hiding my drinking, but the more I drank, the more difficulty I had in hiding my drunkenness—and the more impaired I became, the more I was forced to focus on every word and movement. I deliberated before each sentence, careful not to slur my speech; I grasped the handrail when walking up and down the stairs to avoid a fall; I sucked on mints to hide the smell of my breath.

At the end of dinner, when coffee and dessert were being served, Max and Muriel sat at the end of the crowded table. On a plate before them, I noticed a cloth napkin with two bulges under it. Muriel poked my uncle's arm and pointed to the napkin. Max shook his head no. Again, she pointed to the napkin—this time lifting it up to reveal two dinner rolls with forks in them. He again shook his head. "No," he mouthed. He didn't want to do the roll dance. With a shrug that indicated resignation, my aunt dropped the napkin back down over the rolls. She looked down to her lap and then wiped the tiniest tear from the corner of her right eye.

I recalled the night I'd ruined Max's "weak back" joke, humiliating him. I feared that I had contributed to his decline, that I had somehow taken something from him. I retreated to the kitchen, where I proceeded to drink a half tumbler of bourbon that was left on the counter. I recalled the roll dances of my youth, how I would howl every time the forks crossed legs, how Max would end with a series of leg kicks, a cancan so high and fast that I feared the rolls would fly off and hit the ceiling. I thought about a man's identity, how he tethers to something that he's good at, something that's familiar—and how that something can be torn from him, how his *identity* can be torn from him. And then what's he left with? Sometimes nothing more than a realization that it was all a construct, that it was nothing more than a fake, an illusory salve to help him pass his days without feeling so insignificant. I thought about my own identity, what I clung to—and I wondered what important thing would one day be taken from me.

Chapter 11

~~~~~~~~~

That autumn, my relationship with Missy evolved. The novelty that had once defined our friendship soon gave way to familiarity—an ease that brought us comfort, but at the expense of the nervous anticipation that we had once found so alluring. We settled into a daily routine. Instead of meeting me on the bus each school morning, she would walk the few blocks to the stop in front of my house, two cinnamon buns or bagels in hand, sometimes a thermos of hot chocolate and a couple of Styrofoam cups. We would wait for the bus to come down Lake Shore and, for those few precious minutes, talk about school, our families, the world. Sometimes we spoke about Helen's death, about my suspicions, but she was growing bored of my obsession with something she deemed settled and thus not worthy of debate. "It's like challenging the Pythagorean theorem or Newton's second law of motion," she once told me. "You can spend the rest of your life trying to refute them, but it just won't happen.

She slipped, she fell, she died. Sad but true."

Around that time, Missy began to speak of world events with a passion and depth of understanding that far surpassed my superficial, headline knowledge. One morning, she showed up with a shiny brass coin, a victory medal commemorating Israel's recent defeat of its Arab neighbors.

"Egypt, Jordan, Syria," she said as she rubbed the heavy coin with her thumb, still excited months later. "We beat all of them in six days. Destroyed Egypt's entire air force in an afternoon ... every plane, pretty much. Sharon took the Sinai, they got the Golan Heights, too ... even the Old City. And in *six days*." Missy was filled with patriotism and a feeling of empowerment that she'd inherited from her immigrant parents, who had been expelled from Vienna, stripped of their possessions, degraded, and shuffled between refugee camps. For the Dopkins, more than for my family—who had lived in the States for generations—the Six-Day War was a source of tremendous pride. Jews had finally beaten someone.

"Want me to get you one of these?" she asked, holding the medal up to my eyes.

I thought about my lack of interest in the war and its outcome. "No, thanks."

Missy shrugged, confused no doubt by my indifference. She could not understand how, only two decades removed from the end of World War II, a Jew would not support Israel with the most impassioned fervor.

The day after Thanksgiving, Missy and I had lunch at the Shack: fried shrimp and clams, onion rings, and the most delicious corn on the cob. Thrilled by recent developments on the Supreme Court, Missy was buzzing, her mind and mouth racing.

"Can you believe it? We've got a black justice, Thurgood Marshall ... *and* the *Loving* decision. Imagine that, a man and a wife, white and black, sleeping in their bed in the middle of the night, and these cops ... these goddamn storm troopers from Virginia ... barge in and arrest them! For what? For being in love? Since when's that a crime?" She paused. "Turns out since 1883." I watched as her upper lip twitched in fury, and I admired that she, like my father, was outraged by injustice. "But the court got it right, finally. A unanimous decision, 9-0. That doesn't happen too often, all nine. And what a perfect name for the case ... *Loving*."

While it had always seemed unfair and bizarre to me that people of different races couldn't marry and have children, I didn't yet possess Missy's level of moral outrage. Based on our upbringings, it should have been just the opposite—as I was a child of Newark, where even though we lived in separate neighborhoods, black and white people had comingled, coexisted for decades, and Missy was a product of the suburbs, of a neighborhood without a single black family.

Our relationship with the black community in Newark was largely commercial in nature, with very little social overlap. We worked with them downtown and relied heavily on the entrepreneurs in the black community, the men who owned the car repair shops, the gardeners, the roofers. There was an electrician from Grant Street—a genius with wires, my father said—who installed lights and underground lines throughout our property, illuminating the sugar maples and the Asian pines, the rosebushes and the rhododendrons. Our landscaping was the envy of everyone in our neighborhood. In short, not a day went by when we didn't have some contact with black people. We lived south, they lived mostly north—but there was a regular and mostly civil interaction that facilitated a superficial integration between our worlds. Despite my more frequent contact with the black community, though, it was Missy who at that time had a sincere interest in social inequality. "I guess you're too busy thinking about girls to be thinking about civil rights," she once said, attributing my lack of moral outrage to distorted male adolescent priorities.

"Unanimous is fantastic," I said, "and that *is* a perfect name for the case. *Loving*." I ate a crispy onion ring, eager to move on from such weighty topics. "Speaking of names, I met Dr. Lowenthal's new girlfriend at dinner last night. Her name's Cammy. You ever heard that before? I never met anyone named Cammy."

Missy waved her hand—an expression of indifference, even disdain. She bit into an ear of buttery corn. "Probably short for Camille or Camilla." She smiled, now revealing crooked teeth adorned with a few stubborn kernels. I recalled how, years earlier, she was poised to get braces but her father again lost his job and couldn't afford them. I thought about the prices—emotional and financial—that Missy had paid for her father's volatile nature, his genius. "So what's your point?"

"My point is that it was the same lady we saw in Sid's car, when we were in the bus."

Missy reached across the table and grabbed my last fried clam. "And?"

I leaned close and whispered. "*And* she was wearing the same watch as Helen, I think. The fancy gold one." I was curious to hear her assessment of this potential evidence and hopeful that she would share my growing suspicion of Sid.

She took a sip of ginger ale and swirled the soda around her mouth before swallowing. She smiled again, this time revealing a kernel-free mouth. "Not possible... can't be."

"How's that?" In retaliation for her taking my last clam, I grabbed her half-eaten cob and, like a woodchuck, chewed off the few remaining rows of corn.

Missy glared at me. She snatched the bare cob from my hand and tossed it into the nearby garbage can. "Because there was an open casket before the ceremony, just a few minutes for family and close friends. Not very Jewish, but they did it. I was there with my parents, and I saw her in the casket. She was the first dead person I'd ever seen. Same for you, I guess. Imagine that, what a weird thing for us to share, you and me. She was so beautiful lying there, as graceful in death as she was in life... and that's something you can't teach. It's innate, that elegance... God-given... there or not. Anyway, they had her hands folded over her chest like one of those Egyptian queens. And when I looked in, just for a few seconds because I was nervous, I noticed that she was wearing all her jewelry. The massive diamond ring, the pearl necklace... and the gold watch." She took another sip of soda. "So that watch you saw last night? It's not Helen's. Maybe similar, maybe even identical, but it's not hers."

I must have appeared disappointed, for Missy continued. "It was an accident, you know... nothing more, nothing less. I know it's hard for you to accept, but sometimes the most painful things in life, the most impossible to comprehend, have the simplest, most mundane explanations." She raised her left hand and pointed to her Mickey Mouse watch, then leaned across the table and tapped the face of my own, nearly identical, watch. *"Quod erat demonstrandum,"* she said.

Chapter 12

~~~~~~~

One Saturday evening in December, I was in a particularly dark place. I missed my pals from Newark. As the months passed, our desire to stay connected had waned and our friendships transformed, first into acquaintanceships, and then into what felt like mere memories. I had been seeing my parents less frequently, as my father worked long hours at Saint Clare's and my mother's clothing business was so successful that she had opened a store in Denville. And earlier that day, I stumbled upon something that I had never seen before and that further darkened my mood: I was cleaning out some boxes in the garage and discovered a creased photograph of Helen and Bernice taken at the very moment my sister hit that perfect ball over the net. My mother must have taken the picture and, in too much pain, banished it to a distant, inaccessible place.

I was so depressed by that image—these two great people both dead—that I got drunk. By this time, I had built up my own stash and was no longer reliant on raiding my parents' liquor cabinet. I had befriended the clerk at the local liquor shop around the corner from Tom & Mary's and had persuaded him to sell me booze just before the store closed. Once every couple of weeks, I would pedal over, meet him in back, hand him a few dollars for the booze, fifty cents for the bribe, and ride away with a few half pints. I'd hide the bottles under a loose floorboard in our boathouse and access them under the guise of working on the lures or cleaning reels.

After finding the photo of my sister, taken just months before her death, I drank two shots of gin. Bundled up, I sat on the dock and looked across the lake to my grandparents' house, to the patch of water where I first saw Helen's body. I looked with some hope for Papa's lantern, but saw nothing—of course, I reminded myself, it was off season and they spent most of their time in West Orange. I thought about calling Missy to see if she wanted to catch a movie, but then remembered that she was seeing *Bonnie and Clyde* that night with her parents. I felt alone, detached.

Sometimes, when I was feeling reflective or upset, I liked to take the boat out to the middle of the lake. I'd cut the engine and drift, listen to the sound of the water lapping against the side of the aluminum boat, the squawking of birds, a bass breaking the water's surface. Being on the lake alone often calmed my mind.

That evening, despite the fact that I was buzzed, and that it was cold and dark, I decided that a quick ride on the lake might help clear my head of disturbing thoughts. With a few pulls of the cord, I got the engine running and headed out in the direction of Split Rock. There was a low cloud cover that night—a moonless, starless sky. The boat's running lights weren't working, which contributed to a darkness that, combined with my drunkenness, made navigation difficult. With an abundance of caution, I steered clear of the rocks that dotted the shoreline and the sheets of floating ice. When I was within fifty yards of Split Rock, I turned into the center of the lake and cut the engine.

For a few minutes, it was as if every possible sound was amplified: a heron, rare in winter, flapped its wings above, a fish crested through the water, a strip of ice tapped the side of the metal boat. I felt the cold wind slither over the water's surface. I looked around the lake, clockwise, from First Beach, to Second, to Third. Other than a few sparsely lit homes, the shoreline was dark.

I was enjoying the solitude, the darkness, and my tipsiness. But then, to my shock, a powerful bolt of lightning exploded out of the clouds and struck near First Beach. I had not anticipated a storm and well understood the dangers of being in a metal boat on open water. I pulled the engine's cord—one, twice, three times—but got no response. I looked up to the sky, and another bolt of lightning lit up the night, landing near the clubhouse and splintering one of the willows that twisted and bulged like enormous bonsai. Frightened, I pulled again at the cord until it belched and fluttered, then roared in full engagement.

I set off for my house, my drunkenness only partially offset by the adrenaline that the storm had triggered. I guided the boat around a cluster of rocks near the shore and toward the red light on our distant dock. I revved the engine, which I had illegally modified so that it far exceeded the five-horsepower limit, and made a straight, fast line for home. As I neared, I could hear a dog barking on the shore. The rabbi lived next door, and I could only assume that his alert terrier was reacting to the thunder and lightning. I accelerated, eager to get on solid ground—and out of the metal boat. Just then, yet another flash of lightning hit the water, not far from Split Rock, electrifying the surface of the lake and roiling the water.

I opened up the throttle to top speed. Our dock was in sight. No more than fifty yards from home, a boulder peered out of the water in front of the rabbi's house— it was a familiar boulder that, in my intoxicated and scared state, I had not anticipated. Alarmed, I jerked the engine's handle, turning the boat hard left toward the shore. Moving too fast, I hit the sloping grass full force. The impact threw me from the boat, and I landed bruised but unharmed on the ground. I watched as the boat glided across the slick grass—as it tore into the rabbi's rose garden, slaughtering the prizewinning bushes that he and his wife had spent so many years nurturing. As I lay on the ground and tried to process the scene before me—the damaged boat, the broken gin bottle, the splintered rose-bushes—the rabbi's Welsh terrier approached me with nervous interest. The dog sniffed at my face, licked my cheek—then curled up next to me and snored, her warm snout nuzzled against my neck.

Chapter 13

~~~~~~~~

After my arrest I was charged with several crimes, in-cluding operating a vessel under the influence of alcohol, speeding, and one count of damage to personal property (the prized rosebushes). Rabbi Rabinowitz, understand-ably furious, was nonetheless a spiritual and forgiving man, and he intervened on my behalf, persuading the police to drop the charges if I agreed to two conditions: that I pay him a hundred dollars for the value of the rosebushes and that I attend at least five meetings of Al-coholics Anonymous.

Compensating him for the bushes seemed equitable and carried with it an inescapable logic, one that he sup-ported with compelling opinions from the Talmud. "It's right there in Bava Kamma," the rabbi said, "the first volume of Nezikin." Still, I was not pleased with the idea of going to AA. First, I didn't think I had a drinking prob-lem: I reasoned that I'd just had a few too many drinks and lost control of the boat—and it could have happened to anyone. And at a cultural-religious level, I argued that I couldn't be an alcoholic because we didn't know many Jews with drinking problems. "Our tribe's got a long list of very serious afflictions, but that's not one of them," Papa once said, prompting me to think about my mother's complicated relationship with alcohol.

So while I had no doubt that my actions warranted punishment, I struggled with the requirement that I seek help for a problem I didn't think I had. But as the rabbi was a respected leader in our community and keeping a clean criminal record was paramount, I had no choice but to accept his punishment—which I later came to realize was meted out with the greatest concern for my well-being.

The next week, I went to my first AA meeting at a Presbyterian church in Morristown. My mother drove me there but refused to drop me off at the front steps. Afraid that someone would see her near either a church or an AA meeting (or both), she instead pulled into the parking lot of a diner several blocks away. "I'll meet you here in an hour," she said, ashamed. She took a few steps toward the diner, then turned back to me. "I'll get a booth," she said and, with a flip of her wrist and a pucker of her lips, threw me a kiss.

I arrived as the meeting started and took a seat in the rear of the windowless room, facing the backs of the attendees. The first thing I noticed was the age of the people. Most appeared to be ancient, although I now believe this perception was distorted by my own youth and that most of the group was in fact my parents' age or younger. I had expected most of the people to be men but was surprised to see that many female alcoholics were also attending the meeting. These drunks appeared to be a blend of professionals and blue-collar workers. Also in the group that night was one boy from my high school, a senior I recognized from the football team. He was there at his sober father's insistence, prompted by yet another incident in which the boy drank a bottle of stolen booze and urinated on the living room couch: we nodded to each other but were too embarrassed to say hello.

People raised their hands and, one at a time, spoke about their drinking, their struggles, their recovery. On Missy's advice, I had watched *Days of Wine and Roses*, which proved to be fairly realistic and prepared me for the meeting's tone and substance. I rose after a few minutes, grabbed a cookie from the coffee table, and returned to my seat.

A half hour into the meeting, a man in the front row raised his hand. "I'm Will and I'm an alcoholic," he said. I couldn't see his face from my vantage point, but his voice and his tailored suit were familiar to me. I leaned forward and found an uninterrupted line of sight that allowed me to view this man—who, to my shock, was not someone named Will—but rather the surgeon, Sid Lowenthal.

Lacking the eloquence he had exhibited at Helen's funeral, Sid spoke haltingly. He stammered. How, I thought, could someone be both a respected surgeon and a drunk? How could those two things be reconciled? And why did he identify himself as Will? Was it a pseudonym intended to create an additional layer of anonymity and protect his career? Or was there some deceitful motive involved?

Sid talked with some frustration about his inability to stay sober, how he kept relapsing, and how he'd been "in and out of the rooms" for over two years. He then said something that caused me to rise slightly from my seat: "There's something that's been on my mind, something tough to shake. The truth is that I've done some bad things... some things I'm not particularly proud of... and I'm just not sure how to go about making it right."

I thought of Helen's death; I thought of Cammy and her fancy gold watch; I thought of Sid dressed up as a flashy pimp. And I wondered what was behind his vague confession.

When Sid finished speaking, I feared that he would see me, so I ducked behind a pillar and scooted out of the meeting a minute before it ended. Once outside the church, I raced to meet my mother at the diner, eager to tell her about Sid and the things he'd revealed. I found Lillian sitting in a huge booth, flipping through *Better Homes and Gardens*. Before her was a plate of chicken, stripped to the bone, and two wineglasses—one full and one that had been polished off. She did not look up when I plopped down on the bench across from her. I cleared my throat.

"How was it?" she asked, still with no eye contact, as she dog-eared a page in the magazine.

"It was good," I said. "There's a lot of people who have this, you know. All different kinds of people. I still don't think it's something that I've got a problem with, but I heard some things I could relate to. Some of the feelings... especially about not being good enough."

She smiled inscrutably, but instead of showing interest in my experience, she pointed to a photograph of a modern kitchen—sleek white cabinets, marble countertops, the type of industrial stove you see in a restaurant, and rows of hanging steel pots. She pushed the magazine across the table and at last looked at me. "What do you think of this?"

"It's nice," I said, hurt by her lack of interest in my very first meeting.

"Nice?" She seemed annoyed. "Just nice?"

I turned the magazine around so I could get a better look at the kitchen my mother desired. Other than thinking that it looked expensive, I formed no opinion about it. I didn't care. "It's beautiful," I said.

She tapped the picture. "Terrific, because this is going to be our new kitchen." She flipped the pages until she came to several photographs of a high-end bathroom with a skylight, a claw-foot bathtub, a glass-enclosed shower, a bidet, two sinks, and a heated towel rack. "And this?" she asked.

"Beautiful, too."

She lifted the full wineglass to her lips and drank half. A drop of red wine slipped from her lip and landed on the paper placemat. She wiped it with her thumb and then inserted her thumb into her mouth. "Terrific," she said, "because that's our new master bath."

"Huh," I grunted, saddened that my presence in a church basement, in an AA meeting, was too painful for her to discuss. And I was disheartened that she could be drinking wine at this moment, mere minutes after I had left the meeting. "One down, four to go," I said, an attempt to provide her with some assurance that I would be okay—or, more likely, an attempt to offer myself some assurance at a moment when my mother could not. I was about to tell her that Sid was in the meeting and that he'd said something odd, but I recalled the group's vow of anonymity and feared breaching what appeared to be a sacred covenant. But more than that, as I watched her finish off the wine, I didn't trust my mother with the information.

Chapter 14

~~~~~~~~

To compensate the rabbi for the destruction of the rosebushes, I took as many odd jobs as possible: babysitting,
dock repairs, painting, washing cars. One of the people
I approached for work was Dr. Lowenthal. I hoped to
earn some money from him, of course, but I was also angling for access to his house. Given his relationship with
Cammy and his ambiguous confession in the AA meeting,
what I really wanted to do was search his home. I was
looking for insight into Helen, into their marriage, into
Sid and Cammy; I was looking for evidence that might
help explain Helen's death; and I was looking for peace
of mind, which I'd had little of since I found her body six
months earlier.

Sid eagerly gave me work. "I need the help," he said
with a hearty shake of the hand that revealed his strength.
"It's been impossible to keep everything in order without
Helen, you know. I had no idea what's involved. She was
the one who handled *everything*."

Dr. Lowenthal had a spectacular black Lincoln with a gray interior and a dashboard covered in yards of brushed chrome that, with cotton swabs, chamois rags, and the precision of a watchmaker, I kept in immaculate condition. When Sid was having lunch one day with my grandparents, I searched the Lincoln's glove compartment and trunk for anything that might be relevant to my search, but found nothing. After a heavy rain one afternoon, I climbed a shaky ladder and removed the muck, twigs, and rotten leaves from his gutters. As I ascended, I peered through the windows of the house and looked for something that might suggest some wrongdoing on Sid's part. Again, I saw nothing. A week later, I spent three full days cleaning out his chaotic boathouse, throwing out broken rods, rusted lures, and empty bottles of motor oil—and to my disappointment found nothing of note. During that time, Sid never asked me to work in his home. And in my hyper-suspicious state, I imagined that there might be something inside that he was keen to hide.

A few days before the new year, though, Sid called and asked if I would do some work at his house. "I need you to help me clean out some closets." He paused. "*Helen's* closets ... still filled with all her stuff."

I thought of being inside the Lowenthal home, of at last being close to Helen's possessions and the clues they might offer. "Sounds like I could use a girl's eye," I said, hoping that I could bring Missy along to help me search for clues. "Do you mind if Missy Dopkin joins me?"

"Missy, sure. Smart girl. Isn't she going to Cambridge?" he asked.

"It's on her list, yes. And she's trying to make some spending money."

"Of course, bring her along. With a father like hers, she could use a few extra bucks." I was taken aback by Sid's mean-spirited gibe. I recalled that the two men had once argued about the surgical invention and the split of the profits.

I told Missy about the work, and because she needed cash, she agreed. "But just work. No conspiracy theories, please," she said, reluctant to indulge my suspicions of Sid.

Missy and I arrived at Sid's home later that day. Where most of the homes at the lake were decorated in a more traditional manner, the Lowenthal place was—according to my mother—stylish and sophisticated. The living room was awash in deep blues, enameled whites, and glistening silver. There was a round glass coffee table with sinuous chrome legs. There were bottles of colored liqueur—blue, red, and yellow—reflecting off the wet bar's smoky mirror. I eyed a Lucite ice bucket, next to which lay silver ice tongs. Much of the far wall had been removed, making way for an expanse of floor-to-ceiling windows that permitted a glorious view of the lake.

"Upstairs," Sid said as he climbed a wide, curved staircase. Missy and I followed and looked up to a rococo chandelier that Helen had commissioned from a famous glassblower in Venice. He led us down a long hallway hung with black-and-white photographs of New York skyscrapers, old storefronts, the intricate steel lattice-work of city bridges. The decor and the taste in art was unlike anything I had ever seen, and when Sid noticed me admiring a photograph of the Empire State Building, he said, "Abbott something...something Abbott...she's famous. Helen picked them out. She was the one with the good taste."

He led us into the master bedroom, with its groovy faux leopard rug and matching headboard, then opened a door. He flipped a light switch and gestured for us to enter. When Missy and I stepped through the doorway, we found ourselves inside Helen Lowenthal's enormous walk-in closet. There was an entire rack dedicated to colorful summer dresses, another rack of black cocktail dresses, one for formal gowns—and so on. There was a large custom dresser that ran along the far wall, above which were angled shelves holding several dozen pairs of shoes. There was so much clothing in this closet that it rivaled the offerings of my mother's store.

Sid remained outside. He seemed reluctant to enter Helen's closet, as if he were afraid to be so close to her possessions. "All this ... all this ... I think it's time to get rid of all this," he said. "Ben, I asked your mother to handle it, and she said you'd pack it up. It's fine with me. Take it all to Lillian's shop, to a charity ... anywhere, really. Tell your mother she can sell what's got any value and give the money to the temple, Hadassah ... it's up to her." Sid poked his head into the closet and, as if he'd been hit by a blast of frigid air, quickly withdrew. "I haven't been in here since Helen passed ... left it just like it was, just like she kept it. Too hard, I guess."

Without awaiting our reaction, he left the room— and we soon heard the opening and closing of the front door, the groan of the Lincoln's engine, and the tires on the driveway's slick pavement. Missy and I stood in the closet and looked around. I watched as she ran her fingers across a row of silk dresses, price tags still hanging from several sleeves. I glanced at a few tags and was amazed at their cost. Next, I moved over to the dresser and opened the top drawer. There, lined up by color, were Helen's tennis outfits: white, yellow, salmon, pastel blue. I lifted a sleeveless top from the drawer and held it up to the light, brushing the shadow of a perspiration stain beneath the armhole.

I turned my attention to a row of shoeboxes that were lined up on the floor. I opened the first box, and inside was a pair of high-heeled shoes in off-white silk, the soles of which were in pristine condition. I moved on to the next box, which also contained a pair of brand-new shoes. The third and final box, like the first two, held expensive shoes—sequined pumps with shiny silver heels. Unlike the other boxes, this one had a layer of tissue paper at the bottom, and as I was about to return the top to the box, I noticed something peeking out from under the corner of the thin paper. I removed the shoes and pulled back the paper—and there, at the bottom of the box, was a small leather book. I removed it and opened to the first page, which revealed Helen's name written by hand. I flipped to the next page. There was a date on top—just months before my sister died—and, below it, in what appeared to be Helen's handwriting, a diary entry. I looked around to see if Missy was nearby, as I feared her reaction to what I would do next. She was folding sweaters in the bedroom, applying her customary precision to the task. I turned my attention back to the journal.

I keep getting these damn UTIs and this one's really painful. Sid put me on antibiotics but they don't seem to work. I drank a quart of cranberry juice yesterday, today too, but there's no improvement. It's a bubbe-meise, I think.

Whenever I get these, and it's been happening more as I get older, it makes me really depressed, moody, irritable. I took it out on Sid today, even though he's been really helpful and supportive, which is a relief because sometimes he's an insensitive shit when I'm sick. Surgeons! But I'm just not myself since this came on. The infection and the antibiotics just turn me into a monster. It's hell on my stomach. I feel awful, hideous. I'm going to lie low until this passes. No tennis or bridge this week.

Ashamed of what I'd just read, ashamed of my intrusion into the most private and sensitive aspects of Helen's life, I quickly closed the book and slipped it back under the tissue paper.

Missy returned to the closet and eyed the stack of boxes. "Fancy shoes?" she asked.

"I think so. And there's something else too."

"What's that?"

"A diary. Helen's diary, right here." I tapped the box with the tip of my sneaker.

"You're not going to take that, are you?" Missy asked with the righteous tone that she'd mastered. She had a very strong sense of right and wrong, which she applied to ethical dilemmas both big and small.

"I was thinking about it. Maybe there's something in there, something that could explain what happened."

"Explain what happened?" Annoyed, Missy lifted a hanger from the floor and hung it in the closet. "Well, I think it's wrong. It's her personal stuff, and you've got no right to read it."

I bristled, for I knew that Missy was right. "Well, Doc said we should clear out the whole closet, so ..."

Missy raised her right eyebrow skeptically, thus managing to deliver another lecture on right and wrong. I could tell that she was growing tired of my obsession with Helen. "Let's start getting this stuff over to your grandparents," she said. "It's like Saks in here ... could take us a while."

Missy and I each pulled an armful of patterned dresses off the rack and brought them next door, then returned for another collection. It took us a total of fourteen trips to erase most of the evidence of Helen from the closet. All that remained were the three shoeboxes. As we prepared to gather them and leave, we heard the sound of Sid's Lincoln in the driveway.

A few seconds later, we heard the front door open and then Sid's voice, followed by Cammy's excited cackle. "You upstairs, Ben? Missy?" he called out. "Making progress?"

"All good, Dr. Lowenthal ... almost finished," I replied.

I heard inaudible whispering, followed by Cammy's voice. "It's about time you cleaned that closet out," she said to Sid, showing little regard for the dignified woman who had preceded her. Footsteps on the stairs announced their approach, and Missy and I stood at attention, greeting them as they entered the bedroom. As if enveloped in a swarm of bothersome gnats, Cammy waved her hand in front of her face and pushed past us into the closet.

"It looks so much smaller when it's empty," Cammy remarked, running her fingertips over a bare hanger—and perhaps searching for some residual proof of Helen's existence. "What's that?" she asked and pointed to the shoeboxes.

I glanced at Missy, who was showing signs of discomfort that included misty dew on her forehead and a twitchy bounce in her heels. "Just some old shoes," I said.

Cammy assessed her own shoes. She lifted her right foot and examined the scuffed heel. "I could use some new pumps," she said. Whether she was speaking to Sid or to herself I could not tell.

Sid scanned the closet with a sadness that the vigilant Cammy must have detected, for she winced and departed the small room, shoulders squared. "Nice job, both of you," the surgeon said as he followed Cammy's grand exit, then peeled two fives from a thick roll and handed one to me and one to Missy. "You'll get rid of those shoeboxes, too, won't you?"

Missy glanced at me, then the boxes, then Sid. "Sure thing, Dr. Lowenthal," she said. We gathered the boxes with a controlled haste, stepped down the stairs, and opened the front door. Once outside, we sprinted back to my grandparents' house. There, I placed the two boxes that contained only shoes next to the rest of the items in the living room. Missy and I both looked at the third box—the one with Helen's journal. She glared at me, and I felt the full weight of her moral authority, her recognition that, in this particular instance, she was powerless over my actions. After many years of dealing with a father who acted self-destructively, who behaved in ways that violated Missy's sense of pragmatism, she understood the limits of her influence. Five-dollar bill in hand, she waved goodbye and returned home. I took the box and brought it down to Papa's basement, where I hid it behind a stack of old crates, saving it for I knew not what.

Chapter 15

~~~~~~~

On New Year's Day, Missy and I sat on the lawn in front of the clubhouse, a beautiful Arts and Crafts mansion with a clumpy stone facade. The design of the building—the carved stone, the mahogany molding—suggested that our community was old money, rather than middle-class aspirants. On its first floor was a horseshoe-shaped bar that looked out over a grand lawn and the water beyond: there, the bartender kept bowls of spiced nuts and hard candies that I loved.

It was at the clubhouse—the hub of the lake's social life—where we had dances and parties, including the annual costume gala in which my family once went as "The Typical American Family" (we carried a placard that identified us as such). My father and grandfather each dressed in drag with prairie skirts, wigs, and fake buck teeth, Nana wore a pickle barrel around her torso, and my mother donned overalls and a straw hat and sauntered about with a live goat on a leash, while I was tied to a dummy to create conjoined twins. We came in second place, which infuriated my father.

Missy and I sat on a bench under one of the massive willow trees that lined the shore. Nearby, the tree that was hit by lightning moments before I destroyed the rabbi's rosebushes stood as a painful reminder of that evening. The dead branches had been removed, and all that remained was the tree's jagged, fractured trunk. I looked out over the lake, which was in the early stages of its deep freeze—and as the ice thickened, formed, cracked, the lake emitted a mournful howl, a mystical moan that reminded me of the sounds of a whale.

I drank from a bottle of beer and, the lake before us, watched as the wind whipped a beer can across the surface of the ice. I offered the bottle to Missy, but she declined. She would on occasion share a beer with me, but she had very little interest in alcohol—and the more I drank, the more she seemed to abstain, as if she were trying to convey to me a message of restraint.

Normally bristling with energy, Missy had been subdued for days. "What's going on?" I asked.

There was a small patch of water where ice had not formed, the result of a hot spring below. Missy stood and skipped a flat rock across the water. "That was nine, maybe ten."

I watched the divots in the water recede. "What's your record?"

"Twelve, but I did that when I was eight and haven't gotten close since." She looked for another suitable skipping rock. "Imagine that, peaking at the age of eight. Maybe that's what happened to me."

Missy's negativity—so atypical—surprised me. I

thought about myself at that young age and feared that I had already peaked. "So what's going on? You don't seem yourself lately."

Missy picked up a round, heavy rock that was unsuitable for skipping. She bent down low—waist and knees—to create a flat trajectory and threw the rock across the water. As expected, it hit with a thump and fell to the lake bed.

"Does that count as zero or one?" I asked.

"Zero. It's only one if it elevates after the first point of contact."

"Got it." I took another swig of beer. "So, how have you been?"

Missy turned her back to me. "Well, let's see. My father got fired last week ... again. Can you imagine that? I'm off to college in a few months and he just can't control himself. Always has to prove how damn smart he is. People do what they want, you know, and there's not a damn thing you can do to convince them otherwise. Sort of like you with Helen's journal. There's just no changing a person's mind." She laughed in exasperation and picked up a flat rock. She threw it across the water and counted the skips. "That's seven ... actually six, if I'm being honest. I think I'll be honest. Why not, right? Be honest?"

"I'm so sorry," I said.

"Yeah, well, it's not the first time, and it won't be the last. He always gets another job. It's just the in-betweens that are hard."

I again offered her the bottle, and this time she took it. After holding it up to the weak winter sun, she took a few big gulps. She wiped her lips with the back of her hand and sat down next to me, close enough that our shoulders touched. Even the most minor physical contact with Missy evoked in me a pleasurable sensation and fantasies of a shared future.

"The only thing he's got now with any promise is that invention he's working on with Dr. Lowenthal. The surgical device."

"They came to an agreement?" I asked, recalling how Sid and her father had fought over the split of profits.

"Fifty-fifty," Missy said with the pained, outsized pride that a child has in even the most modest accomplishments of a struggling parent.

"Well, I hope it works out," I said, a tepid encouragement that was dampened by my suspicion of Sid.

Missy frowned and wrinkled her nose, as if she had detected a foul odor. "You're not still conjuring up ridiculous theories about Dr. Lowenthal, are you?"

"I wouldn't call them ridiculous. I just don't think he behaves the way a widower should behave … not the way you act when your wife dies."

"How the hell do you know how someone should act when their wife dies? There's no prescribed method of mourning, no defined expression of emotion … maybe some societal expectations, but that's all just nonsense. People can grieve however they want." She was angry with me. "And I think you're being stupid. He's a good man who lost his wife and you shouldn't be messing around, especially after what you've done."

She was referring, no doubt, to my boating accident and my subsequent arrest. Missy had wounded me. And as she took a swig of beer, I wondered if she viewed any threat to Sid as a threat to her father's business venture, to her family, to her own future—and if her self-interest had at last trumped her morality.

We sat in silence and watched the lake. We inhaled the vestiges of burning pine that drifted over from the clubhouse chimney and listened to the lake's rusty, wintry groan. I turned my head and looked at Missy. I considered her pain—the pain of her father's unemployment, his chronic underperformance, the fear, the instability that grips us when we are forced to accept that the people we idolize have let us down.

"Sorry about that," she said. "I took that out on you. It's just brutal when the people you love break your heart. Brutal. It's unavoidable, I'm afraid." She kicked my foot. "It's going to happen to you one day, too, you know. *Someone's* going to break your heart."

As Missy picked up a stone and threw it at the willow's fractured trunk, I wondered how and when my heart would be broken—and who might break it.

Chapter 16

~~~~~~~~

In late January, Sid Lowenthal asked me to prepare his house for spring. He had work for Missy, too, but she declined, citing a busy schedule. The truth behind her decision, though, was that she had become exasperated by my refusal to accept that Helen's death was accidental—and she knew that any work in Sid's house would prompt yet another theory on my part that she would deem meshuga, crazy. So, with Sid and Cammy away in Fort Lauderdale for some doctors' convention, I worked alone.

I dusted off the deck furniture that was being stored in the basement and arranged for the air conditioners to be filled with Freon. I removed, cleaned, and replaced the home's window screens—and when I did so in Sid's bedroom, I glimpsed Helen's walk-in closet, now filled with Cammy's flashy clothing. I recalled the beautiful dresses that Helen wore, the matching tennis outfits. I shuddered at the thought of having taken her journal and, then, invading her privacy by reading the first entry.

As I wandered through Sid's empty home, I searched for clues that might help me understand Helen's life and death—and for anything that might explain Sid's vague confession at the AA meeting, some evidence of a transgression big or small. I lifted sofa pillows, finding only a few coins and a mascara brush; in the basement, I found a bag of Helen's old makeup and a few pretty bottles of perfume; unsure of my own intentions, I flipped through Helen's dusty novels, still stacked in the study in a manner that suggested they too would soon be sold off, thrown out, or banished in some other undignified way; most disturbing, there was only one photograph of Helen in the entire house—a faded picture of Helen and her two young daughters in front of the Central Park carousel. There was little remaining evidence of Helen's brilliant life, and I clenched my jaw in anger at the purge of Helen's possessions. Although I found no clues that could explain our neighbor's death, the almost complete erasure of her memory left me feeling even more uneasy and suspicious.

That night I sat at the dinner table with my parents, eager to tell them how Cammy had taken over Sid's home. Lillian was in one of her foul moods, prompted by my arriving thirty minutes late for dinner. The three of us were sitting in the dining room, which overlooked the water. My mother poured herself a gin on the rocks—no mixer—and drank it before we finished our first course: a homemade mushroom barley soup with chunks of stringy brisket.

Lillian had a tendency to think of people in the most black-and-white terms: saints or sinners, good or bad, brilliant or stupid. Her worldview was binary, with no nuance, and often her opinion of a single person fluctuated between the extremes. "Hands down, Helen Lowenthal's the best ladies' tennis player in all of New Jersey," she'd said after Helen gave Bernice that memorable lesson—until Helen didn't attend my bar mitzvah, at which point my mother said, "Helen's okay for here, for our little piece of the world, but there's a dozen ladies in Westchester alone who'd beat her in straight sets." And so she would swing—high to low, low to high.

She was particularly sensitive to the comings and goings of those she loved. To be a half hour late (which I was the night of this dinner), to cancel plans at the last minute, to decline a lunch invitation, to be independent of her, emancipated, to *leave*—these were the things that triggered in her an intense sense of abandonment. Hence, I believe, her reaction when Helen didn't show up at my bar mitzvah. Every April, she would become agitated when my father traveled to a medical conference in Miami Beach, accusing him of infidelity. "Which little tramp nurse caught your attention this year?" Lillian would ask. She would later claim that she was joking, but there would be not a hint of humor in her voice.

Lillian's spasms of anger and criticism were infrequent, and for the most part she was upbeat, but I lived in a state of near constant trepidation, never knowing if some minor transgression on my part would forfeit my standing as her little prince and result in my vilification. Each time I did something wrong—like destroy the rabbi's rosebushes and get arrested—and yet remained her special boy was for me a moment of affirmation, evidence that she loved me and always would, that I would not be rejected for my failings. There were times when I thought that my propensity for trouble was a misguided way of testing my mother's love, for if I could be very bad and still remain in her good graces, then maybe our bond would remain secure, sacred. But as I watched Lillian redefine her closest friends as villains, and then as friends again, I feared that my next mistake would send me into exile.

"How was your day?" my father asked, slumped over his soup at the dinner table. He appeared to be tired, caving in upon himself as a result of the psychic weight he had carried around for years—not just the death of his daughter but also the strain of being married to Lillian.

"Not bad," I replied. "I've been doing work for Doc to make some extra money. It's not too hard and he pays good."

"Well," Lillian corrected.

"Pays *well*." I recalled the large walk-in closet. "But it was pretty upsetting, what I saw." My mother eyed me over the lip of her raised glass. "There's hardly a thing of Helen's in the whole house. One photo from years ago, that's it. There's nothing else. And those fancy paintings that Helen bought in New York? They're gone too. Cammy's got all of her crap in the closet. She just moved right in and took over the place. Even Helen's tennis trophies were boxed up with a bunch of trash. It just makes you wonder, doesn't it?"

"Makes you wonder what?" my mother asked, sounding a lot like Missy. I was afraid to reveal my suspicions about Helen's death. "*Ben*," Lillian said. She rapped her knuckles on the table, commanding me to proceed with caution.

I looked at my father, who nodded for me to continue.

"Well, I've just got a lot of questions about how Helen died. I mean, it just seems really hard for me to believe that she just slipped off the dock and hit her head, drowned. She was a real athlete, perfect balance on the court. She hardly ever drank much. Everyone knew that. So how'd she fall in the water and drown? And then the next thing you know, just a few months after Helen dies, Sid's with another lady. *Cammy.* You've seen her, loud and flashy and the opposite of Helen." My father nodded in agreement. "And then she moves right in to their place, takes over like she owns it, and wipes out every memory of Helen? That's just not right, for either of them to do that. Like I said, makes you wonder."

"Wonder *what*?" my mother said angrily.

I glanced at my father, who winced in discomfort. "Wonder if, I don't know, wonder if maybe Sid had something to do with it ... and Cammy too. They have the same watches, you know, Helen and Cammy."

Before I could continue, Lillian slapped me across the face. "How dare you," she yelled. "Pillar of our community, famous surgeon, terrific father, husband. And you, with your stupid little conspiracies, defaming a man of his standing. How dare you. What gives you the right!" She grabbed my glass of soda and sniffed it. "If I didn't know any better, I'd say you're drunk."

Always my defender, Abe intervened. "Lillian, *please*, don't hit the boy. I thought we agreed. Ben's just being silly, a teenage boy with lots of fanciful ideas. And remember it was a trauma for him ... finding Helen the way he did. He hasn't been right since that day. He didn't mean anything by it, right, Ben?"

I rubbed the left side of my face, which was stinging

from Lillian's perfectly landed slap. I had seen enough of
my mother's anger over the years to know when to back
off. "Right, Dad ... just some silly ideas, crazy ideas. I
don't even know why I said that."

Lillian took an aggressive gulp of gin and licked her
lips like a haughty cat. She glared at Abe. "And you,"
she said. "Always choosing his side. You got a wife,
remember?"

"It's not about sides. The boy didn't mean a thing.
Like I said, he's just a silly boy sometimes."

"Dad's right," I said with the understanding that he
needed to undermine me in order to defend me.

Sensing what she viewed as an opposing alliance, Lillian undertook her customary preemptive abandonment.
She got up from the table and stared down at us. "I see
what you're doing," she said, now slurring. "Don't think I
don't know. Always ganging up on me ... a sick little collusion the two of you have."

Uncomfortable, my father repositioned himself in
the chair. "Lillian, we're not doing anything. There's no
collusion, no sides here." I watched as he pondered his
next words. "I think you're in one of your moods," he said,
leaning back to await my mother's predictable response.

Lillian straightened and took down the remaining gin.
"One of my moods?"

I could tell that my father was considering whether
to retreat or advance. "Yes, Lillian, one of your moods."

Having seen her in this state several times per year,
my father and I both knew how Lillian would react to his
defiance. "Abe," she said to my father with a grin that projected arrogance and command, "I think it's best if you
sleep on the couch until you get your wits back."

Not surprised, he nodded. "Fine, I figured as much." As my father removed a folded kerchief from his pocket and wiped his brow, I tried to make eye contact with him, to express in some subtle way my support for him, but he was so ashamed that he turned away.

Lillian snapped her fingers, spun on her heel, and with an inappropriate swing in her gait retreated to their bedroom. She made a grand display of slamming the door, locking it, ensuring that we knew she had eliminated the possibility of rapprochement. Soon, the wan light of the television seeped through the crack under the bedroom door while a muffled, mechanized laugh track created an ironic score for our suddenly tense household.

Abe and I sat in silence for a minute or so until he rose from his seat, his slouched posture suggesting some disappointment in the arc of his life. "Think I'll go into town and pick up some ice cream," he said and again wiped his damp brow with the kerchief. "Sweets are always good for times like this, right?"

I smiled.

"Any preferences?" he asked.

I shook my head no.

"Then mint chocolate chip it is. And I'm going to get a pint for your mom. Coffee crunch ... her favorite. Who knows, maybe she'll come around."

My father was prone to carrying out kind acts designed to placate my mother—all of which were futile. I once read that trying to satisfy a person like Lillian was like trying to fill the Grand Canyon with a water pistol. *Impossible.* I was poised to tell him how foolish his kindness was, how ineffective, how he could never bring her consistent happiness—and how she would never treat him the way he deserved to be treated. But to say such a thing, to bludgeon him with the most obvious logic, would have been cruel of me—and fruitless too. For reasons that I have never been able to understand fully, he tolerated their dynamic. He was invested in believing that she could change for the better, and I've often thought that for him to admit the contrary would be to admit that the most important decision of his life had been flawed—and that every result of that union, me and my sister included, might contain the seeds of that flaw.

After he pulled out of the driveway, I went into the den and prepared the couch. I had undertaken this task several times in the past, for allowing my father to set up his own exiled bed saddened me. I first removed the cushions and stacked them on the floor, then put a fresh case on a clumpy old foam pillow. I laid down a sheet and a soft blanket and, with some pride, stepped back and examined my work. There was a tiny buckle in the blanket, and like the most fastidious innkeeper, I flattened it out. "There," I said to myself. From the pillowcase, I removed a piece of lint—a nest of pearl-gray fuzz attached to the crisp linen by only the thinnest single filament.

As was often the case, my father returned to the bedroom the very next night. Lillian was a master at creating separation, enforcing it on her own terms, then facilitating a détente that not only eradicated her very role in the rupture but also implied some magnanimity on her part. This time she did not say a word to restore harmony. Instead, she made breakfast for us and then walked over to the couch; she stripped the sheets and blanket, removed the pillow, and replaced the cushions. She signaled that her grudge was, for now, over.

Once my father got off the couch and slid back under the covers of the marital bed, what often followed was an extended period of normalcy. During these long stretches of what appeared to be genuine contentment and partnership, it was impossible for anyone on the outside to appreciate our family's sporadic bouts of tumult—and even difficult for me to recall those short bursts of dysfunction. Whether our dynamic was normal or not, I did not know. Despite the occasional blip, though, I believed that we were a functional family.

Chapter 17

~~~~~~

On Valentine's Day, when I considered purchasing a gift for Missy but was dissuaded by the inevitable awkwardness that would result, I awoke early to a still, dark house. My parents were asleep and an erratic wind slapped a rope against our flagless flagpole, breaking the eerie quiet. Surprisingly alert for such an early rise, I attempted to fall back to sleep, but with each passing minute my acuity increased and I soon gave up hope.

As I lay in bed, I thought about my old friends from Newark. The ones who'd moved to the Oranges, Livingston, Short Hills, and Millburn had the good fortune of being accompanied by waves of other émigrés from Weequahic. We were the only family to move to Red Meadow, and I found myself yearning for some connection to my old community—and as I listened to the sound of the rope slapping against the flagpole outside, a sense of loneliness and disconnection consumed me.

In this state, an array of disturbing thoughts formed

and battered my brain. I thought about the AA meetings I had attended and how, after that first meeting, I did not see Sid again. I mulled over the possible explanations behind his confession that night. *Cammy*, I thought. Perhaps he was confessing to an infidelity but nothing more. Or maybe his confession had something to do with Helen's death. I looked around my room and thought of my mother's volatile temperament, my stash of booze in the musty boathouse, my affection for Missy and the fear, the acceptance really, that I would always lag behind her. I thought of the unexplained lantern lights and Helen's diary. So relentless and chaotic, and yet so ethereal, were my thoughts that I could not focus on one for more than a few seconds before it evaporated and was supplanted by the next intrusive thought—only to resurface moments later in slightly different form and substance, a detail added or omitted, a fact's significance elevated or demoted, my perspective more or less pessimistic.

"Enough," I said to myself, frustrated by the clutter that was occupying my brain. I considered what might have a palliative effect on me—something light and easy, untainted by the heaviness of my thoughts—and the only thing I could think of at that moment was sports. The Knicks had played the San Diego Rockets the night before, and it was the first game in weeks that I had not listened to on the radio. I'd been following the Knicks closely that season, excited by a young team filled with so much talent: Willis Reed, Bill Bradley, Walt Frazier, Cazzie Russell. ("They've got a Jewish coach!" Papa would say every time I mentioned one of my favorite players; it was, it seemed, the only thing about the team that excited him.)

So, with the Knicks in mind, I got dressed, put on my shoes, and stepped out of the house. From the doorstep, I could see the paper in the center of the driveway. I noted with admiration that Missy had once again delivered the paper on time, perfectly positioned and wrapped so well in plastic that no amount of rain or snow could dampen it. In addition to her intelligence, I thought, she had a job that required her to get up an hour earlier than everyone else. And while some of us did odd jobs on the weekends, Missy was the only kid I knew who worked *during* the school week—a consequence of her father's bouts with unemployment.

My parents appreciated her punctual delivery, but what I most enjoyed were the secret notes she often hid for me in the sports section. Every morning, I would flip through the pages and look for cryptic words and numbers embedded in advertisements, photos, and statistics. In a Tigers-Indians box score, just below Chico Salmon's dreadful batting line, she once penciled in *27.10.1914–9.11.1953.*

"What's that?" I asked her later that day at school.

"Dylan Thomas," she said. "Birth and death, the way the Europeans write it. I'm not sure why we write it month, day, year. There's no logic to it … backwards. It should go sequentially, by unit of time, shortest to longest. Day, month, year."

Another time, the morning after Missy's father was fired yet again, I noticed the tiny letters *ILRMLBSIBMH* written under a team photo of the New York Rangers.

I tore out the photograph and later that day waved it in front of Missy's face. "And what's this?"

She looked unsure—a rarity for her. "I love Red

Meadow Lake," she said, "but sometimes it breaks my heart."

I thought about my own evolving relationship to the lake. "Is that meant for you or me?" I asked.

"Both of us, maybe."

On that Valentine's Day when I awoke early, I tossed the newspaper to the kitchen table and removed a carton of orange juice from our new refrigerator. As my mother had proclaimed after my first AA meeting, she had completely renovated our kitchen, re-creating the same one that was profiled in the glossy six-page spread in *Better Homes and Gardens*. Our new kitchen, with its futuristic appliances and shiny tile, granite countertops, and breakfast nook, was the talk of the lake for several weeks—until the butcher and his wife sparked an even greater level of architectural envy by installing a bowling alley in their basement.

I sat down at the table and, without even looking at the front page, flipped to the sports section and searched for a Valentine's message from Missy. Sometimes her coded messages were obvious, but more often they were subtle and difficult to locate. That morning, I scanned the photographs, articles, advertisements, and box scores in search of Missy's handwriting, but found nothing. Disappointed, I turned to the first sports page and saw that the Knicks, my favorite team, had beaten the Rockets. I checked the scores from the high schools in other Essex County towns: Bloomfield, Glen Ridge, Montclair, the Oranges, even the Caldwells. After consuming most of the sports section, I again scanned the pages to see if I had missed a note from Missy. Weequahic had played Mount Pleasant the night before and there, in the article's margin, was a message from Missy. She had written the letters *IHVD*. I laughed, for I shared her sentiment: *I hate Valentine's Day.*

Below an article about the West Essex High School basketball team, Missy had written me another note. *Most madness is self-inflicted*, it said. *Let Helen be.*

Chapter 18

~~~~~~~~~~

In the middle of March, Papa and Nana threw a lavish party in honor of their fiftieth anniversary. They rented out the entire clubhouse and invited more than two hundred guests, a crowd mixed with friends from Red Meadow and Weequahic, with clients and work associates, with family members close and distant.

There were third cousins from Baltimore whom I hadn't seen in years, including a pompous boy my age. My mother pushed the two of us together and said, "You two are blood and you're the same age, so you'll have lots in common." And then she drifted off to the dance floor, leaving me and this distant cousin to stare at each other in competitive silence and then withdraw in relief to opposite ends of the room. I was impressed by the boy's refusal to pretend that he had even the slightest interest in me—as I felt the same way.

There, crammed into a sleeveless gown covered in gold sequins, was Myrna Mandel, Papa's plump secretary who knew more about his professional life than anyone in our family; she stood by the side of her husband, a man whose social awkwardness manifested in a perspiration that discolored the back and armpits of his khaki suit. Bonnie Schwartz, the most beautiful woman at the lake, posed at the bar and awaited her martini, while her husband half-heartedly flirted with the hostess—a college girl who carried a tray of pigs in a blanket and deli mustard. I was baffled that a man with such a pretty wife could show interest in another woman.

Uncle Max and Aunt Muriel were there too. I noticed that they were trying to hold on to their wineglasses, napkins, and lit cigarettes, while at the same time dipping latkes into a bowl of applesauce. As something was bound to fall, I offered to help. Max gave me his glass, and Muriel handed me her Newport, burned almost down to the filter. Their hands now free, they each devoured several potato pancakes before turning their attention to me. I gave Muriel a kiss on the cheek, which was painted with several layers of powdery makeup. When she turned to wave to the rabbi, I coughed and quickly wiped the bitter-smelling rouge from my lips.

Max looked at me and, rather than hug me as he had done since the earliest days of my youth, extended his hand as if he were greeting a stranger. "And you would be?"

I laughed, thinking that he was joking. "Benjamin," I responded with a grin and extended my hand.

"Benjamin? Huh, I don't believe we've met." He spoke with an earnestness that frightened me.

"It's a pleasure to meet you, Max," I replied, playing along with what I continued to hope was his shtick.

"Are you from around here, Benjamin? From here in Atlantic Beach?" he added, referring to a Jewish community in New York that I'd never visited. He again spoke with such seriousness that I began to question if he were indeed joking. Max's sense of humor was not one that involved staying in character too long; he favored one-liners over comedic tales. "In and out, in and out," he once told me about his approach—so his commitment to this feigned cluelessness surprised me.

I giggled, but Muriel was not amused. "Honey," she said, pinching her husband's elbow, "you know who this is. It's Benjamin ... Abe and Lillian's boy. Louie's grandson." She took the cigarette from my hand. "You've known him since he's *this big*." She dipped and dropped her hand below her knee.

"Okay, okay," he said.

Muriel looked at me. She scraped her top front teeth over her lower lip and painted them with a blur of scarlet. She then smiled wearily, thus revealing to me yet another secret about my uncle. My thoughts turned to Max's older brother, a Newark cop who suffered from a progressive dementia so severe that at the end of his life he was reduced to a stammering, infantile state, one in which he was entirely dependent on caretakers for even the most basic tasks. Spanning the width of that generation—male siblings and cousins—and then back several more, there was a familiar pattern: the men on my mother's side were likely to be afflicted with a pernicious senility that ruthlessly destroyed their faculties.

Max looked at his wife, then at me. "Of course, of course. Benjamin. Well boy, you've turned into a fine young man, haven't you." I don't believe he recognized me, but was merely following Muriel's direction.

My aunt pressed close and squeezed his arm. "Your uncle's delivering a toast tonight," she said to me with pride and with some trepidation. "And he'll also introduce the show," she continued—a reference to the skit my mother and her two cousins had written and would perform. "Isn't that right, honey?" She kissed Max on the cheek.

With watery eyes and a vacant look on his once expressive face, he said, "That's right, that's right ... a toast. A toast tonight."

I was nervous about the state of his mind and his ability to entertain a crowd. "I'm looking forward to it, Uncle Max," I said. I asked myself why Muriel would expose him to potential embarrassment, but as I now look back on that evening, I believe that she, too, was unable to let go of the identity that we were all invested in: Max the Entertainer.

Resplendent in his tailored suit, Sid Lowenthal stood nearby and, after chatting with the butcher, approached us. He held a lowball and, given his attendance at the AA meeting, I was curious if it contained alcohol or soda. "Muriel ... Max ... Benjamin," he said. He gave my aunt a kiss on the cheek and shook Max's hand, then mine. "What an evening," he said. "Fifty years."

"Fifty years," Max repeated. "A miracle."

Just then, Cammy danced over to Sid, grabbed him by the hand, and led him to the dance floor. "Sorry," she called out cheerfully to us as she twirled about.

"Sorry ..." Max muttered. He snatched a Swedish meatball from a passing tray. "You know the surgeon's a killer, Ben ... a stone-cold killer."

"Max!" my aunt cried.

Was it possible, I thought, that Max knew something about Sid, about Helen's death?

"He *is*. Just last week a patient died on his operating table," my uncle said. "Went in alive... came out dead. Sounds like murder to me."

Muriel placed her hand on Max's back. "Come now, honey, you know what happened there. That was fifteen years ago. Not last week. And it wasn't Sid's fault. It was that anesthesiologist from Millburn who made the mistake. I think Freed was his name. Sid got cleared by the medical board, and Freed got suspended. I remember it from the papers. These things happen, Max. Surgery's a dangerous thing."

From across the room, my aunt and uncle eyed the hostess with the tiny franks, and they darted after her like hungry jackals. I turned and saw Missy and her parents standing next to an ice sculpture of a fish: it looked like a mutant carp, a scary thing with an enormous head, sharp dorsal spines, and two stumpy appendages extending from its sides. Missy noticed me and waved, then, with a roll of the eyes, pointed her thumb in the direction of the strange ice sculpture melting over her shoulder. "A coelacanth," she declared.

The din of the party was interrupted by the sound of one fork, then several, then an orchestra of forks tapping against glass—and as the frequency and volume of taps built in a crescendo, the conversations declined until the room was quiet.

I looked up to see Max standing on the band platform at the front of the room, glass in one hand, fork in the other. Satisfied that the room was still enough for his toast, he slid the fork into the breast pocket of his suit jacket, the tines peeking upward, and placed the glass on top of the snare drum. And after turning on the amplifier and setting it to seven—two higher than was normal for this system—he cleared his throat and lifted the microphone to his mouth.

"Welcome, friends, family..." A feedback shriek blared from the speakers, causing the guests to wince and cover their ears. Max paused, and I looked to my father, who made a frantic gesture with his hands, an indication that I should fix the problem—so I scampered up to the stage, stepped behind my uncle, and adjusted the amplifier. Confused by the noise and my movement, Max continued, this time at a tolerable volume. "Welcome, friends, family, and *freeloaders*..." He paused, expecting to be rewarded with laughter, only to be met with a pitiful quiet. He looked around the room, at the people who had enjoyed his jokes for decades. "I welcome you all to this, the golden anniversary of the esteemed Mr. and Mrs. Louis B. Fox."

From my position on the side of the platform, I could see that Max was reading from a card cupped in his right palm. He'd always prided himself on memorizing the words, the inflections and timing of his jokes, on improvising when circumstances—a broken microphone, a heckler—called for a change, and seeing him read his lines further clarified to me that all was not right, that his mind was in rapid decline.

Max fidgeted with the card and tried to hide it behind the cuff of his shirt, but with his hands shaking, the card popped out and fell to the floor. He looked at it, then over to me. There was desperation in his plaintive gaze, an understanding, a concession perhaps that the few days that lay ahead would never be as good as the many days behind. In his moist eyes, I saw a forlorn plea for help—a supplication for more time.

Trying to make myself less noticeable, I bent down at the waist and crossed the stage. I picked up the card and turned my back to the audience so they couldn't see what I was doing, then placed the card in my uncle's coat pocket. From my spot on the side of the stage, I saw my father across the room; he raised a thumb in acknowledgment of the mitzvah—the good deed—I had done.

At our family's major celebratory events—anniversaries, bar mitzvahs, graduations, weddings—we had a tradition that often overshadowed the reason for the event itself: a satirical musical skit that poked fun at our middle-class Jewish lives. That night, my uncle pulled the card from his pocket and, without even attempting to hide it, announced the skit. "Now, performing an original number ... 'Three Hundred Down and Fifteen a Month' ... the beautiful, the fabulous, the talented Fox girls!"

As Max stepped to the side of the stage, his foot caught in a tangle of electrical cords and he fell forward, regaining his balance only at the last moment by grabbing the edge of the upright piano. He reached for his bruised shin, which had cracked into a speaker. "Fuck ... *fucking fuck*," he growled. I extended my hand, held his elbow, and led him off the stage.

"Thanks," he said. "Thanks, Jeffrey." To correct him would have been too painful—for him and for me.

From the other side of the stage, my mother and her two cousins approached. They stepped up on the stage in age order, oldest to youngest—Selma, Lillian, and Norma.

For weeks, the three cousins had been writing and practicing the skit at my mother's shop after hours, and they'd managed to keep it a secret from all of us. So when they turned to the audience dressed as hoboes—their hair in feral disarray, skirts soiled, bare feet caked in dirt—the crowd howled in delight.

"And a-one and a-two and a-three," my mother called out, snapping her fingers with each count. On three, the ladies leaned close together, their cheeks pressing, and sang: "Three hundred dollars to buy the lot, three hundred dollars to grass the plot, three hundred dollars for railroad fare, three hundred dollars to fog the air ..."

The ladies were mocking the unexpected costs of homeownership at the lake, and it was the reference to spraying with mosquito-killing pesticide that most amused the crowd. The next day, the *Rockaway Record* ran a photo of the cousins dressed like vagabonds, an honor that my mother would often recall with the pride of a minor celebrity.

At the end of the skit, after the applause and laudatory howls subsided, Max ascended to the stage in choppy steps. He appeared grumpy and irritated, and he scowled at my mother. It was as if he were jealous that their act had been received with such fanfare, a reaction that he could no longer elicit.

Max held the microphone in one hand and the top of the stand with the other. He looked out over the crowd. I expected that this would be the moment he'd call Nana and Papa up to the stage and toast them. Instead, he continued to gaze blankly at the celebrants, above them, through the tall windows, out to the stiff, drooping limbs of the willows and the frozen lake in the distance.

My aunt took two steps toward the stage. "Max," she pleaded.

He held up his hand, a signal for Muriel to stop. He tapped the microphone, filling the room with a percussive thump. "You know, you know, I almost filled in for Milton Berle once," he told the baffled crowd. "Or was it Danny Kaye? Sid Caesar? Muriel, who was it? Red Buttons? Was it Red? I don't remember." He glared at his wife, who was so dismayed that she did not respond. "I don't remember. Red, Danny, Sid, Milty. I don't remember... I don't *fucking* remember. Does anyone here remember? Muriel? You were there... who was it?"

"Milton Berle," she whispered.

"Not Mel Brooks?"

"No, not Mel Brooks. Same initials, though. Maybe that's why you're confused."

"Well, fuck Mel Brooks... and fuck Milton Berle and Danny and Sid and fuck Red. Fuck all of 'em!"

Her mouth agape, Muriel reached for her husband's hand. "Max... Max, *please*."

My father darted up to the stage and whispered something into Max's ear, something that made him laugh and surrender the microphone. Abe then guided my aunt and uncle through the nervous crowd and to the front entrance. Before stepping out of the clubhouse, Max stopped and turned, waving grandly in my direction, and with a finality that has haunted me to this day.

"He's a killer," he called out to me—and pointed to Sid Lowenthal. "Trust me, I know things." Uncle Max rapped his right temple with his knuckles. "Doc's a stone... cold... killer."

I watched as Muriel, with the utmost care, escorted

Max to the passenger seat of their car and then got behind the wheel. I pressed my face against the window as they pulled out of the parking lot—red lights disappearing around First Beach. I felt sick; I felt somehow complicit in his breakdown. My palms turned clammy, my breathing quickened. Distressed, I ran to the bar and stole Bonnie Schwartz's martini while she was searching the room for her philandering husband; and after downing that drink, booze-soaked olives included, I pulled a cigarette butt from a half glass of discarded Scotch and drank that too.

That was the last time any of us would see Uncle Max. Later that evening, he would pin his old Grossinger's Hotel name tag to his lapel, put on the sequined turban that he wore when entertaining guests by the pool, and, with an old microphone cord, hang himself from a ceiling pipe.

Chapter 19

~~~~~~

A few days after Max's funeral, my family gathered for a Sunday lunch at Paul's Diner in Mountain Lakes—a simple place right on Route 46 that had been around since the late 1940s. My mother dipped three french fries into a bowl of gravy and, working her way around the table, pointed to each of us: Nana, Papa, me, and my father

"It was a fall," she said. "I spoke to Muriel, and that's what we'll tell everyone . . . a fall. There can't be any mention of what happened. Not the turban, not the cord . . . nothing."

Lillian's directive confused me. "How did he fall?" I asked as she stuffed the fries into her mouth. "How should we say he fell? Down the stairs? Off a ladder?" I was bothered by our family's commitment to hiding our tragedies and magnifying our successes.

A bit of gravy dripped down my mother's chin. She chewed furiously, wiped the gravy from her lips with the back of her hand, like a sloppy man, and then looked at me as if she could not comprehend my idiocy. "How did he *fall*? Down *what*?" She reached for another trio of fries. "What does it matter? I don't know...the basement steps? If you say 'a fall,' no one's going to ask you what kind of fall. Who do you know who's so rude that they'd ask how a person fell and died?"

I shrugged and drew on my straw. I tried to pull up some of the thick milkshake, but a ball of ice cream stuck to the bottom and prevented the liquid's flow. After lifting the straw and bending my head low and to the side, I opened my mouth wide and sucked in the chunk of mint chocolate chip, thus further aggravating my mother. "Yup, bad form," I agreed. "A fall makes sense." I sucked again on the straw. "But how about a heart attack? Seems like everyone's having a heart attack these days." In search of support, I looked around the table. Everyone but my mother looked down to their plates.

Lillian drew the blade of her knife across the table's edge. "A *fall*," she snapped, ending the discussion.

Defeated yet again by my mother, overwhelmed by the force of her personality, I turned my attention to the meatloaf and mashed potatoes before me. A deep sadness arose in me, and I moved the food around the plate with my fork. As I sat with my family in silence, my thoughts again turned dark and varied: the disconnection from my old Newark friends that widened with each passing month, the violent swings in mood to which my mother was prone, her need to hide from the world our family's misfortunes, and of course my role—real or imagined—in Max's decline, his death.

Lillian had an inexplicable need to withhold bad news, an obsession with transforming even the most minor adversity into something more palatable. Was it the result of an insecurity that threatened her, threatened her sense of self, her esteem? Or was there some strange competition with others in which she, unaware, was the only participant? Did it stem from her father's financial crisis, the one that defined her childhood? Or was it Bernice's illness and death that caused this shame? I did not know, but as we came from a people who had suffered for so long, who so easily discussed our centuries of hardship, our misfortune, and our survival, her refusal to acknowledge our own family's setbacks suggested to me some deeper psychic malady.

My mood sank deeper. I cut off a piece of lukewarm meatloaf and put it in my mouth. Whether it was my sadness or the consistency of the meat, I found the food revolting and spit it into a napkin, prompting yet another critical look from my mother. I wanted to get up and leave, to run far away from my family—Lillian, in particular—but we were too far from Red Meadow to walk. I felt trapped. Stuck in this booth, stuck in this restaurant, stuck in this life, I pushed my plate into the center of the table and leaned over my milkshake in defiance.

"Ben!" someone called out to me from the pastry case. I looked up and was surprised to see Missy waving at me. She beamed. "Number forty-three," she yelled, a counter ticket in her hand. I glanced at the sign above the counter and saw that she was next in line.

"Excuse me, but Missy's here," I said to my father, who sat at the end of the booth and blocked my exit.

"Benjamin, we're not finished here," Lillian said. She pointed to the uneaten food on my plate.

Abe must have sensed both my melancholy and the

antidote for this melancholy—Missy—for he stood and allowed me to pass. My mother, threatened by the formation of even the most minor alliance, bristled with anger.

"I'll get a ride home with Missy," I told my parents. As I left, I snatched a handful of my mother's fries, further provoking her; my father smiled at my puckishness, a transgression for which we both knew he would be punished—perhaps with yet another banishment to the couch.

As Missy and I stood in front of the pastry case, my family was in the process of leaving and, as was their custom, making a huge scene. They never could get out of a restaurant—or for that matter a house, beach, theater, hardware store, funeral parlor, even a bris—without a big production. My mother was kibitzing with the young waitress, lecturing the poor girl about romance, telling her that her boyfriend—who had just dropped out of trade school—was a no-good bum and that she should leave him.

Papa was going over the check yet again, calling out to anyone who would listen, "Who ordered the sausage? I didn't see any sausage. You have any idea what they charge for sausage?" Nana and Papa had somehow gotten their gloves mixed up, and I watched as my grandfather tried to pull a pair of slender, mink-trimmed gloves over his meaty hands. The manager watched in bafflement, confused no doubt that this group was capable of functioning in society.

Missy poked at the glass, instructing the girl behind the case. "I'll have one of those bear claws," she said, "and two of the linzer tortes and ... and one ... make it two of those black-and-whites in the back." She turned to me.

"You like black-and-whites?"

"I do."

"One more cookie, please," she told the girl. "Actually," she said to me, "I think it's probably *blacks-and-white*. Maybe that's the right way to say it ... like *attorneys general*? It's hard to tell which one gets the plural. *Blacks* or *whites*? I think it's one or the other, but not both." She took out a pen and scribbled on a napkin. She held it up. "*Black-and-whites* looks right to me. What do you think?"

I shrugged and watched as my family moved in a pack through the dining room and out to the parking lot. I watched through the window as Papa stood by the side of his Bonneville and handed the mink gloves to my grandmother, receiving in return his own leather ones. I watched the four of them hug and kiss goodbye, then get into their cars.

After the counter girl finished packing the pastry order, she handed Missy two white boxes tied in thin string, which we took over to the cashier. As Missy paid, the manager—a cigarette bouncing off his lower lip—ran past me, through the front doors, and out into the parking lot. He waved a manila envelope and raced after Papa's car as it pulled out of the lot, but my grandfather didn't notice the man in the rearview mirror and made a sharp left out of the driveway, west on 46.

The manager, apparently exhausted from this shortest of dashes, raised his arms, placed his palms behind his head, and puffed out his chest to encourage the flow of oxygen—impeded, I suspected, by the burning cigarette that remained stuck to his lower lip. He dropped his arms, slapped the envelope a couple of times against his thigh, and trudged back to the diner. When he entered, he noticed me standing next to the cashier.

"Young man, I didn't even see you there. Could've saved me a sprint outside." He extended the envelope to me. "This was on the floor, under the table. Someone must've dropped it... one of your family, I figure."

I examined the envelope, which was sealed and free of writing and type. "Not sure whose it is, but I'll bring it home and see."

I pinched the envelope under my arm and grabbed a handful of mints from the dish next to the register. On the ride back to the lake, I sat in the passenger seat while Missy drove. I held the two boxes in my lap. Missy's proximity, the pressure of the boxes, and the vibrations of the car on the road—in particular, a series of potholes on Mountain Avenue—threatened a potentially embarrassing tumescence, but I managed to fill my mind with enough dark thoughts—the simultaneous deaths of my parents, thermonuclear war, a family of ducklings being crushed by a train—that I preempted any noticeable movement.

After Missy pulled up to my driveway on Lake Shore, I stepped from the car and centered the pastry boxes on the passenger seat. She looked at me in her knowing way. "Weirdo," she said, which left me wondering if she'd been reading my mind.

The driveway was empty, an indication that my parents hadn't come straight home from the diner. As I'd been doing for the last several weeks with a frequency that bordered on maniacal, I stopped at the mailbox on the way to the house and pulled out a bundle of letters and catalogs. We were in the middle of college acceptance season, and I was desperate to learn if I'd gotten into

NYU. Over the preceding weeks, each day had brought no news from the school and mounting acceptances for my classmates, triggering in me a series of low-grade anxiety attacks—clammy hands and racing heart—from which I could obtain little relief.

I had become enchanted by New York, by Missy's version of the city, really, with its many pockets—its inviting cafés and bars, cozy nooks, hidden fireplaces—cramped, dark sanctuaries in which one could read and write, drink and think; a jumbled mass of humanity that by virtue of its chaos and size gave birth to innumerable refuges for the creative, the damaged, the odd. Given my fascination with the city, I was eager to start my new life in the Village.

As Missy drove away, I flipped through the stack of bills, catalogs, and letters until I came across an envelope with the purple NYU logo. My hands damp, my eyes dancing, I tore it open and scanned the first few lines with excitement. The words *pleasure, invitation,* and *honor* indicated that I had been accepted! Euphoric, I ran to my room and jumped on my bed as if it were a trampoline. I bounced so high that my head hit the ceiling and, slightly dazed, wondered when my parents would return so I could tell them the good news. I thought about how happy Missy would be. She had applied to Stanford, Harvard, Princeton, Oxford, and Cambridge—and was accepted to all of them. Cambridge had offered her a generous scholarship, which, given her father's precarious financial condition, determined her choice. And for the past several weeks, she had been waiting eagerly for me to get a letter from NYU.

I imagined my collegiate life in Greenwich Village,

then tossed both the acceptance letter and the envelope from the diner on the side table. I lay down on the bed. Exhausted, perhaps by the marvelous news or perhaps by my mother's latest infuriating attempt at revisionist history, I quickly fell asleep. I awoke several hours later, arising in a state of sweaty confusion, unsure of the time or even the day of the week. I glanced over to the clock beside my bed and saw that it was almost dinnertime.

I leaned over and grabbed the acceptance letter, reading it again, admiring the signature of the dean of admissions. I was exhilarated by a lofty goal accomplished and, guided by this achievement, imagined what path my life might take, what academic accomplishment, what lucrative career awaited me. I thought about the girls I would meet at college—different colors and religions, poor ones, rich ones, girls who'd gone to private schools like Newark Academy, maybe even a shiksa from some fancy boarding school in New England; I thought about the places where I could drink—dark Irish pubs, trendy cafés, music clubs like Cafe au Go Go; I thought about the different paths that Missy and I were taking; but mostly, I thought about the freedom I would at last enjoy, away from my family and my insular community.

I tossed the NYU letter on the side table and lifted the other envelope—the one from the diner—up to the ceiling light. Curious, I tore it open and removed several sheets of paper, which after some examination appeared to be a document relating to Dr. Lowenthal's surgical practice—a settlement agreement of some sort among Sid, an insurance company, and the New Jersey State Board of Medical Examiners. I read the letter: there was a red stamp at the top that said *Draft*, a reference to an expensive fine, and a mention of a possible suspension if the surgeon failed to comply in the future. I read further, to the part that described *billing irregularities* on the part of Sid's medical practice. The surgeon had an impeccable professional reputation, so the allegations in the letter surprised me and deepened my growing suspicions of him.

I noticed that Papa's name was at the bottom of the letter—cc'd under the signature line. As Papa was Sid's accountant, I assumed that my grandfather had dropped the envelope at the diner. I wondered about my grandfather, the man whom I had long worshipped and considered a model of integrity and sound judgment. I pictured him trudging through the water and carefully lifting Helen's dead body onto the mossy embankment. And then I thought about the lantern lights during the storm and how he had denied flashing them. I had a fleeting, dreadful thought: What if Papa wasn't the man I thought him to be? What if he knowingly represented clients who, like Sid, did bad things? Ashamed of these thoughts, I considered the argument that Papa would make: as an accountant, he was responsible for advising clients who made mistakes and helping them get out of trouble. "Just like a lawyer, but with numbers," he once told me.

From my bedroom I could now detect the presence of my parents: the smell of chicken, carrots, and potatoes being broiled in our new restaurant-style oven—a cozy, homey smell that to this day engenders in me bittersweet feelings of the security, coupled with achy loss. I took the letter and the envelope into the living room, where my parents were sipping their favorite cocktails: a dry gin martini for my mother and a Moscow mule in a chilled copper mug for my father.

Lillian and Abe lounged on the crushed velvet sofa while Tom Jones's "Delilah" played on the phonograph. I could tell as soon as I entered that they were intoxicated; their voices were loud, their laughter excessive, their physical presentations sloppy and uninhibited. My mother's blouse was open an extra button, revealing to my distress her bra strap, and the wings of my father's dress shirt fell over the front of his slacks. Another sure sign of drunkenness, they appeared to enjoy each other, so much so that Abe's future banishment to the couch seemed impossible.

As I watched them drink and smoke, laugh and flirt like young lovers, they appeared more human to me—less parental. I waved the acceptance letter and snapped it in the smoky air. "Great news!" I yelled, which prompted them to separate—perhaps from the embarrassment of having been observed—and turn to me. "I got into NYU!"

My parents shrieked and, cigarettes and drinks in hand, ran toward me. Together they hugged me, and I could feel not only their love but my father's cold copper mug against my neck and the smoke from Lillian's cigarette burning my eyes. They exulted in my success.

"I *knew* it," Abe exclaimed.

"I'm so proud," my mother declared with moist eyes as she poured a half glass of wine for me. "Just because it's a special occasion," she said, "and only a few sips."

As was my nature, I finished the wine in three gulps and enjoyed the rapid change in my body chemistry. My mother downed her martini in celebratory fashion and refilled her glass, and I watched in awe as she quickly finished the new drink. As she teetered on her heels and placed the glass on the table, I noticed a slight shift in her personality, in her carriage. "You know," she said, "I could've gotten into NYU too." She tried to start another cigarette, but couldn't get the lighter going. "It's just that I didn't have the chance. I was smart enough to get in, and had the grades too. It was just the money. You both know what happened when Papa's partner stole that money. But I could have got in. I mean, if you and your father could get in, well..."

"I know, Mom. I know."

My father put his arm over Lillian's shoulder and comforted her—and I understood what had just happened. Once again, my mother had made something that wasn't about her into something that was *all* about her.

My moment diminished, I looked down at the envelope that I'd gotten at the diner and held it aloft.

"What's that?" she asked.

"The manager at Paul's gave this to me, said it was under the table after we left and figured one of us dropped it." I handed the envelope to my father. "Looks like Papa's... something to do with Sid."

Curious, Abe began to open the envelope, but Lillian snatched it from his hand. My mother flipped through the documents, then took a languorous drag of her cigarette. "I'll let Papa know he dropped them," she said in an informed manner that suggested some prior familiarity with the envelope's contents. She fanned herself with the papers and stared at me. She seemed annoyed either by me or by the document. As if she were trying to determine whether I was friend or foe, she quietly assessed me, then picked up the phone and dialed my grandfather. "Ben gave me an envelope," she said. "Something to do with Sid's practice." Lillian raised her hand to her mouth in a manner that suggested she'd just remembered something important. "Okay, okay. Yes, I figured as much." She paused to listen to Papa, and from across the room I could hear his muffled and indecipherable voice. "Uh-huh... uh-huh... okay," my mother said.

Lillian put down the phone and addressed me. "Papa said thanks for bringing these back." I sensed in my mother disingenuousness, an evasiveness that arose whenever she sought to hide our family's flaws. I watched as she marched down the hall, slapping the envelope violently against her thigh—and I wondered why this document had so irritated her.

Chapter 20

~~~~~~~

In early May, just weeks before the lake would be infused with the vital energy of the seasonal residents, the *Rockaway Record* ran an article about an "environmental incident" at nearby Hope Pond. According to the report, a stone quarry adjacent to the pond had released a toxic stew into the once pristine water.

My father was the first in our family to read about the accident, and he feared that the quarry's harmful effluents might contaminate our lake. "That's how we get most of our water, you know," he said. "The little creek that lets out at Second Beach? You know the one ... all that water comes from Hope Pond, feeds the whole lake." I knew the creek, for Missy and I often caught crayfish and minnows there with a net, and sometimes even a towel. Abe continued to read. "PCBs, petroleum, ammonium nitrate fuel oil, unidentified chemical solvents, it says here ... but says the quarry contained the leak and there's no harm to people or wildlife." He tossed the paper to the table and clenched his jaw. "That's bullshit, you realize ... total bullshit. They say that every time they screw up, all these corporations. Only a few specks and couldn't hurt a fly. Next thing you know, everything's dead."

My mother snatched the paper from the table. "Don't be so dramatic. You're always making something out of nothing."

"Something out of *nothing*?" he responded. "Don't be so *dramatic*?"

"They're hardworking people at the quarry, you know, and people make mistakes sometimes."

"They shouldn't make a mistake like this," Abe countered.

Lillian's smile was imperious. "You ever make a mistake?" She challenged him with a tone that signaled imminent cruelty. She raised her eyes to the ceiling, mimicking some deep reflection. "Ever misdiagnose someone?"

Stung by her implication, Abe turned red: we all knew that he'd been sued for malpractice once in his career, twelve years earlier when he failed to detect a malignant lump in a patient's throat. Wounded, livid, he rose from the table and strode down to the dock, where he sat on a chair and smoked a cigar. As he puffed away, I imagined that the smoke gathering around his head and integrating into the dense fog might very well have been pouring from his ears.

Within days of the *Record*'s report, we learned that the spill had, as my father feared, infected our lake. The first sign that something was wrong was when Nathan Gold was puttering along on the *Ark*, from the clubhouse toward Split Rock. As Nathan described the encounter, he stood behind the wheel and saw something floating in the water before him. He cut the boat's engine and glided toward this white thing, which he first thought might be a garbage bag or a tarp of some sort, only to realize that a mute swan was dead. As he recounted this story, I thought of Helen's body and wondered why one's natural instinct on seeing something dead in the water is to seek the most benign explanation.

"It's the chemicals," my father said.

"Maybe the bird had a heart attack," my mother countered. "Ben here seems to think everyone's got to have a heart attack sooner or later."

"Maybe it fell down a flight of stairs," I said.

The next day, several dozen sunfish—their milky eyes dangling from the sockets, their gills blood red—floated up on First Beach, a rotting, stinking mess that terrified the children and forced the beach's closure. My father raised his eyebrows when he heard the news. "Look who's right this time," he said to Lillian, tired of her righteousness.

Lillian hated to be challenged, to be reminded of even the slightest imperfection; she was incapable of laughing at herself. "A broken clock's right twice a day," she replied and turned her back on Abe.

For the next week we stayed out of the water and watched the sick lake from a safe distance: there was no swimming, no fishing, no boating. Gone was the dance of slicing, swerving motorboats, sailboats, canoes, and pontoon boats; gone were the swimming races; gone were the fishing rods that hung over the water like the bent branches of old willows.

Instead of participating in the lake's social and natural ecosystems, we instead became spectators. We were worried caretakers of a sick patient, checking vital signs obsessively: the water's smell, its pallor, its hue, the movement of fish beneath the water's surface, the lap of water against the retaining wall (its pulse), the condition of a pickerel frog when it leapt from the toxic water and sought refuge in the thick reeds. Each day, the patient showed marginal but steady improvement. The smell slowly turned less chemical, more organic, more musky; the water's clarity—a result of the death of much of the lake's flora—devolved back into a comforting, familiar murkiness; the fish regained their speed, their thickness, their sheen. By Memorial Day, the lake had returned to a state approximating normalcy. And although we could not forgive the rock quarry for the damage done, we did move on—and we gave little thought to the quarry until the moment when ignoring it would later become impossible.

Chapter 21

~~~~~~~

Missy called me a few days after the lake was contaminated and invited me to take a ride with her into the city. "It'll get our minds off the lake," she said. "Those bastards at the quarry screwed it up. Screwed *everything* up."

"Sure," I said, recalling the image of a dead mallard duck that I'd seen floating near First Beach.

"Village?" she offered. "Central Park?"

I thought about NYU, about the adventures that awaited me. "Village," I said.

On the ride to the city, I was so distracted by fantasies of my college life that I didn't realize where we were until Missy held out her hand. "Split the toll?"

I looked up to see that we were on the helix that led down to the Lincoln Tunnel's ugly mouth. Surprised, I pulled a quarter out of my pocket and handed it to her. "So where do you want to go? Where in the Village?"

"I've got a few places in mind. There's a vintage place on Bleecker. Remember the one? Bleecker and

MacDougal. Last time we were there, they said they were getting some leather jackets ... leather bomber jackets. So I want to stop by. And then let's walk over to Patchin Place. Have you heard of it?"

I felt the same surge of shame that arose every time Missy knew something that I did not. "I haven't. Is it a restaurant? A bar?"

One of the things I loved about Missy was her purity. She was so modest that she assumed others knew as much as she did. So, when she asked fellow students arcane physics questions or referred to obscure poets and Renaissance sculptors, she fully expected that they would have the answers. And when she was met with slack jaws and vacant gazes, she responded in such a measured, sincere way that the uninformed never felt inadequate.

"Patchin Place is where E. E. Cummings lived for many years. The poet. He and his wife lived there. I think her name was Morehouse, Marion Morehouse. She was a model, you know. I haven't been there, to Patchin Place, but I read about it. It's supposed to be a charming little street, right off Sixth ... Sixth Avenue, not Street."

Missy found a parking space on Bleecker, around the corner from the clothing store. "I know your mother calls it vintage, but it's really just old stuff from dead people," she said as we entered the store. On the far wall was a rack of used leather jackets. "Come with me." She grabbed my hand and pulled me toward the rack. There were a dozen or so in a variety of styles and colors: black, brown, tan, even a small red-white-and-blue one, motorcycle jackets, bombers, three-quarter length, and one cut like a peacoat. "Try this," she said, pulling out a Steve McQueen–style motorcycle jacket with reinforced shoulders.

I put on the jacket, rolling my shoulders forward, extending my arms until it fit just right. "How does it look?" Missy smiled. "You look tough. *Good* tough."

Encouraged, I turned around and faced a full-length mirror. I was surprised by the change in my appearance. Not at all fashion-minded, I tended toward khakis and button-down shirts, jeans, T-shirts, and sweaters. But the cut of the jacket, its heft and style, its scuffed rawness, gave rise to a feeling of coolness, of potency. The padded shoulders offset my narrow frame, the worn elbows suggested fights waged and crashes survived, the dangling waist belt foretold the need to harness up for a high-speed ride.

"I like it," I said and turned to look at my profile in the mirror. "How much is it?"

Missy reached for the tag. "Fifteen dollars."

I pulled a twenty out of my pocket and showed it to Missy. From the work I did for Sid, I'd made enough not only to pay back the rabbi but also to save some extra spending money. "Why don't you try one on? How about the red-white-and-blue one?"

Missy put on the jacket, which looked like something Evel Knievel might wear. Cut low at the waist with narrow shoulders, it fit perfectly. "You're getting that," I said and guided her over to the mirror. "There's no way you're leaving without it."

I could tell from the slightest flourish that Missy, too, felt empowered by the leather jacket. She lifted her right wrist and tugged at the price tag. "Twenty dollars," she lamented. Given her family's financial struggles, she could not afford the jacket.

I snatched another twenty from my pocket and passed

it in front of Missy's eyes. "I'm flush, and it's my birthday present to you."

She laughed. "That's two years in a row you've given me a present. So, thank you for that. But out of curiosity, do you have any idea when my birthday actually is?"

I recalled the house dress I gave her last summer— blue with sunflowers. "I have no idea."

"Ides of March," she said. "That should be easy for you to remember."

I paid for the jackets and then, in our new leather armor, we strutted around the Village. I'd brought a flask of apricot brandy with me, which I drank as we walked to the poet's home. I offered it to Missy two or three times, but as expected she declined. As we walked, we each benefited from an added kick in the step, a verticality to our swagger, a confidence that was the result of our leather jackets.

"Over here," Missy said, pointing to a small lane. "That's Patchin Place." She led me through a wrought iron gate and into the block-long enclave, a tree-lined sanctuary only feet from the noisy street. At the end of the cul-de-sac stood an old-fashioned gas lamppost, and over the southern building line rose the clock tower of the Jefferson Market Library.

"When I think of poets, I think streams and meadows … not this," I said.

"I think you can be a poet anywhere." She pointed to a three-story building on the left: Cummings's number four. "And this could be the best place, right here. Maybe it's the dissonance, the noise that inspires … more than peace and quiet, even. Although they say he hated noise."

We sat on the stoop of the poet's old building, the

arms of our leather jackets pressed close. "Let's listen for what he heard," Missy said.

There was a yapping Yorkie at the end of the block; from nearby Tenth Street, two drunks argued over a pint; a siren Dopplered up Sixth Avenue; the wind tossed a paper bag over our feet; Jimi Hendrix's "Little Wing" poured from an open window above.

I pointed to the window. "You think Cummings would've liked Hendrix?"

"Definitely," Missy replied. "Listen to these lyrics! Cummings would've *loved* him."

The front door opened behind us and an elderly woman stepped out of the building. Missy and I moved to opposite edges of the stoop to let her pass, and we watched her trudge down the street, toward the gate. "You think she knew Cummings?" Missy asked.

"No doubt." I took another swig of brandy. I'd made my way through half the flask, and I felt buzzed, peaceful, uninhibited. With my motorcycle jacket and my apricot brandy high, I was free from the self-doubt that often crippled me with attacks of anxiety. I moved back toward Missy, so that our arms were again touching.

What happened next was something I would long regret. Missy turned to me when the pause after "Little Wing" gave way to "The Wind Cries Mary." She made a pitter-patter motion over her heart, indicating her love of the song, her love of Hendrix. So intoxicated was I by the romantic setting, the music, my closeness to Missy, and the alcohol that—without even the slightest reflection—I leaned over and kissed her on the lips.

I had given so little thought to this risky maneuver that any reaction by her would have surprised me. Best, of course, would have been an enthusiastic kiss in return; next, maybe a nervous but willing peck, followed by an encouraging smile. Missy's reaction, though, was instantaneous and severe. She gasped and pulled her head back, so hard that she hit the metal railing on the stoop. After staring at me with disgust, she stood and hovered over me. She tugged angrily at her leather jacket—my gift to her—and I feared that she would remove it, throw it to the ground.

"It's time we head back," she said. She stomped toward the gate at the end of Patchin Place without even a glance in my direction. I followed in silence—to her right and several feet behind—until we reached the car. I took my seat on the passenger side and replayed my ill-advised kiss, over and over, as we drove to the lake in silence. I cringed in shame, but I could not muster the courage to discuss it, to apologize, to express my regret at having done something that had damaged what I only then realized was a fragile friendship, one predicated on honoring unspoken boundaries.

Missy didn't talk to me during the hour-long ride back to the lake. She drove in her usual focused and disciplined way: hands on the steering wheel—ten and two—with regular glances at the side and rearview mirrors. After winding through the dark, curling roads of Red Meadow, she dropped me off at my house on Lake Shore, the Dodge's wheels rolling, kicking up gravel, before I even closed the door. That night, I lay in bed and rued my clumsy kiss. I cursed myself. I considered my behavior—what I had done to cause the worst of all possible reactions. Was it simply the fact that I had kissed her? The crossing of a line that was obvious to her but invisible to me? Or was it because I was drunk when I did it? Was she hurt that I didn't kiss her sober, that I was not fully present?

During those final weeks before graduation, Missy had been driving the short distance to school instead of taking the bus. Every weekday morning, she'd pick me up at my house and drive the few minutes to school. The morning after the kiss, I stood at the top of the driveway and, with little hope, awaited her arrival. I checked my watch and saw that it was three minutes past eight—three minutes later than her usual pickup time. Missy was the most punctual person I'd ever met, arriving five minutes early for meals, classes, doctor's appointments, tennis lessons, fishing contests, and anything with a starting time. So I resigned myself to walking up to the corner of Lake Shore and Wenonah to catch the yellow bus. As I walked up the hill, a car slowly passed me on my left: Missy's Dodge. My instinct was to wave to her, to catch her attention in the rearview mirror. But ashamed, I lowered my head and continued toward the bus stop.

I was looking at the ground, not ahead, and didn't realize that Missy had stopped the car on the graveled edge of the road. So immersed was I in my shame that I almost walked into the car's rear bumper. I was only a few inches from the belching exhaust when I looked up to see Missy staring at me through the rear window, her body twisted, her right arm over the top of the passenger seat. As I approached, she leaned over and opened the door for me. I took a few deep breaths—an attempt to slow my heart rate, to ease my anxiety. I sat down and closed the door, my moist palm sliding across the handle.

"Morning," I said, appreciative of her magnanimity.

"Good morning," she responded, the first words she had spoken to me since Patchin Place. "How was your night? Sleep well?"

"Terrible. You?"

"About the same." She pulled the transmission into drive.

I rehearsed my next line, choosing brevity over an epic apology. "Sorry about yesterday... sorry about that. That was stupid of me... so stupid."

Missy paused at a stop sign and waited, so long that a car behind us honked, then pulled around. "Do me a favor?" she demanded.

"Anything."

"Don't ever do that again... not when you've been drinking. It doesn't feel good. For other girls, maybe it's fine... but not for me. Especially with you... with your issues... your issues with booze and how we get along."

I again cursed my bad judgment, my impulsivity. As I glanced at Missy's clenched fists on the steering wheel, I thought of her father and the many problems that his mercurial nature had caused. I admired Missy's clarity, her pragmatism, a commitment to protecting herself from harm. I admired the boundaries that she defined and enforced.

"That's a promise," I said.

Chapter 22

~~~~~~

Sid Lowenthal's oldest daughter was getting married at the clubhouse on Saturday night, and many of our friends and family had arrived for the festivities. I vowed to avoid alcohol after my foolhardy attempt to kiss Missy—and the wedding dinner was my first test of abstinence. I wasn't an invited guest that night, but working as a busboy to make extra cash. I was tasked with cleaning up after cocktail hour and bussing the tables, so I had many opportunities to steal an abandoned drink. But when tempted to knock back the final drops of a lukewarm martini left by the always gorgeous Bonnie Schwartz (her bronze lipstick beckoning me from the glass's edge), I thought of my sloppy, drunken kiss and the shame that followed. I thought about the consequences of my drinking and, mortified, poured the booze into the sink.

Missy didn't attend the dinner, but I found myself scanning the crowd for her nonetheless, seeking the comfort of her face and the palliative effect that she had on my neurochemistry. Nathan Gold's daughter, Becca, saw me from across the room and waved. She was working the coat check that night, and when I waved to her in return, she left her post and crossed the room to greet me. We had known each other since our earliest days, and there was a notable photograph in the family album that showed the two of us at my second birthday, smooching as if we were lovers.

My relationship with her over the years was governed by benign indifference. I found her to be a likable girl, sweet in personality and unremarkable in appearance; we had just enough in common to maintain an uninterrupted pleasantry, but not enough to forge a deeper friendship or romance. Since we were members of the same insular community, though, I felt an obligation to support her. So, when kids from a Bergen County swim team mocked her pudgy physique at a state meet, I intervened in her defense, threatening to punch anyone who disparaged her. As I look back now at my friendship with her, I am ashamed to admit that until that evening, she didn't mean much to me as a person; she did, however, mean a lot to me as a Weequahic girl and a member of the Red Meadow Lake Property Owners Association. She was one of our own.

"How's the night going?" she asked near the end of the evening. "Nice party. I always love working the weddings ... rehearsal dinners too."

"Okay, I guess ... slow," I said, eyeing a half-filled glass of what looked like a Manhattan. I leaned against the wall and watched as the celebrants enjoyed their chocolate mousse, mandelbroit cookies, Maxwell House coffee, and after-dinner drinks. Sid Lowenthal and Cammy crossed the room and approached the head table. On the way, they passed my parents. I watched as Sid's smile disappeared upon sight of Abe and Lillian, and as he passed them with barely an acknowledgement. As I had in the past, I wondered about their relationship, which appeared to be civil, yet distant and cool.

Sid stood behind his daughter and tapped his glass with a fork, indicating his desire to make a toast to the newly married couple. As his daughter, Laurie, blushed, her husband placed his arm over her bare shoulders. I recalled an image of her at Helen's funeral just months earlier, when she was grief-stricken, broken—and here she was in a flash, pretty and self-assured, getting married. I marveled at the resilience of human beings, our ability to persevere, even to regenerate after the most devastating losses.

Sid was a tall, athletic man with a genius for a tailor and a powerful, unaccented voice that carried a room. As an adjunct professor of surgery, he was accustomed to delivering lectures to medical students, teaching residents, and speaking at academic conferences. So, when he stood in front of the large room, surrounded by his family and closest friends, we expected nothing less than a compelling, eloquent toast—and he did not disappoint. He described the marvel of Laurie's birth, how she was two weeks late, reluctant to enter the world—how she came out feet first. He described her calm, considerate nature, evident from the very first days of her life, when she slept through the night and rarely cried. He talked about the velocity of a life, how the speed with which she went from little girl to bride defied the laws of physics. He discussed his growing affection for his son-in-law, Joseph Vogel, a medical student training to be—like him—a surgeon. Most moving was his description of Helen, how she was a strong and beautiful woman who passed on to her daughter some of her finest traits: style, athleticism, kindness, service to others. "We all wish she could be here tonight, to see this ... to see Laurie looking so beautiful, so happy. But she's here somehow." He looked around the room, then up, as if searching for evidence of his dead wife's spirit. "That, I believe."

Sid seemed so kind, so sincere, that I began to doubt my suspicions of him.

"L'chaim," he whispered, his voice shaking with emotion. He raised his glass high and squared his shoulders. "L'chaim!" he yelled—a cry of joy, of anguish, of hope.

"L'chaim," the room roared back. Sid took a moment to enjoy the harmonic power, then leaned down and kissed his crying daughter on the cheek. I watched as he lifted his champagne glass to his mouth and took several lusty sips: unable to maintain his sobriety, he'd again fallen off the wagon.

The crowd had begun to return to their dessert and coffee when something unexpected occurred. Sid and Cammy appeared from my vantage point to be engaged in a minor argument. She tried to stand, but Sid guided her back down to the chair. She slapped at his dissuading hand and rose to her feet, causing him to drop his face into his hands as she tapped a wineglass with a fork. Sid and his daughter looked up to Cammy with alarm, an indication that her toast was not part of the dinner plan.

"I'd like to say a few words too," she said, so loudly that some of the older people cupped their ears. She wobbled a bit in her high heels and grabbed Sid's shoulder for balance. "Sid and I couldn't be happier that Laurie and Joe found each other. Of course, parents want their children to find the perfect mate, someone who treats them with love and respect, and we think Laurie's found that in Joe. So, we can sleep easy at night knowing that we've delivered her into capable hands."

I looked over to my father, who appeared to be irritated by Cammy's toast. And when I scanned the room, I sensed that many others too were annoyed. Having discovered Helen's dead body, I felt a unique closeness to her—and I was protective of her and her legacy. Cammy's words infuriated me. She was not a true member of our community, but rather a recent interloper who had replaced one of the most admired women at Red Meadow Lake. Her toast, filled with first-person plurals and parental implications, struck us as presumptuous

"L'chaim," she called out, glass up high.

"L'chaim," a few people responded with little gusto.

Cammy's tone-deaf toast put a damper on an otherwise festive evening, and people soon began to say their goodbyes. When a line started to form in front of the unattended coat check, Becca Gold ran back across the room. But before she returned to her post, she pulled me aside. "I stole a bottle of wine," she said. "French. You want to go over to First Beach after and have some with me?"

I was surprised, as I'd never known Becca to take risks of any kind. I considered the vow that I had made to myself, how I wouldn't drink alcohol. And then I thought about how good that first drink felt, that warmth that poured down my throat and into my gut—the chemical change in my body. I watched as one of the guests finished off a glass of wine and then lit a cigarette. "Sure," I said, surrendering to my urge.

When all the guests were gone and Becca and I had finished our work, it was almost midnight. She came into the dining room as I was breaking down the final table. "You ready?" she asked. She held up a bag that contained the wine bottle.

I turned the bridge table on its side, folded the legs, and leaned it against the wall. "Done now."

It was late June and the air was cool for that time of year. The walk from the clubhouse to the beach was only about fifty yards and took us over a small dam, one that allowed a thin sheet of water to drain from the lake. Sometimes, a minnow would slide through the dam's grates and flop about on the wet deck below, and I would watch with some sadness as it pounded its tail and arched its spine in a desperate effort to return to the water. A poorly maintained chain-link fence surrounded First Beach, and we slipped through a large hole near the concession stand. We sat down at a picnic table under a covered structure that resembled a carport, and from the bag Becca pulled out the bottle and two Dixie cups.

"I loosened the cork at the clubhouse ... thinking ahead," she said proudly and poured the red wine into the cups. "Cheers."

"Cheers." I had known Becca for many years, but this was the first time I could recall ever being alone with her. "You do this a lot?" I asked, pointing to the bottle.

With her fingernail, she scraped a layer of wax from the side of her cup. "Now and again."

I sipped the cabernet, which tasted different, less candy-like, than the sweet concord wine on which I first got drunk. "Me too. Now and again."

She smiled, as I had achieved some level of local infamy for getting drunk and destroying the rabbi's rosebushes.

The moonlight illuminated Becca's puffy face, and I took in her features: a crooked nose that her mother wanted her to have fixed (but which pressure she proudly resisted), a high, broad forehead that captured a disproportionate amount of her face, and fair but oily skin with a red blemish on her right cheek. As I examined her, she seemed to understand my scrutiny, for she pulled a clump of hair from behind her ear and draped it over her forehead. She looked down to the table, and I sensed in her face not resignation, but an acceptance of who she was and would be; and when she shrugged as if to say, *What you see is what you get*, her comportment suggested that she would not be tormented by a life of constant striving.

She filled our cups. She took a sip and burped, then covered her mouth in embarrassment. "Excuse me," she said, her cheeks turning red. "That always happens to me when I drink wine. Red, not white."

"Happens to me too," I said, lying to make her feel less uncomfortable. I held my hand up to my mouth and jerked my shoulders to mimic a burp.

Becca pressed her leg against mine. She raised her cup to me, and we toasted silently. I drank some more and began to experience that magical chemical change—and I recalled a lady at an AA meeting who said that *one drink is too much and a hundred are never enough*.

With the wine almost finished, Becca picked up the bottle and moved to my side of the table. She sat down and leaned close, and I found that her warmth comforted me. She lifted the bottle to her lips and gulped, then held it up to the moonlight. "Just a little left," she said, and handed me the bottle. I thought about wiping the top with my sleeve, but feared that to do so would insult her—so I put the bottle to my mouth and finished off the wine.

"It's almost like kissing," she offered.

"What is?"

"My lips on the bottle...then yours."

"I guess." I was relieved that I hadn't wiped the bottle.

With an assurance that surprised me, Becca placed her hand on mine. Rather than withdraw it or even acknowledge the contact in any way, I remained still. The weight of her plump hand soothed me, grounded me, and we looked out over the lake, at the clubhouse—the lights of each room being extinguished in sequence by the caretaker. We took in the moon's glow off the sheer face of Split Rock in the distance. I was peaceful, serene, and I compared this pleasing sensation to the anxious impulsivity that guided me to kiss Missy.

I became aware of a sudden desire to kiss Becca, to hold her pudgy face in my hands, to touch her breasts, to taste the wine on her breath—to eradicate the memory of Missy's rejection. I turned to her and stared into her wishful eyes. As I hadn't in that moment on the poet's stoop, I thought about the consequences of both rejection and acceptance. But before I could consider these consequences in greater detail, before I could touch my lips to hers, Becca again surprised me. She lunged forward, wrapped her arms around me, and kissed me in the most aggressive way—her tongue deep into my mouth, her lips pumping like a baby on a bottle.

We soon found ourselves flopping about on the cool sand, her hands going to places that at first frightened me and then, when I relented, brought me a release that

I had felt only with alcohol. I placed my hands under her sweater and maneuvered to unlock her complicated bra, but just as I was on the verge of accomplishing a minor engineering miracle, a flashlight darted across the beach.

"Ben," the caretaker called out. "That you? And who's that with you?" Becca turned her face away from his flashlight, and I sat up to obstruct the caretaker's view of her, to protect her in some way. "Beach closed. Out of here ... both of you!"

He turned and walked back down the path to the clubhouse, across the small dam, his flashlight bouncing with each choppy step. Becca and I stood and brushed the sand from our clothing. I left my shirt untucked, hanging out over my waist, in an effort to hide evidence of my arousal. I gathered the bottle and cups and tossed them in the bin behind the snack bar, and we slid back out through the opening in the fence. As we walked down the path, Becca reached for my hand. I squeezed her meaty palm, unafraid for once that my palms would dampen and reveal my stress.

I looked to our left, toward something that caught my attention across the dark water. In the vicinity of my grandparents' home, I saw what looked like two flashes of light—the click-click flash of a lantern. I thought at about the coded communication that that Papa and I had used for years. Two flashes: *Come over, the fish are biting.* I stopped and let go of Becca's hand, then stood up on a small boulder to get a better look.

Becca tugged me off the rock. "Come, come, take me to the car."

We took a few steps down the path, away from the lake, and then I stopped to look back toward Papa's house.

The flashing lights were gone. I thought about my mental state since I'd found Helen's body: my drinking, the boat accident, the rosebushes, my imprudent kiss on Patchin Place, my obsession with these damn lantern lights. I feared that I was going mad. Seeking some grounding, some connection to another human being, I reached out and held Becca's hand. We walked across the street to the parking lot, where only two cars remained. She leaned against the side of her Olds and pulled me toward her. She kissed me again, but this time tenderly, slowly, without her earlier abandon. I kissed her back with the same kind of affection and tenderness—and for a few moments I felt secure, safe, sane.

In the distance we heard the caretaker's voice, and his flashlight soon found us again.

"Ride home?" Becca asked.

I feared that to accept Becca's gesture would somehow bind me to her. Years later, I would reflect on that summer as marking the start of a painful dynamic between me and the women I loved: to my detriment, I would long seek those who, like Missy, were unavailable to me, and I would shun those good souls who, like Becca, would give me everything. "Think I'll walk home tonight," I said.

She shrugged in her accepting way and gave me a quick peck on the lips. In seconds, she was in her car and out of the lot, on her way back to the festive home of Nathan and Bea Gold—captain and first mate of the *Ark*.

Chapter 23

~~~~~~~

Papa called the next day to let us know that he was having his basement refinished—new carpeting, a wet bar, couches, a pool table, and a television—and that we should come over and clear out anything we'd stored there. My mother had a few boxes of summer clothing that hadn't sold, and my father mentioned a set of golf clubs he'd put there years ago when Lillian had objected to the frequency with which he played. When I heard the news, I thought immediately of the shoebox that I'd taken from Helen's closet, and the diary inside.

"I'll get everything," I offered.

"And how's that?" my mother asked. "You going to bring everything over on your Schwinn?"

Her sarcasm annoyed me. "I'll call Missy. She'll drive."

"Good, because I've got a couple of large boxes ... or maybe it's just one ... down on the right, near the tool room. They're marked *Summer Schmattas*, I think. At least that's what I remember. And your father's golf clubs? Who knows? And no loss if you can't find them. The last thing he needs is to spend half a day on the golf course when he's got a practice to build. Sid Lowenthal? He can afford to play golf, but not your father."

I fumed at Lillian's disparagement and turned to walk away from her.

"How was it working the party last night?" she asked. "Sid take care of you?"

"He sure did," I said, declining to tell her exactly how much Dr. Lowenthal had paid me.

"And how about the Gold girl? Rumor has it you two ran off to First Beach after the party."

I was again amazed at the speed with which gossip spread through our small community. I thought about Becca and her sweet face, our kiss and how we flopped about on the cool sand. I recalled the flashing lights near my grandparents' house. "Mom," I asked, "did you see any lantern lights last night ... outside? After the party?"

My mother shook her head. "I didn't. Where were they?"

"It was hard to tell. Papa's, maybe."

Lillian tugged at her right ear. "Your father and I were asleep five minutes after we got home, as soon as our heads hit the pillow. Probably just people out celebrating after the party, having a nightcap on the docks." She smiled out of context, as if a pleasurable idea had just occurred to her. "Or maybe it was you having the nightcap ... seeing things that weren't there," she said, unable to resist the opportunity to debase.

Later that afternoon, Missy dropped me off at the end of Papa's driveway, and I asked her to pick me up in an hour. My grandparents had a beautiful double lot on West Lake Shore with a long driveway carved into the woods, and as I walked through a tunnel of darkness created by the dense canopy, shafts of sunlight filling the voids, I looked up to see a turkey vulture sitting high up on a gnarled bough. The scavenger looked down at me—black feathers and the red, wrinkled face of a grim old man. The sight of this bleak bird caused me to quicken my step until I came to a clearing before the house, where I could see that Papa's car—the gunmetal-gray Pontiac Bonneville—was not in the driveway. I looked back at the buzzard, which continued to stare at me with its awful, creased face and its evil white tooth-beak. "Fuck," I muttered. I rang the doorbell and waited. No answer. I looked back at the bird, which held its stare like some ancient Egyptian sculpture. Again I pressed the doorbell and, hearing nothing, peered through the side window into the still house. I could see from the darkness inside that no one was home. I stepped down off the front porch and looked for the vulture, but the great bird was gone.

Papa always kept a spare key under a lumpy, odd-looking rock by the boathouse, so I walked around the back, retrieved the key, and let myself into the basement. I first went over to the place where I'd hidden Helen's shoebox and was relieved to find it right where I'd left it. My mother's box—labeled *Summer Schmattas*—was in front of the tool room, just as she had recalled. Helen's shoebox was nearby; I removed her diary, slipped it into my pants pocket, and dumped the shoes into my mother's box. After bringing the schmattas outside, I returned for Abe's golf clubs. I had to search through the crowded dusty room but after a few minutes was able to locate the bag, which had fallen down and lay flat beneath an old desk. I pulled out a sand wedge and took a couple of swings in the cluttered space. On the third swing, this one looser and freer than the first two, I managed to crack the club into the head of a tacky porcelain dalmatian, decapitating it in splendid fashion. My heart racing, I paused to listen for the sounds of someone in the house and, hearing nothing, lifted the dog's head from the floor. I cupped its ears and looked into its sad eyes. I tried to balance the head on the cracked neck, but it would not hold, so I placed it under the desk and hoped that many years would pass before Nana noticed the damage.

Before taking the golf bag outside, I reached into my pocket and felt Helen's diary. As was often the case with me at that time in my life, I was torn between the conflicting forces of reason and impulse: there was what I knew to be right, and then there was what I knew to be wrong but nonetheless wanted, the needs and urges that cried out for satisfaction. I recalled the shame I felt when I read Helen's first diary entry—the one about her urinary tract infection—and also Missy's admonition when I removed the diary from the closet. I then felt a pang in the gut, the manifestation of an instinct that something was not quite right, that some elusive and frightening truth was beckoning me. And just as when I'd quickly broken my vow of abstinence and drank with Becca on the beach, impulse again prevailed.

I opened the journal and read the next entry.

Feeling better at last! I need to figure out what's causing the UTIs. Maybe the long bike rides. Not peeing enough? Dehydrated? Stress.

Spicy foods. Who knows? We did have Indian in Edison last week. It certainly isn't sex that's causing it, because Sid hasn't been too interested lately. We go through these phases, on and off for years. Kids, work, life, stress. But it all seems to work out eventually. I was well enough to play tennis today. I hit with the rabbi for a half hour, ran him around the court. Then gave that sweet Baum boy a lesson. He's a good kid, Ben. I also spent some time with his sister. What a tragedy, poor Bernice. And what a crazy disease. Aging before our eyes. Sid said it's really rare and she doesn't have long to live. Maybe just a few months. Years at most. So sad for all of them. I can't imagine how Lillian holds everything together. She's such a strong woman. The little girl hit a ball today, a perfect topspin forehand that had us all in tears. G-d bless her.

Helen's reference to our family surprised me and again brought up the most tender feelings for her—and for dear Bernice. As I ran my fingers over Helen's handwriting, struggling to connect with her *and* with Bernice, I heard the raspy throat of the Bonneville's engine and then the slamming of car doors.

I shut the diary and returned it to my pocket. I eyed the dalmatian head. After what sounded like grocery bags being dropped on the kitchen table, I heard Papa's voice through the floorboards above. While he spoke in a loud and animated manner, the distance and the ceiling above muffled his voice, and I could not hear what he was saying. I soon heard another man's voice, which I identified after a few seconds as that of Sid Lowenthal. While his voice, too, was muffled, I could tell that they were having a disagreement. I could not imagine what might cause these two men to find themselves in conflict. Was it something to do with Helen? An argument about Papa's accounting work for Sid? Some kind of boring dispute between neighbors?

I heard the front door being opened and then slammed shut. I ran over to the basement door and peered through the glass panes to see Sid trudging through the dense brush that separated the properties. I listened as Papa's heavy steps made the floorboards creak above me.

Troubled by this inexplicable conflict between two men who had little reason to disagree, I sat on a torn armchair from which sprouted tufts of stuffing. I looked down to the floor, to the dalmatian head and its sad eyes. I felt cramped in the cluttered room, claustrophobic and trapped. Papa's footsteps grew heavier, louder, closer— and then they stopped. I could feel him standing directly above me, the floorboards bending, arching toward my head. A puff of dislodged dust floated downward and coated my face. Suppressing a cough, I lifted the heavy golf bag and hastily carried the clubs to the door, where I again peered through the glass. Seeing neither Sid nor Papa, I ran around to the side of the house and leaned the clubs against my mother's box. I then jogged over to the boathouse and replaced the key under the lumpy rock. When I turned around, Papa was standing on the elevated deck looking down at me, hands on hips.

I waved a sweaty palm. He did not respond, but rather continued to stare at me with a numb expression that I had never before seen on him. I waved again. "Hi, Papa!"

I yelled.

He made a motion that directed me to approach him, which I did with tremulous fear. "What are you doing, Benjamin?" he asked. He leaned over the deck's railing and glared at me.

"Just getting some stuff from the basement. Mom sent me. I picked up Dad's golf clubs and some old clothes." I stepped back and shielded my eyes from the sun. When I did so, I thought I saw Nana float across the plate glass window like an apparition, a feather duster in her hand. "I've got it all on the side yard. Missy's coming to pick me up soon."

Papa waved to the Golds as they puttered by on the *Ark*, with "A Beautiful Morning" by the Rascals announcing their merry mood. "Missy?"

I took a few steps closer. "Yes, Missy Dopkin."

"Of course. Poor thing, cursed with that father of hers, the crazy engineer ... the genius. It's not all smarts, you know. You can have an IQ up to here"—Papa raised his hand above his head—"all the way up here and still not make it." He looked over to the side yard. "You need some help with that stuff?"

"I'm good, thanks," I said, afraid that he would see the diary poking out of my pocket.

"Okay, fine. You put the key back?"

I pointed toward the boathouse. "It's under the rock." I neared the deck and extended my hand upward.

Papa leaned down, put his hand through the slats of the railing, and held my hand in the loving way that had always defined his affection for me. "Ben, did you hear anything when you were in the basement?"

I resisted the urge to withdraw my hand. "Like what?"

He squeezed hard. "Like talking. Me and Dr. Lowenthal?"

"Nothing, Papa."

He stared at me with a probing skepticism, and I felt as though he were trying to assess my truthfulness. "Okay," he said, releasing my hand. "Okay."

I walked around the side of the house and stood next to the items I'd taken. In the trees above, the grim vulture glared down at me with its scavenging menace. Frightened, I pulled a club from the golf bag and waved it in the bird's direction. The vulture blinked and appeared to smile sarcastically, then launched off its perch and flew toward the water, its thick wings pounding the air with little of the grace exhibited by the egret on Split Rock. To my great relief Missy soon arrived, and we packed up the car and drove around the lake to my house.

After Missy dropped me off, I stumbled down the driveway with the bag of clubs over my shoulder and the box of clothes in my arms.

"Papa called," Lillian said in a solemn tone when I opened the door. Given the argument that I'd just overheard and Papa's chilly behavior afterward, I feared what he might have said to her. I felt my gut rumble as she sipped a gin on the rocks. "He said you destroyed the dalmatian ... decapitated it," she deadpanned in a way that indicated some perverse pleasure in my wrongdoing.

I exhaled. "Pitching wedge ... and I wasn't even drunk."

After dropping the clubs and the clothes in our garage, I returned to my room. I closed the door, locked it, and removed the diary from my pocket. I scanned the room for a hiding place—somewhere safe from my mother's inquisitiveness, safe from her insatiable need to know everything about the lives of others while hiding the truths of her own life. Beneath my bed was a metal locker in which I secured my prized possessions: my Sandy Koufax rookie card, a tennis ball autographed by my favorite player, Arthur Ashe, my bar mitzvah program, a photo of me and my old buddies from Weequahic, my stamp collection, and a mint two-dollar bill from one of the last runs in 1966. I placed the diary in the box and pushed it under the bed, deep into the corner where Lillian was unlikely to see it. I wondered if I would one day read another journal entry, or instead destroy the diary or, perhaps, find some innocent way to return it to Sid—who, according to Missy, had become the journal's rightful owner.

I thought about the most recent entry that I had read: Helen's talk of UTIs was too personal for me, too intimate, but her mention of my family—me, my mother, and Bernice—had, I felt, given me some moral argument to keep reading. She was, after all, talking about *us*—and perhaps, I reasoned, she was speaking to me from the grave.

Chapter 24

~~~~~~~

Missy and I spent our last few weeks together enjoying the lake's simple pleasures. We met every few days to fish off the dock, to putter around the lake in the motorboat, or to laze in front of Tom & Mary's, where we drank bottles of cold Yoo-hoo and talked about our increasingly near futures away from the lake—and away from each other.

One muggy afternoon, we sat on the bench in front of Tom & Mary's and drank Yoo-hoos. "You excited about going to England?" I asked, believing in all seriousness that she might one day marry British royalty.

She ignored my question. Instead, she sipped her Yoo-hoo and turned to me with a look of sublime satisfaction. "These are so good. When I was little, I had this fear that all the things I loved ... wax lips, Yoo-hoos, fishing for sunnies, skipping rocks ... the lake ... I was afraid that all the things I loved wouldn't mean much to me when I got older, that I'd outgrow them." She finished off her bottle. "Maybe in a few years it'll happen, but not yet."

I looked at my bottle, which was still three-quarters full. I concluded that I no longer liked this chocolaty drink. Although I'd enjoyed it for many years, the truth was that I'd come to dislike the taste—a cheap imitation of the chocolate milk that Nana made with fresh milk from O'Dowd's, melted Swiss chocolate, and rich whipped cream. I wiped the perspiration off the bottle and took the shallowest sip. "It *is* good."

Missy rolled her eyes and reached for my bottle. I surrendered it, impressed yet again by her trenchant insight. She raised the bottle, but before the glass touched her lips, she wiped the opening with the palm of her hand. Deflated, I thought about Becca's comment when we shared a bottle of wine and tumbled to the sand on First Beach: *It's almost like kissing.*

"I am . . . looking forward to England, that is," Missy said, almost apologetically.

I always knew Missy was destined to do great things that would take her far away, but I was disheartened when I'd first heard of her plans to study abroad, plans that were so clear and unequivocal, so distant. "That's fantastic," I said with that shameful, unspeakable pain we sometimes feel when a friend prospers.

"Thanks." She dropped both bottles into the can at the end of the bench. "The only problem is the money. They gave me some scholarship money, but not the whole thing. So, I'm not sure how long I can stay there." Missy's father had recently been fired for yet another insubordinate outburst aimed at someone who could not comprehend his genius. "I'll start and we'll see how things go . . . see if that device my father and Sid are working on takes off. Fingers crossed."

Just then, Pearl Lipsky's shimmering bronze Seville blew through the stop sign at the corner and accelerated hard right into the parking lot before us, so fast that the force of the turn caused the car's chassis to slide out, cartoon-like, over the tires. Missy and I jumped up and ran in opposite directions, and we watched—hearts racing—as she came to a halt mere inches from the bench. So small was Mrs. Lipsky that we again could see only her shock of salmon-colored hair above the steering wheel and, waving to us with no appreciation for the terror she'd just caused, a wrinkled hand adorned in gold rings and bracelets.

She stepped out of the car with a grin of the kindest oblivion. "Be a doll," she said to me, "and come help me with the bags. They've got it all ready inside."

"Sure, Mrs. Lipsky." I followed her into the store and caught Missy winking at me as I passed. On the counter were several bags waiting for Mrs. Lipsky, and while she paid I took the bags out to the car and placed them on the rear seat.

Missy and I returned to the bench and sat close to each other, just as we had on the steps at Patchin Place. "You're a mensch, you know." She leaned in to me.

Mrs. Lipsky stepped out of the store and shuffled to her car. She peered through the rear window and counted the bags. Satisfied, she approached me. "For you ... such a good boy," she said and handed me a nickel.

I was embarrassed that she had given me money for such a small task. "Thanks, Mrs. Lipsky."

Missy and I watched as she returned to the car and pulled onto Upper Mountain with such reckless and lane-crossing abandon that she nearly clipped, in order, a landscaper's truck, an oak tree, our classmate Byron Fein, and a family of ducks that appeared to recognize the imminent danger and waddled furiously to safety.

"What are you going to do with all that cash?" Missy joked.

I bit the coin as if it were a gold doubloon. "Buy you a ring," I said on impulse, cursing myself as soon as I said it.

Missy frowned. "You can't get much of a ring with that now, can you?"

I ran my fingers across the face of the nickel. I felt sad, as if I had again disappointed her. "Not much." I put the coin in my pocket. "Not much at all."

That night, I emptied my pockets on the kitchen table: a few pieces of Bazooka gum, a crumpled one-dollar bill, and the nickel that Mrs. Lipsky had given me. My father was sitting at the table nursing a lemonade and reading a medical journal. He looked up at me and then down to the pile of things I'd tossed onto the table. Something caught his interest, and he squinted and leaned forward. After pushing the pieces of gum to the side, he lifted the nickel and examined it, turning it front and back, front and back.

"You know what you've got here?" he asked.

"A nickel?"

"What you've got is a 1937-D three-legged buffalo ... and in very good condition. Look here." He held the coin up and pointed to the front of the buffalo. "See, it's missing its front leg. You can see a little bit up top and the hoof at the bottom, but there's no leg. The mint made a mistake with the die, but a few of 'em got into circulation."

"And?"

"And it's worth a whole lot more than a nickel. It's

very rare, collectible. I think people pay a lot for these. Fifty... maybe a hundred dollars?" Abe handed me the coin.

"A hundred dollars!" I held the coin, rubbed it, studied the missing leg.

"Where'd you pick it up?"

"Pearl Lipsky gave it to me."

We heard the front door open, and my mother called out to announce her arrival. She entered the kitchen and gave me a hug and a kiss, then bent down and, with what appeared to be sincere affection, kissed my father on the cheek.

"Look what Ben got," he said, pointing to the nickel.

I handed the coin to Lillian. "What's so special about it?" she asked.

"It's a three-legged buffalo... very rare," I said with the authority of a skilled numismatist.

"It's worth a lot," Abe interjected. "A hundred dollars, maybe."

My mother curled her lower lip, an indication that she was impressed. "Really? Where'd you get it?"

"Pearl Lipsky gave it to me, as a tip. I carried her bags to the car."

Lillian frowned. "Did she know it was so valuable?" she asked.

"I don't know. I doubt it. I mean, she didn't say anything when she gave it to me... didn't say it was special or anything. She probably thought it was just a plain old nickel." I thought about the oddness of a world that randomly assigns value to some imperfect things and yet punishes others with comparable flaws.

Lillian pinched her chin, an affectation that presaged

her piousness. "You've got to bring it back to her," she ruled as if she, too, carried Nana's moral gravitas. "You've got to tell her it's got value she didn't understand."

My father leaned back in his chair and studied her. "Lillian," he said, "the boy's had some good luck. Let him enjoy the rewards of it."

"It's not good luck," she countered. "It's taking advantage of someone who's got no idea they're giving something valuable away. And that's not right ... to take advantage of someone's ignorance."

Abe drank the rest of his lemonade, and his face turned red. He appeared irritated. "Take advantage of someone's ignorance?"

Lillian, hypersensitive to even the most subtle shifts in mood, braced for conflict. "Yes, take advantage of someone's ignorance."

"Like you do at the store?"

Lillian flinched. "What do you mean by that?"

"I don't know, how about that Kelly bag you picked up from the old lady in Montville? How much did you pay for that? Five dollars? And sell it for twenty?"

"Thirty," Lillian replied curtly, with a hint of pride in the higher price.

"Even worse. See, she had no idea what it's worth."

"That's right, Mom, it's the same thing. Same as you do with the clothes." I felt emboldened by my father's logic. "I think you're being a hypocrite."

"A hypocrite?" Lillian slapped the nickel against the table. "It's different, now take it back to Pearl and let her know!" She exited the kitchen with dramatic purpose, walked down the hall, and slammed the bedroom door to indicate the anger to which she felt entitled.

That night, I called Mrs. Lipsky and told her about the three-legged buffalo and how it could be worth a hundred dollars. She spoke loudly, and I pictured her phone's mouthpiece slathered with the glistening bronze lipstick that matched her Seville. "Oh, Benjamin, don't be silly. A nickel's a nickel. You keep it and get whatever you can for it. Buy yourself something nice . . . or something for that lovely Dopkin girl. So smart, but the things she has to go through with that father of hers."

After thanking Mrs. Lipsky for her generosity and telling my father that I could keep the nickel, I knocked on my mother's door. "It's me, Mom."

"If you're prepared to apologize, you can come in. If not, I'm watching TV."

I opened the door and entered. Lillian was lying on the bed in a fluffy robe. She smoked a cigarette, and by her side, on the blanket, were a *TV Guide* and an ashtray. "I spoke with Mrs. Lipsky," I said. "I told her all about the three legs and how the nickel's worth a fortune. I offered to give it back, but she wouldn't hear of it. She told me to keep it."

Lillian gave me a skeptical look. "Fine, now you get to enjoy the money and you can do it with a clear conscience. It's a good lesson for you . . . one to remember. Always have a clear conscience." Her hypocrisy enraged me. She lifted the *TV Guide* and opened it. "Anything else you want to say to me?" she asked, her eyes fixed on the evening's show schedule.

I knew from prior experience that my mother was requesting an apology for challenging her, for the minor alliance that my father and I had presented to her. In the past, I had accommodated these requests, even when I believed that I'd done nothing wrong. I had capitulated for many reasons, but mostly because I feared that she would withhold her love for some period of time (a day, a week?) or, worse, that she would make a decision to no longer love me. But after going through these cycles with her for so many years, twisting and contorting in all sorts of ways to satisfy her whims, I had come to believe that losing her love—or some portion of it—was a price I might be willing to pay for some tranquility. Just weeks away from going off to college, I felt strong, brave.

I stood up straight, shoulders back. "There's nothing else I want to say."

She sat up in the bed. "Nothing?" she said, eyebrows raised. "You think it's okay to call your mother a hypocrite. Well, I think you've got plenty amends to make. Isn't that what those miserable drunks in the church basement taught you? Making amends?"

I experienced a surge of anger—and a desire to hurt her in some brutal way. I thought about her volatile behavior, how she would banish Abe to the couch, about her sick need to hide our family's warts and promote our good fortune. "Nope, I've got no amends to make to you. Maybe to some other people, but not you. *Never* you."

Lillian dropped the *TV Guide* to the floor. She looked at me with shock, as if I had violated a sacred covenant, as if she recognized that a shift had just occurred—a permanent, irreversible shift in which power had been lost and power gained. It was a shift that saddened me, for it meant a disempowerment of the most important woman in my life, a separation, the loss of a flawed maternal shield behind which I nevertheless took frequent comfort. I now believe that it was at this moment that one version of me ended and a new one began.

"Watch yourself, young man," she said, rising from the bed. "You're misunderstood ... very confused. You haven't been yourself since you found Helen." She tapped her right temple. "A little meshuga."

I heard my father's footsteps approach and took a step back, away from her. She nodded to me—a cautionary nod. As she placed her right index finger to her lips, indicating that this conversation was to be our secret, Abe entered the bedroom and looked at us. "Everything okay?" he asked.

Lillian smiled. "Everything's great. Right, Ben?"

I struggled to speak. "That's right, Mom."

That evening, my father and I had dinner by the water's edge, while my mother ate a chicken pot pie on the bed and watched *The Carol Burnett Show*. It was a muggy July night, and without the desire to either cook or go out, we resigned ourselves to leftovers from the Denville Shack, the tastiness of which declined, it seemed, the moment we removed the food from the premises. Just one day old, the cold fried chicken was unappealing, its skin dotted with globules of solidified white fat; the biscuits were dense and dry; the coleslaw tart and sodden. We would get little pleasure from the meal.

Abe tossed a piece of biscuit into the lake, and we watched the fish devour it. "You fight with Mom?" he asked.

"Yup."

"Figured."

Given the conflicts with Lillian, neither of us was in much of a mood to talk. We sat at the picnic table and picked apathetically at our food. Behind us was our pretty home and, inside, the woman we both loved but who brought us an intermittent pain that only he and I could truly appreciate. We were bound together by the many forces that connect father and son, not the least of which was the love and the pain inspired by this complicated woman: we were bonded by a shared trauma.

Before us was the lake. I looked west to Second Beach, then to my grandparents' white dock. On the other side of the ridgeline was Hope Quarry, which I could not see but which had infected our lake with its poisonous emissions. The setting sun dropped over the ridge, into the quarry's screaming maw, and released a creamy, opalescent light that did not so much reflect off the water's surface as it infused the lake with a violet-marigold-fuchsia glow. I located Split Rock off to the right and searched for the regal egret. As I had not seen the bird in weeks, I feared that it too had become disenchanted with Red Meadow and had moved to distant waters. Above a cluster of reeds, a cloud of fireflies performed a frantic light show before extinguishing their flames in unison and disappearing from view.

"Don't mind your mom," my father said.

I pulled a piece of puckered skin from a chicken leg and draped it on the side of my plate. "I won't. It's hard sometimes, though." I opened a can of cola. "Has she always been like this? Since you first met?"

He blinked as if he were formulating his response, uncomfortable with the words he was considering. "I didn't see it when we first started courting, but it came out after a while ... after we got married. She was always a bit volatile, but things got a lot worse when your sister died." My father reached across the table and took my discarded chicken skin. "And what can you say to a woman when her child dies? Nothing. You just have to accept that this is the way it's going to be. A woman just doesn't recover from something like that, you know."

I feared that Lillian had never allowed my father the space to grieve Bernice's death, that she was unable to acknowledge anyone's pain but her own. "Neither does a man," I said.

He bit into the chicken skin and, disgusted, spit it on the grass. Then he looked back to the house and scraped his lower lip with his thumb. He appeared concerned, and I imagined that he dreaded what awaited him. "Let's head back," he said. "Don't want to upset your mother any more."

We gathered the dirty plates, the soda cans, the utensils and walked arms full up to the house. As we passed through the porch on the way to the kitchen, I could not help but notice the living room couch—made up by Lillian with two white sheets, a shabby blanket, and a clumpy foam pillow.

Chapter 25

~~~~~~~~

Later that night, at around eleven, I stepped out of my bedroom to use the toilet. There was a stretch of a few feet in the hall where an archway opened a line of sight into the living room. As I approached, I vowed not to look in that direction, for I knew that the image of my father on the couch would sadden me. I was able to pass without looking and reached the bathroom. There, I pissed, brushed my teeth, and examined myself in the mirror. For years, people had commented about my resemblance to my father: we shared the same wiry physique, the same round eyes, crooked nose, and thick lower lip. But as I looked at myself, turned my head from side to side, ran a hand through my shaggy hair, my lips pulled back, teeth exposed in a forced smile, I noticed hints of my mother: a critical squint of the eye, as if the sun were shining bright, a flaring of the nostrils that suggested intense focus, a pinprick dimple on either side of my mouth. And I trembled at the thought that this burgeoning similarity in appearance might also indicate a similarity in constitution.

On the way back to my room, I again resolved to look away from the living room, to ignore the evidence of Lillian's madness. I kept my eyes trained on the bedroom door, but just feet away I heard a noise in the living room: the crackle of my father's transistor radio. I looked to my right, through the archway, and saw him lying on the couch, the radio next to his ear, a flashlight on his shoulder illuminating an open book.

"Dad," I whispered. He did not answer. "Dad," I repeated.

With no response, I approached him and stood at the foot of the couch. He was asleep. From the radio, I could hear the muffled call of the Yankees-Indians game, Bob Sheppard announcing Joe Pepitone in the bottom of the ninth. I moved closer to him and looked at the book that lay open on his chest. He was reading a novella written by a famous writer from our Weequahic neighborhood. I loved the book for its courageous examination of what was really happening in our insular Jewish world, including the growing divide between upper and middle class—but my mother loathed it, disgusted at the manner in which the author portrayed our community, at what she perceived as high treason in literary form.

Moving slowly, I lifted the book from my father's chest, folding the flap over the open page so he would not lose his place. I removed the radio from Abe's pillow, turned it off, and placed it on the floor. Next, I picked the flashlight from his shoulder, and when I did so he twitched like a dog caught in an awful dream. At last, I raised the blanket over his shoulders and pulled the bottom down to cover his bare feet. *I tucked my father in.*

When I returned to my room, I found myself tormented by the events of the evening, subdued by a range of white-hot emotions that scorched my weak soul. I closed my eyes and tried to sleep, but my heart raced. My mind played a repetitive loop: Helen's body, the lantern lights, Sid's ambiguous confession. And then my mind for some reason latched on to the image of the three-legged buffalo—that mutated, deformed beast, valued only because of its rare manufacturing flaw. I thought about the promise I had made to Missy, to wake up early and help with her paper route. I feared that I would oversleep. And in this distressed state of mind, there was only one thing for me to do. Drink.

I sneaked out of my bedroom, out the front door like a stealthy burglar so that my parents wouldn't hear me, and down to the boathouse. Once inside, I lifted a bucket of old reels from the wooden floor and removed the plank that covered my stash. With only the moonlight as a guide, I could not see what was in the dark pit, so I reached down and felt inside. There were several empty bottles—fifths of Scotch and gin. I moved them around until I felt the bottle, the Gilbey's vodka I'd purchased earlier in the week.

From the moment I ran my fingers over the bottle's smooth shoulders, I experienced relief, the anticipation of a transformative chemical change. I sat on the steps of the boathouse, facing the water, close enough that I could detect its sweet musk and hear the gentle ripples crest and surrender, crest and surrender. I drew the bottle to my lips and drank—and drank and drank until, in less than ten minutes, I'd finished the entire half pint. Where minutes earlier my mind was astir with dark thoughts and, for my father, feelings of empathy that staggered me, the alcohol cleansed my mind. I felt tranquil, at peace, happy. I felt connected—but to what, I did not know.

I lay on the grass and looked up at the few striving stars, at the towering oaks and their gnarled, geriatric branches, at a milky onyx canvas, at a bleak, lunar sky. I began to feel unstable on the ground, a sensation of oscillating movement—a boundless rotation, a galactic drift. I closed my eyes and reached for something that might tether me, ground me—something that might pull me back from this alcoholic dream. I reached for an exposed tree root. I reached for Missy. Missy on her bicycle; Missy lecturing me about Middle East geopolitics; Missy teaching me how to bag a newspaper; Missy marveling at Dylan Thomas's barstool fall; Missy in her red-white-and-blue leather jacket; Missy on E. E. Cummings's stoop, "Little Wing" calling from an open window. I re-created my kiss, but with a different result. I wrote a new narrative—a pleasant narrative, a false narrative. And with my hand clamped to the tree root, I fell asleep.

I awoke several hours later, not as a result of the morning light or the cries of the cantankerous crows, but from a gentle kick to my ribs. I opened my eyes and saw that Missy was standing above me, a bagged newspaper in her hand. She dropped it to the ground next to me and pointed to something near my head.

I turned to see a mound of vomit on the grass and, inches away, the empty bottle. I sat up. "What time is it?"

"It's twenty minutes past when you were supposed to be at my house."

I scanned the scene before me. A theatrical, dry-ice fog hovered over the lacquered water; drops of dew slid off the oak leaves and plip-plopped to the ground; sparrows and robins, blue jays and cardinals sang their morning song—their back-and-forth playground song; a coal-black turkey vulture, still and focused, watched from above with grim prescience.

I looked back to Missy. "I'm sorry," I said. My stomach rumbled so loudly that I put my hand to my belly. She looked down at me not with justifiable revulsion, but with a sadness, an acceptance that terrified me, for I knew that any chance I'd had of kissing her before we left for college was now gone. After this, there was no way she would ever touch me: she was too smart to put herself at risk.

"Yeah, well..." She bent down and picked the newspaper off the ground.

I pushed myself up and attempted to slap my pants and shirt clean. "How'd you find me?"

"I didn't want to call...too early, and I didn't want to wake your parents. So I loaded all the papers in the car and drove over here. I parked on the side and was walking around to tap on your window when I looked down to the water and saw you lying there...right there in that ugly yellow shirt."

I looked down at my shirt, at the vomit stain on my sleeve.

"Come on," she said. "I need a thrower."

We drove around to the west side of the lake: Jackson, Miami Trail, Algonquin, Brookside. Often when we delivered papers, Missy would put on the radio and chat away, but this morning both she and the radio were quiet. My head hurt and my stomach churned with each bend and bump in the road, although the silence and the cool morning air helped clear my mind. I watched the fog, like hot breath on a freezing day, rise off the asphalt. I reached out, spread my fingers wide, and tried to catch the elusive mist in my hand. Every time we neared a customer's house, Missy would slow down—almost to a stop—and I would toss the paper out the window to the driveway, careful not to leave it too close or under a parked car.

We approached Sid Lowenthal's house. At the end of the driveway, on the edge of the road, was Helen's treasured '65 Mustang—with a *For Sale* sign on the windshield.

"Look at that," I said, woozy and nauseated. "She loved that car and now he's selling it." I gripped the armrest. "It's just strange behavior and not very respectful."

"Just deliver the damn paper," she said with uncharacteristic impatience. "I'm tired of all your anti-Sid talk." Over the preceding weeks, Missy had grown even less sympathetic to my suspicions. She didn't have many important memories of Helen, and while her death was troubling to Missy, it didn't evoke in her the sorrow that afflicted me. As I considered Missy's fear that she might not be able to afford Cambridge, I continued to be concerned that her father's burgeoning business relationship with Sid was playing some role in her irritation.

I tossed the paper through the open window and, my coordination shot from the hangover, missed the driveway by several feet. We both watched as the paper landed with a thump mere feet from the Mustang. "I think it would be weird if he *didn't* sell it," she said. "You do know he's got to move on ... no choice but to move on."

I shivered at Missy's pragmatism. We continued in silence, and when we reached 33 Miami Trail, the home of Doris and Hyram Eichler, she stopped.

"They still want it on the stoop?" I asked.

Missy nodded. "Dead center."

I stepped out of the car, and my sudden rise caused some adverse physiological reaction, some shift in blood flow or pressure that made me light-headed. Fearing that I might faint, I put my hand on the car for support and slid down until I was sitting on the curb, my back pressed against the door.

"You okay?" Missy called out.

I raised my arm and waved so that she could see my hand through the window opening. "I'm fine."

I took a few deep breaths and gathered the strength to stand. I was frustrated that I could never remember the pain of a hangover *before* I drank, that the previous hangover seemed to have no deterrent effect. Rising to my feet was no easy matter, and during the few seconds of my ascent I experienced all of the following: the urge to vomit; a dreamy, otherworldly sensation that would normally presage a fainting spell; a pain in the temples so sharp and punishing that I feared my eyeballs might implode; the desire to return to my seated position; the desire to assume a fetal position; and, at last, the desire to wedge my head under the front tire and have Missy hit the gas.

Somehow I persevered and not only rose to my feet but started to walk. The Eichlers, who were rumored to have won the lottery, had filled their driveway with almost every conceivable type of vehicle: two new cars, a golf cart, a camper, a motorboat on a trailer, and a minibike. Given my hungover state, the driveway appeared to be an impenetrable obstacle, and I was forced to rotate shoulders and hips in a serpentine through the narrow gaps and alleys that separated the vehicles.

When I reached the Eichlers' stoop, I tossed the paper to the top step—a foot right of center but close enough, I decided. Rather than try to maneuver back through the forest of chassis and bumpers, tires and antennae, I took a shortcut straight across the lawn.

"That wasn't right," Missy said when I got in the car. "Going on their grass. It's newly seeded, you know."

She didn't need to explain further: in my haste to finish the paper route, I had shown little respect for the Eichlers' property. "I'm sorry."

"And did you put it dead center? On the stoop?"

"Yes," I lied.

"I don't believe you."

We drove back around the lake, again in silence, and Missy dropped me off at my house. When I entered, I was surprised to see that the couch had been restored to its normal state, with no evidence that it had been converted into a makeshift bed. My parents sat at the kitchen table, eating breakfast and reading the newspaper. They appeared to be in fine spirits, as if the prior evening had not occurred: my mother had cycled rapidly through this most recent spasm of rage.

Chapter 26

~~~~~~~~~~

Near the end of the summer, shortly before my matriculation to NYU, my grandparents hosted a barbecue. The theme was patriotism, and it was a festive, well-attended celebration. We decorated the property with red, white, and blue streamers, with the Stars and Stripes, and with Israeli flags. "Americans first, Jews second," Papa used to say.

The butcher and his wife were there, as were Cammy and Sid. Even Missy's parents stopped by for apple pie and sangria. Her father was in an unusually good mood, with lots of backslapping and enthusiastic handshakes. After too many failed jobs, he'd recently admitted to himself that he was constitutionally incapable of working for another human being, and he'd set up his own company: Dopkin Labs was located in an old garage in Dover and was filled with crazy contraptions in varying stages of development, assorted engineering relics, schematics and plans, even a stuffed fox. He at last had free rein to be a mad scientist, to rant and rave, to sulk and brood, to turn moments of inspiration into ideas, into *things* like surgical devices—and this freedom, although it had not yet translated into financial success, lifted his spirits.

Sid was not his usual composed self at the party. His attire, normally crisp and well executed, suggested some shock. His linen shirt was creased, one cuff of his trousers drooped over his ankle, and a shaft of his pomaded hair sprouted from his scalp like the sprig of a spring tulip. I watched from across the lawn as he talked to my grandfather under the rust-red leaves of a sugar maple, and I thought that his disheveled state might be a symbol of his guilt. As the surgeon spoke, Papa nodded in a comforting manner. Their conversation must have caught Nana's attention, for she crossed the lawn and joined them—and soon she, too, nodded in assurance. The three of them sat down on lawn chairs, with Sid speaking and my grandparents appearing to ask questions. I looked around for Cammy, who sat on the dock doing her nails, a bottle of polish by her side, her feet doing a playful kick in the water. My mother must have noticed the three of them sitting together under the tree, for she soon approached the group. Sid appeared to stiffen a bit when my mother joined the conversation. He took a step back from her and directed his words to Papa, who placed his hand to his mouth as if he were shocked by what he'd just heard. After about ten minutes, Papa said something that caused the doctor to roll his eyes and sigh as if he'd been forced, for his own good, to capitulate to some irresistible force. The conversation ended, and before Sid walked away—through the brush and back to his house—Papa rubbed the surgeon's shoulder.

The party broke up at around nine, and I began to help put the property back in order: picking up discarded soda cans, snatching cigarette butts from the grass, folding and stacking the chairs. Missy was there, too—hired by Nana to clean the kitchen and bathrooms at the end of the night. She stepped out of the house after finishing up and, with the five-dollar bill that my grandmother had given her, waved goodbye to me. I waved back with the sad recognition that I would see far less of her once we went off to college.

My mother asked me to help her pull streamers off the sugar maple, and while we cleaned off a low branch, I asked her about the conversation that had occurred under that same tree. "It's nothing," she said, but I could tell from her abruptness that she was withholding the truth. Since the night that I argued with her about Pearl Lipsky's nickel—when I called her a hypocrite and refused to apologize—her interactions with me had been civil, yet cautious, distant.

"Come on, Mom."

Lillian would not reveal a single negative detail about her own family, but she was not as principled when it came to the adversity of others. Not wanting to miss out on an opportunity to gossip, she looked around to make sure that no one was nearby. "It's Helen."

I looked up to see that Cammy had returned to retrieve her forgotten purse. Her gold watch glistened in the moonlight. "What about Helen?" I asked.

"Sid got a call from the medical examiner. Turns out that the lab botched the toxicology when she died. Somehow they made a mistake, mixed up a sample or something. How that happens is beyond me, but they just figured it out. What do you know but Helen was pretty drunk ... a lot more booze than they initially thought ...

even too much to drive a car. I guess that explains the fall. Poor lady was just too tipsy and fell into the lake." Lillian stood on her toes to try to reach a dangling shred of bunting, but she fell a few inches short. Flat-footed and satisfied by my greater reach, I snagged the paper and pulled it from the tree. "I'm not surprised, really," my mother said with what sounded to me like glee. "She was always a little too perfect to believe."

I thought about Helen—how perfect she was to me. "Yeah, well," I said, unsure how to respond to Lillian's snippy tone.

I moved over to a row of bushes that bordered the Lowenthal property and pulled a balloon out of the branches. I picked up a plastic cup and a smoldering cigarette. As I turned back to the house, I noticed something on Sid's property: the lamppost on the side of his house was flickering. One flash, then another. Then a pause. One flash, then another. With a sickening feeling, I thought of the lantern lights that had tormented me since that summer storm. I pushed through the bushes and stood in front of the lamppost. I examined the rusted metal and the cracked glass.

Sid stepped out onto his slate patio and waved to me. "There's a short in there somewhere," he said, pointing to the lamppost. "It's been on and off for months. I had a guy come fix it ... *try* to fix it. It was working for a few days, I think, then back to this." I heard Cammy call to him from inside the home. He shrugged and stepped inside.

As I walked back through the bushes, I thought about the people who feared that I was not myself since I'd found Helen's body, how Papa, Lillian, Abe, even Missy, were concerned about my mental health. I thought about the lantern lights—two flashes—that I'd been seeing, how they had taken on a mysterious meaning, how they implied some deception on Papa's part—how I had somehow created a dark narrative around them. I looked at the flashing lamppost, and I recalled Missy's words when I was disturbed by Cammy's watch: *Sometimes the most painful things in life, the most impossible to comprehend, have the simplest, most mundane explanations.*

I trudged back to Papa's house, a balloon floating above my head and a five-foot-long streamer stuck to the sole of my sneaker—and I feared that I was, indeed, going mad.

After helping Nana and Papa clean up the mess from the party, I drove the boat back across the lake to our home. I lay on my bed and considered the mounting evidence that for months I had been unstable, shaky, suspicious, disconnected from reality. I thought about the absurdity of my quest to understand Helen's death. As usual, Missy was right and I was wrong.

I turned on my side, and when I did so my wallet fell from my pocket onto the floor. When I reached down to pick it up, I noticed my strongbox, which I hadn't opened since I put Pearl Lipsky's nickel inside. I grabbed the box from under the bed, opened it, and looked through my belongings: the baseball cards, my stamps, the Weequahic photos, the nickel with the three-legged buffalo. And then there was Helen's diary, which no longer represented the possibility of some insight into this woman's life and death, but rather had become a symbol of my shaky mental state, of the pain that I had caused in furtherance of my outlandish suspicions. I wondered if, as Missy suggested, I should give the diary to Dr. Lowenthal or if I should destroy it without saying a word. At that moment, humbled by the realization that the lantern lights were nothing of the sort, I was committed to the future preservation of Helen's privacy, and I dropped the diary back into the box.

Without knocking, my mother threw open my bedroom door. She scanned the room, and her eyes soon settled on the strongbox.

"What's that?" she asked.

"Nothing. Just where I keep my important things ... my private things."

"Your *private* things? Really." She peered into the open box. "What's that? A diary?"

"That's mine." With my foot, I pushed the box back under the bed.

"I didn't know you kept a diary."

My boldness had been increasing as my move to college neared. "There's a lot you don't know."

"Apparently." She ran her finger over my dusty bookshelf and frowned. "When you're finished with your private little things that no one else is allowed to see, make sure you clean up this pigsty. I want it immaculate when you leave for school." She closed the door and left me alone in the room. I reached down and lifted the locker. After reorganizing the various items, I decided that, as Missy had advised, I would return the diary to Sid with some benign explanation—perhaps that it had gotten mixed up with Helen's shoes and was only recently discovered. I looked out my window, across the lake, at Sid Lowenthal's flickering lamppost. Two flashes in the darkness, right next to Papa's house—and I laughed at my faulty imagination.

Chapter 27

~~~~~~~

Two days after the party, I was preparing to go over to Missy's to say goodbye, as she was leaving that night for England. We were ending one phase of our lives, and given the distance that would separate us, I wanted to bring her a gift, something to remember me by. For years I had been collecting first day covers: new stamps, stuck to envelopes and dated the first day of issue. One of my favorites was a stamp of Henry David Thoreau from 1967, which commemorated his 150th birthday. The etched image of him—bearded, feral, asymmetrical—was unusual, conveying a certain madness that I found compelling. He looked like a modern-day hippie. I knew that Missy loved Thoreau and his iconoclastic ways, and I decided to give her the collectible.

I pulled my locker out from under the bed and opened it. Inside were my valuables, as well as Helen's diary. Between the mystery of the lanterns being solved and Missy's move to England, I felt a certain sense of closure, and my old curiousness about Helen's diary seemed to have lifted: the past, I thought, was at last behind me. I removed the Thoreau envelope, which was in pristine condition, and pushed the box back under my bed.

As I walked over to Missy's house, the thought of her imminent departure evoked in me a feeling of melancholy, a dread at the awesome velocity of time, and a sad admission that I was powerless to elicit in her the same kind of romantic affection that I had long felt. I walked up the driveway and saw Missy standing near the garage. She was eyeing a wasp's nest—a striated, taupe, football-shaped thing—and holding up a can of pesticide. She blasted the nest with a stream of poison, then ducked behind the wheel of the Dodge to await the death flurry that would soon pour from the nest. Frightened, I darted over to the car and knelt next to her.

"Hey," she said without turning to look at me. "You know, I feel some compassion, some sadness whenever I pull a hook out of a fish's mouth . . . but not with these bastards. Both living creatures, so there shouldn't be a difference, right? Maybe it's because they sting, but I don't care much for these wasps." We ducked as a sick one buzzed overhead and then fell dead on the hood of the car, a quick spasm before going still. "Maybe I should care more about them." She stood, gave the nest another blast, and again retreated to safety behind the car. "But I don't give a shit."

I had never seen Missy this cold-blooded. "You okay?"

"Not really."

"What is it?" I had assumed, incorrectly, that she would be in fine spirits, excited to leave the lake and start her collegiate life in England.

"Let's start with the fact that the world's gone mad. MLK, dead. RFK, dead. The Russians invading Czechoslovakia. And this insane war. I mean, what are we even doing over there? It goes on and on, I'm afraid." A poisoned wasp buzzed on the ground before us: Missy stepped on it and twisted her shoe to ensure its death. "And on a personal level, things blew up between my father and Sid last night. There's no repairing it. And I can say with absolute certainty that this is the first time it wasn't my father's fault. Turns out Sid's a real prick. First he changed the split... the profit split... and then he dropped out entirely. And now he's claiming that he has exclusive rights to the patent... says my dad has no rights at all. Sid's hired a lawyer, an aggressive one, to go after my dad." Missy sprayed the nest again. "So much for going off to Cambridge on a happy note."

"I'm so sorry, Missy."

"Yeah, well..."

As the poison began to take greater effect, dozens of dying wasps fled the nest. Some fell dead quickly, landing on the ground right under the nest. Others—like disabled prop planes—floated, rotated, and wobbled a few feet before surrendering and crashing downward. After a few minutes, the activity ceased.

"All clear," Missy said, moving away from the uncomfortable topic of her father. We stood, and she turned to look at me. "You grow? I think you got taller... just in the past few weeks."

"Possible," I said, pleased.

I noticed a tiny flake of crust in the corner of her eye. I reached out and wiped it off with my thumb. Missy flinched. "What's that?" she asked.

"Just some schmutz." I looked over at her mother's station wagon and saw several suitcases in the back. "What time you leaving?"

"Early evening." She stepped back and again studied me. "Yup, you got taller. No doubt."

I handed Missy the first day cover. "This is for you. I know how much you love Thoreau."

She was so accustomed to my clumsiness, always anticipating my selfish impulsivity, that she was startled by the thoughtfulness of my gift. "This is *amazing*," she said. "The stamp is incredible. He looks positively deranged in this drawing... in the best way possible." Missy stepped forward and gave me a hug. She held me tight for a few moments and then kissed my cheek. Fearful that I might again offend her, I stood motionless, sheepish.

Missy withdrew and spun toward the Dodge. "I've got something for you too. A couple of things, actually." She opened the rear door and lifted from the seat a bagged newspaper and a book. First, she handed me the paper. "I know how you love the sports section," she said. I thought of the many secret notes she'd passed to me in the box scores, and I just knew there would be one last message in these pages. Missy then handed me the book. "I couldn't decide between Dylan Thomas and E. E. Cummings... but Cummings is a bit more special... a bit more special for us." She handed me the book. "Patchin Place and all." I recalled that drunken moment when I kissed Missy on the steps, when she recoiled. "That was a special day," she concluded with a sincerity that touched me.

I admired the generosity with which she exonerated me. I felt loved. "Yes it was," I replied. We said our goodbyes, and I walked back home—paper and book in hand—with the painful understanding that our time together had come to an end.

Chapter 28

~~~~~~

Two days before I went off to college there was another accident at the quarry: a massive containment facility ruptured and released over a million gallons of chemicals and explosive fuel oil into Hope Pond. The poison then traveled via the narrow, winding rivulet that acted as a conduit to Red Meadow, and again contaminated our beautiful lake. But unlike the relatively minor spill months earlier, this one was massive. So great was the volume of pollutants that the lake's water level rose several inches—and so lethal and combustible was the effluent that the ecosystem of the lake was harmed beyond our collective comprehension.

Fish bobbed lifeless on the water's surface, their eyes swollen, engorged with dark blood, their gills agape as if they were seeking to expel the poisonous stew from within, scales peeling from their bodies like layers of old paint. The egret—the majestic bird that stood guard atop Split Rock—floated past me as I stood on our dock, its once white feathers now a bacterial green, its neck bent in a peculiar way, like the curve of an old lamppost. As the dead bird passed, one black eye looked at me, and I thought I saw it blink. The toxic waste decimated the mussels that had long thrived in the dense silt, propelling them to the surface, their shells ajar, their veiny pulps dangling like umbilical sacs.

And then there was the smell. I was able to pick up only remnants of what once was—fleeting whiffs of the water's algal musk that had since my childhood been a sensory tether to the lake, an unconscious connection, a register of time and space, people and place that grounded me in a familiar context. It was a smell that brought me comfort. But overpowering that smell was now something different, something unstable, volatile, accelerant, even hellish—something that reminded me of the lighter fluid we used on the grill. As I leaned over the edge of the dock and looked downward, I experienced a sense of foreboding, one that reminded me of that flash of incipient rage in my mother's eyes whenever she felt outnumbered.

I inhaled the tart chemical smell and picked up a flat rock—a perfect rock for skipping. I got low, bent at the knees and waist the way Missy did, and launched the rock at the water. Given my smooth mechanics and the size, weight, and shape of the rock, it should have skipped six, eight, maybe ten times. Instead, the rock hit the water, took one small leap, and disappeared.

I picked up another stone—a round, heavy one the size of a plum. I threw it high and watched its lazy arc, watched as it hit the water like a fist to a fleshy gut. As the ripples of concentric circles emanated from the point of contact, as they extended out into nothingness, absorbed and consumed by the sick water, the sense of foreboding became clear to me—for what I had believed could never happen suddenly appeared to me as a possibility, and maybe more. I looked around the empty, poisoned lake, as still and deathly as if it were the middle of the cruelest winter, and I feared that Red Meadow Lake was done with me—and that I was done with it.

The day after the spill, our community gathered in front of the clubhouse. There, the chief of the Rockaway fire department informed us that a state agency would clean up the lake and that we could not have any contact with the water for the foreseeable future. To live in our homes, to walk on our lawns was safe, but we were to stay off the shore, the beaches, and the docks. There was to be no swimming or playing in the water, no fishing or boating. "Keep your dogs out of the lake," the captain directed. "And this next point is important, very important. Absolutely nothing that can cause a spark or a flame...no cigarettes in the water, cigars, no charcoal or ash from the grills. Don't start a boat engine. Nothing."

"Why's that?" Pearl Lipsky asked, waving a wrinkled bronze hand adorned with gaudy gold bracelets and sparkling rings.

The captain looked over to the lake and then back to us. "We're just not sure what could happen if a lighting agent came into contact with the water." I assumed that he was lying, that he had already tossed a lit match into a water sample and knew exactly what would happen.

So we kept our distance from the lake, never venturing too close to the shoreline or stepping foot on the dock. We ate our meals in the house, behind the screens of the porch, or on the picnic table that we had moved away from the water's edge. As if the lake were a sick and contagious loved one, we watched it with concern, the men in their protective white suits working their hoses, their screens and hydraulic pumps.

As we approached my last day at the lake, Lillian's mood deteriorated on an almost linear basis, and the closer we got to my emancipation, the more temperamental she became. She would argue with me about the smallest things: how many pillowcases I should take to college, whether I had eaten the last apple in the fruit bowl, if I had enough typewriter ribbon to last the semester. There seemed to be nothing I could do to satisfy her. Lillian, so fearful of being left alone by the people she loved, was the master of preemptive abandonment: she was going to push me away before I left on my own. As my father once said to me, *she leaves us before we leave her... even though we're not going anywhere.*

After berating me about not yet having packed my valise for college, my mother went out for a few hours to shop in Morristown with Nana. I decided to surprise her with a kind gesture, an attempt to soothe her prior to my departure. Our home was in general orderly and clean, although it often needed some refreshing at the end of the summer. During that period of peak activity, an accumulation of muddy shoes and wet bathing suits, fishing poles and blades of grass, dead tennis balls and dirty towels gathered in our home. I looked around the house and saw that, indeed, the place was approaching a state of disarray.

I started out in the kitchen, tossing out a moldy peach and a tub of cream cheese that was covered with puffs of fuzzy green. In the pantry, I found an opened box of egg matzo that was two Passovers old and an even older box of breakfast cereal. I threw out a carton of eggs from O'Dowd's because there were tiny cracks in the speck-led shells. I went through the house and cleaned out the ashtrays, many of which contained mounds of lip-stick-smudged butts, with a few of Abe's gnarled cigar nubs. There was a pile of bedding in the laundry room, and I ran a load in our brand-new washing machine, which my mother had just purchased from Karl's in Bel-leville. The one room I did not enter was my parents' master bedroom, for to clean their room would require a level of intimacy that made me queasy.

The final room I cleaned was my own. I made the bed with a bit more precision than usual, stacking the pillows and tucking the sheets into tight hospital cor-ners. I cleared the desk of stacks of paper, including the newspaper that Missy had given me—which was still in its bag, unopened since we'd said farewell. Curious to see what message she'd left for me, I removed the newspa-per, turned to the sports section, and there, in the broad margin under the Pirates-Mets box score and then up the side of the page, was Missy's note—not coded as usual, but cryptic nonetheless.

Don't fret, my friend. I'll be hiding messages in the cricket scores and sending to you from Mer-rie Olde England. In the meantime, think of Edgar Allan Poe, whose ghost will haunt your Greenwich Village lairs. It's right there in "The Purloined Letter." Sometimes the thing we're looking for is right under our nose, but it's so obvious that we just can't see it. I'm afraid that's what happened with me and Helen. I've come to believe that your views of Sid were saner than I first thought, and mine were blinded by, well... by things that I'd like to put behind me. So there you have it, Ben. Carry on. Until we meet again...

I folded the paper and slid it back into the plastic bag. I repeated Missy's words: *Your views of Sid were saner than I first thought.* I felt vindicated, victorious: at last, I was right and Missy was wrong. She was still far too smart for me, but perhaps I had closed the gap just a little bit.

The last thing for me to do was vacuum my room. Earlier that summer, Lillian had installed an expensive central system, one with outlets in every room. I ran the vacuum's head over the carpet, and each thump and tinny click brought me satisfaction—a paper clip or staple or eraser head being sucked up, shot through the tube at high speeds, transported, weaving through a network of rubber intestines, and deposited into the system's basement bowels, united with the filth of every other room in the house.

I vacuumed the thick pile carpet, moving from wall to wall, under the desk, until I reached the bed. I got down on my knees and ran the vacuum along the dusty carpet until I hit my locker in the far corner. I would soon be leaving the lake, but would take with me my most treasured mementos: old photos from Newark, my stamp collection, Pearl Lipsky's nickel, and the Sandy Koufax rookie card, among others. I reached for the box and pulled it toward me, opening it to reveal the valuables that I had saved, kept close to me. I ran my fingers across the items and recalled how each one came into my possession: some purchased, some gifted to me, and some, like the Lenni-Lenape arrowhead I found in the woods behind First Beach, acquired through the natural rhythms and adventures of life.

And then there was the item that I had, in effect, stolen: Helen's diary. As I removed the diary from the box, I thought of Missy's final words to me, hidden in the margins of the sports pages. I thought about her reference to Poe and "The Purloined Letter." I thought about the things that are right in front of us that we cannot see: the surgeon dressed as a pimp, Cammy's watch, Helen's Mustang put up for sale, the cruelty with which Sid treated Missy's father. And it occurred to me that what I was looking for might be right in front of me, right in my hands.

I examined the diary's weathered leather cover, tracing my finger around the circular stain of a coffee cup. I pulled on the silk ribbon that hung from the book's spine and, as I had done so often, flipped a mental switch. Rather than move on with my life, rather than leave the lake and our dysfunction behind, some intuition, some force compelled me to do something that just moments before had seemed abhorrent. I closed the door to my room and opened Helen's diary. My hands trembling, I flipped through pages and pages describing tennis matches, mah-jongg games, and boring lake gossip. I opened the locker and prepared to put the diary away when I noticed an entry that was dated the *very day* my sister died.

I saw something horrible today. Unspeakable. I went next door to drop off the platter I borrowed from Harriet. I knocked on the door and there was no answer so I walked around back. When I went past the side of the house I looked into a window and saw some movement inside. I stopped and there was little Bernice on the bed. On her back. Lillian was standing over the girl. She was holding a pillow on the poor girl's face. Holding it down with force. I saw Bernice's legs kicking. She was trying to push the pillow off with her hands. I was about to knock on the window but before I could do anything Bernice stopped moving. Lillian lifted the pillow and I saw the girl's face. She was dead! No movement at all. Lillian killed her. Killed her own daughter. I panicked and ran away. The girl was dead. There was nothing I could do. When I got back home I looked back and I think I saw Lillian in the window staring out at me from the living room. I think she saw me! I think she knows I was there. A couple hours later word was all around the lake. Bernice died of her disease. Of natural causes. Quietly in her sleep was what people were saying. Maybe I was wrong. Maybe Lillian didn't kill her. Maybe they were just playing or something. But I know what I saw. Lillian was smothering the poor girl. She looked dead to me. I'm so confused. I don't know what to do. Oh G-d. Sid won't be home until tomorrow. Away at a damn conference again. I tried calling him but no answer at the hotel. I'll talk to him in the morning. Oh G-d.

My hands shook, my palms and brow became clammy, my heart raced. I struggled to breathe. I was having a full-blown panic attack. What I had just read was terrifying, incomprehensible. Bernice had been suffering for weeks before her death, and my mother had told us all that she and Bernice were over at my grandparents' house when my depleted sister decided to take a nap—and when my mother went to check in on her an hour later, Bernice was dead. Lillian said she'd passed peacefully, in her sleep, that God had at last relieved her suffering and taken her to a safe place.

I thought about my mother's love for Bernice—a love that, while complicated by the financial pressures my sister's illness placed on the family, was purer, steadier, and less complicated than the love she extended to me and my father. I thought about the days after Bernice's death, how my mother sobbed with such violent abandon that she was unapproachable, unable to function, consumed by a pain so vast that we feared she might require hospitalization. I reread a portion of Helen's entry: *Lillian killed her. Killed her own daughter. Impossible*, I thought. Helen was wrong; there was no way that my mother could do such a thing. *No way.*

Trembling, I read the next entry, which was from the day after Bernice died.

I told Sid what I saw. He was stunned. Horrified. He said that no one has the right to take a life, no matter how hopeless the situation. Not a doctor, not a mother, not the government. He says it should be a natural process. The girl was gravely ill, he said, and wouldn't have lived much longer, but only G-d gets to decide when it's time. And I agree. He said I should confront Lillian and tell her what I saw. Maybe there's some innocent explanation. Maybe I didn't see things right. But I know what I saw. Sid says I should talk to her. Tell her she can tell the police and Abe or we will. He wanted to go with me to talk to Lillian, but I said it would be better if I did it myself. Lady to lady. I'm praying that I'm wrong. I hope she can tell me it didn't happen, that I didn't see what I saw.

With the belief, the *conviction*, that Helen must have been mistaken, I continued to the next entry—written a few weeks after Bernice's death.

I ran into Lillian at the synagogue this afternoon. She was dropping off her daughter's old clothing for the annual drive. I asked her if we could talk about something important. We sat in her car and I told her what I saw. Her putting a pillow over Bernice's face and the little girl struggling to get free, then going still. Lillian didn't seem concerned at all when I told her. It was like she knew this conversation was coming. She seemed prepared for it. Cool and calm. She said that all I saw was her and Bernice playing around, having some fun ... wrestling, tickling ... and right after that Bernice took a nap. She was dead a half hour later, nothing to do with their high jinks, she claimed. I said it sure didn't look like that to me, but then I started to question myself. Maybe they were just playing around? I told her again what I saw. That she was holding a pillow over Bernice's face and that her girl didn't move after that. Lillian went from being very calm to aggressive in a split second. She said she knew Sid was padding his medical bills. She didn't tell me how she knew, but she must've heard it from her father. I thought Louie would've been more discreet. Aren't accountants supposed to protect their clients' secrets? Not even tell a family member? That's the problem with everyone working together. Jersey Jews. We all know each other's business. She said if I ever told anyone about Bernice then she'd make sure everyone at the lake knew about Sid. She threatened to ruin his reputation. His career. Maybe call the cops. She said, you and your husband keep your mouths shut. Well, I got the hell out of that car fast. I didn't feel safe with her.

Just then, I heard my mother's car in the driveway, the slamming of the door, the opening and closing of the trunk—and then her heels on the front walk. I heard a thud—the fall of a full grocery bag on the walk—and my mother screamed, "Fuck!" I considered my mother's explanation, her defense: that she and Bernice were just playing around. I recalled the many times that Lillian would tickle my sister, how they would have pillow fights, how Bernice would cry out in joy, reveling in the delight of our mother's touch and playfulness. And as to Lillian's threat to reveal Sid's misdeeds? I had often seen my mother move quickly from defense to offense in the cruelest ways, in particular when she felt wrongly accused, so her attempt at intimidation did not surprise me.

I flipped through the diary, looking for anything that might relate to Lillian or our family. After that last entry, though, Helen's writings appeared to focus on her children, her travels, her home, and the quotidian frustrations of her comfortable life. I turned to the final entry in the journal, written the day I found her body in the lake.

I begged Sid to clean up this billing mess and it looks like it's finally behind him. It took him years to settle the damn thing. He says it may take a couple more months to get it papered and signed, but they've got an agreement in principle. He came clean to the insurance companies and the authorities. He'll pay the money back, which isn't much, pay a fine and he agreed to put in better billing procedures. Best of all he keeps his medical license. He feels good about it and so do I. It was terrible judgment on his part... padding the bills... and I don't know what the hell he was thinking. Sometimes a person you respect does something so stupid and senseless that you just can't understand why. I'm disappointed in him. I didn't think he'd be the sort of man to defend himself by saying "everyone does it," but that's what he was thinking. It wasn't even a lot of money... a little here, a little there. Just Sid being a little too clever, thinking he's so smart. Anyway, it's behind us now and he promised he won't take any chances like that again. A few hours after we found out he had a deal, I was over at the courts. Lillian was playing a round robin and we started talking. I wanted her to know that she didn't have anything over us anymore. I never forgot the threat she made after Bernice died. And when I saw her I said, "Just so you know, Sid settled that billing problem. Or maybe you already knew that from your father? Sid's got no exposure anymore. Releases from the insurers and the state. So that threat of yours? The one you made to me in the car way back when? Well it's irrelevant now. You can tell whoever you want for all I care. You've got nothing over us now. And for what it's worth, I know what I saw. That was no tickling, no playful pillow fight. That was something else entirely. One of these days, Lillian, you're going to be accountable for what you did. And I'm going to make sure of that." Well, I never saw someone get so angry so fast. She poked her finger in my chest and said, "Like I told you, Bernice and I were just playing around... a little fun with the pillows. That's all you saw, and if you tell anyone about that you're going to pay a very serious price. The worst price, I promise." She was staring at me like she didn't have any fear. Angry but calm. I ran off the court and went right home. I called Sid at the hospital but he's in the OR. I'll tell him what happened as soon as he gets home tonight and we'll figure out what to do. Drive over to the police station or maybe tell Abe what happened?

Feeling that I might vomit, I lifted the trash can and hung my sweaty face over it; I retched violently, but nothing came out; I rapped my knuckles on the desk until they were raw and red; I took a few swings of my old wooden tennis racket, then cracked the frame on the edge of the desk. I heard Lillian's voice in the house. I placed the diary back in the box, hiding it under my collection of valuables, then frantically pushed the box back under my bed.

Before me was the tape recorder on which I practiced my debate skills, and on an impulse—a nervous reaction to the horror of what I had just read—I violently smacked the play button. The machine's speaker projected the recording of our final debate at Morris Hills, one in which we successfully argued against a compulsory military draft. NYU had a debate club, one of the finest in the country, and I planned on trying out for the college team. One of my weaknesses was a lack of confidence when I ended sentences, a propensity to finish on an up-note, which had the effect of weakening my arguments, turning what should be a declaration into a question. Over the summer, I had been working on this flaw, recording my voice over and over, replaying the tape until I ended each sentence with resolve, with force: I was trying to become stronger, more confident, more *adult*.

Over the sound of my recorded voice I heard my mother on the other side of the door. "Benjamin! Are you in there?"

I tapped the stop button on the machine. "In here, Mom." I retched again.

Lillian opened the door and took a step inside. "Who cleaned up the house? Was that you? Or your father?"

I did not know if I was to be praised or punished. "It was me," I said.

My mother smiled, and I trembled at the depravity that often existed behind her most benign expressions. "What a lovely thing for you to do." She looked around my room, and I thought I saw her glance under the bed. In search of dust, she drew her index finger across my bookshelf. "I think the house was in good shape before, you know, but very nice of you nonetheless."

Lillian lifted one of my pillows and held it in both hands: she shook it, punched it, tossed it in the air, and fluffed it up. She placed the pillow back on the bed and, after a wink in my direction, turned and left the room. I closed my eyes. I pictured my mother, clutching a pillow. And then Bernice, lying on her back, kicking her thin legs, fighting to breathe. I retched—then vomited into the trash can.

Chapter 29

~~~~~~

That afternoon, I bicycled wearily over to the other side of the lake to say goodbye to my grandparents. I was so shaken, so confused, by what I'd read in Helen's diary that I had trouble controlling the bike, and with my thoughts on my mother instead of the road, I hit a patch of gravel and tumbled to the ground. I wasn't badly injured, but my knee was scraped and bleeding. As I continued my difficult ride to the other side of the lake, the sun bore like a laser into the pulp of the poisoned lake, and I wondered if the light and heat, the intensity of the sun, could itself trigger a conflagration.

When Nana saw me limp up the front steps with dirty hands and a trickle of blood on my leg, she took my hand and led me into the master bathroom as if I were still a boy of five. She remained, as she always would, my safe place.

"Are you okay?" she asked with a tone that suggested I had been gravely injured.

"I'm fine, Nana. Just a little fall on the bike."

"All right then, why don't you get cleaned up ... and then we've got some things for you. There's some aspirin, right there on the counter if you need it."

In the bathroom, I turned the knob and placed my hands under the chilly water. The unpleasant temperature caused me to rush, to apply only the smallest amount of soap and wash my hands quickly. My grandmother passed the bathroom, and the familiar smell of her rose petal perfume reminded me of my haste. From the hallway, she said, "Remember to use warm water and take your time." I recalled a moment in my early youth when I stood in front of this very sink and Nana stood behind me, how she adjusted the knobs until the water was warm, how she took my hands in hers and rubbed them with soap—how protected I felt. "I will, Nana," I said. With a few streaks of mud still on my hands, I turned the knob for the hot water, enough to mix with the cold and create a warm, soothing stream. I rubbed my hands together, lathered up, and took my time under the water, rotating my hands, enjoying the warmth, enjoying the care, the wisdom and protection of my grandmother. I then massaged my bleeding knee with soap and warm water, cleaning the dirt out of the wound.

Before I returned to Nana and Papa, I looked around the bathroom. There was the strip of wallpaper I'd torn off when I was a little boy, a transgression that had provoked my mother's ire; there was the Delft windmill by the sink, a porcelain tchotchke that I had long admired; a glass atomizer held Nana's rose perfume; on the sink was Papa's blood pressure medication. In the trash can I noticed a few of Papa's dirty pipe cleaners and that morning's sports section. On the far wall was a medicine cabinet. I opened it, revealing a jumble of vitamins and antacids, creams and ointments, cold medicines and analgesics. There was an old bottle of Valium prescribed to my grandmother, which surprised me. When I read the label, I saw that it was prescribed just days after Bernice's death: Nana must have needed some relief to get through that terrible time. I thought about taking one to calm my own raw nerves but, out of deference to my grandmother, decided against it.

As I placed the bottle back in the cabinet, I heard footsteps coming down the hallway. "Benjamin," Nana called out, "are you okay in there?"

"I'm fine, Nana. Be out in a sec."

My knee aching, my mind awhirl with thoughts of Helen's diary, I moved to the living room, where Nana and Papa were waiting for me. On the coffee table were several gifts in honor of my matriculation to college: a framed photograph of me, as a young boy of eight, a fishing pole in one hand, a tiny bass dangling from the hook, and my proud grandparents by my side; an envelope filled with spending money; a cigar, Papa's favorite from the Dominican Republic; and a burgundy leather briefcase with a shoulder strap.

"Don't forget us," Papa said sadly, as if he could foresee the final arc of his life.

Nana flicked at his shoulder. "Don't be silly, Lou," she said. "Ben won't forget. He'll be an hour away... an hour and a half, tops."

"Depends on the traffic," Papa said. "Once took me two and a half to get to the East Side... but I think there was a parade, some sort of parade. Puerto Rican, I think.

Is that right? Do the Puerto Ricans get a parade? I don't think they should have their own parade. Jews too. I don't think we should get a parade. All it does is cause traffic and make people hate us even more."

Nana frowned at Papa as he put the gifts in the briefcase and handed it to me. We walked outside to my bicycle, and I hugged them. Papa first, and then Nana opened her thick arms—and I fell into her fleshy, perfumed embrace.

By the time I returned home, Lillian's mood had changed for the worse. Abe was on call that weekend, and he'd been summoned to the hospital for several hours. My mother was in the kitchen, an open bottle of gin on the counter. I looked around for her glass but didn't see one, and I feared that she was drinking straight from the bottle. She was a hyper-observant woman, able to pick up on even the most nuanced gestures and signals—a sensitivity that was an element of her mental condition—and I believe she too realized that a bottle without a glass would attract my attention. She opened the cabinet and removed a tumbler, then filled it with gin, leaving just enough room at the top for a few ice cubes.

As if she were drinking water, she took a few easy sips and then sneered at me. "So, you think I can't keep a house? You think I'm not fit? That we live in a hovel?"

I looked around the kitchen that I had cleaned earlier. "No, Mom, I was trying to help out ... do something nice." I noticed a few coffee grounds on the counter that I'd missed. "You keep a perfect house."

"Was this your father's idea?" she asked, unconvinced, and stepped toward me. "Did he tell you to clean up?"

I thought about Abe's periodic banishment to the

couch. "Dad had nothing to do with it. I figured you'd be happy... and I just did it."

Lillian shook her finger at me. "Don't pretend that you were doing something nice. I know an insult when I see one." She turned her back to me, opened the refrigerator door, and peered inside. "Where are my eggs?" She opened and closed the dairy drawer. "Where are my eggs?" She slammed the door, devolving into one of her dark and terrifying moods. "Where are my fucking *eggs!*"

I stood up and backed out of the kitchen. I'd heard her swear like this in the past, and her profanity often foretold an uncontrollable, expansive rage. So flooded with emotion was she during these outbursts that not only could she not edit her words, but she could not even remember them afterward. And when later confronted with the cruelty of her attacks, she would deny it with all the righteous passion of the wrongly accused.

Driven by fear, I retreated to my room and decided not to emerge until my father returned from the hospital, until he was there to protect me from this madwoman. I knelt down next to my bed and pulled out my locker. I opened it and saw the old photos from Newark, my stamp collection, the valuable nickel, my treasured baseball cards—but I had a sense that something was missing. I pulled everything out of the box, one by one, and spread the items out on the bed. I gasped audibly. Almost everything was there, right where I left it, but the one thing that was missing was the most important, the most irreplaceable: Helen's diary was gone. I felt sick. I lay flat on my stomach and reached frantically under the bed. There was nothing there. Someone had taken Helen's journal—and I knew who it was.

Armed with a mental wiring that all but ensured her own survival, Lillian had outwitted me—and with her sickening theft of the diary, any evidence of her potential wrongdoing was now gone. Demoralized, I sat down at my desk. I could hear my mother bizarrely whistling "Happy Together" in the living room. She then started speaking on the phone—loud and giddy—about Bonnie Schwartz's ruby necklace and the butcher's beautiful new home in Coral Gables. "A pool, a tennis court, *and* a full-time maid," she said. "Cuban or Dominican, I heard. They're so good, the Hispanics."

I couldn't stand to listen to her voice any longer. I hated her mood swings, her proclivity to focus on the superficial to the exclusion of what was important, her breezy racism, her *phoniness*. To drown out her voice, to distract myself from her madness, to soothe myself, I reached instinctively for the only thing that might work: Missy's voice. I hit the rewind button on the machine. The beginning of the tape contained Missy's winning final argument in the state semifinals—her compelling case against the legalization of prostitution. I listened as Missy cited the transmission of disease, the exploitation of women, the abuse of minors, and damage to the institution of marriage. I listened to her clear and confident voice, her crackling intelligence, her measured passion— and I reveled in the thunderous applause that followed her closing argument. I felt as if Missy were there with me, in my room, comforting me in her own principled and pragmatic way.

A knock on the door startled me, destroying the fleeting solace of Missy's voice. Heavy, sharp, definitive: it was Lillian's knock. I shivered at the thought of Helen's words, at the possibility that my mother was depraved, murderous. I glanced at the recorder, and I had an idea. I reached over and pressed the record button. As I placed my baseball hat in front of the machine to hide the blinking red light, Lillian entered the room, her silhouette framed by the doorway. She clutched Helen's diary.

"Hi, Mom," I said, alarmed by her imposing energy, by her possession of the journal. I feared that she would hear the machine's low, jerking hum, but the roar of the neighbor's lawn mower obscured it.

She tossed her purse to the bed, sat down on the mattress, and placed the diary beside her. She crossed her legs. "Where did you get this?" she asked. From her skin, from her mouth, poured the junipered stench of gin.

"I found it in Helen's closet... in her closet when I was cleaning up."

She lit a cigarette and took a perfunctory drag. "And why, might I ask, would you steal a dead woman's most personal writings?"

"I didn't steal it. Dr. Lowenthal was giving everything away... said we could sell it, give it to charity, whatever... and he told me to make sure the closet was cleaned out." I looked at the diary, at the chipped polish on Lillian's fingernails. "I brought all the clothing to Nana's, then the shop, just like he said, and that's all that was left."

After just a few puffs, Lillian put the cigarette out on the marble base of my baseball trophy. She lifted the diary and flipped through the pages, shaking her head in condemnation. "*Diary of a Madwoman*, they should have called this." I could tell from the assurance with which she spoke, her derision, the odd confidence in her comportment, that Lillian was entering one of her uninhibited states. She removed a tube of lipstick from her purse and ran the tip across her lips. When she was finished, she folded her lips over her teeth—top and bottom—and with a blotter removed the excess lipstick. She examined her work in a compact mirror and, with her index finger, wiped away a small blotch of red that had spread beyond the boundaries of her lips. "Did you read it?"

"No," I lied without hesitation. "I didn't want to invade her privacy. I was going to return it to Dr. Lowenthal."

Lillian stared at me, as if she were assessing my authenticity. "You know Helen was a drug addict," she said. "A pill fiend and not much better than those junkies your father used to treat on Broad Street."

My mother's nasty, unsubstantiated attack infuriated me. "I don't believe it. That's a lie... not Helen." I looked over to the tape recorder and, behind the hat, saw the dull red light indicating that it was recording.

"Well, she was a no-good drug addict... a junkie. Bonnie Schwartz thinks Helen stole some of her sleeping pills after seder two years ago. Can you imagine that? Stealing pills on a holy day? That's the kind of lady who ends up dead in a lake."

I thought about Helen, about the care with which she taught my sister how to play tennis, her quiet philanthropy, the courage with which she confronted my mother. I thought about the toxicology report, which showed only alcohol in Helen's system. "I don't think she was the type of woman who'd steal anything," I said.

Lillian stood up from the bed and looked down at me. She flicked the cover of her lighter and fired up another Pall Mall. "So now you're the arbiter of right and wrong?" she said calmly. "Is that what I'm hearing? The same little boy who couldn't get top grades at Weequa-hic, a drunken fool ... embarrassed our entire family ... destroyed the rabbi's rosebushes ... and ended up in a *church basement!*" She took a drag of her cigarette and released a cloud to the ceiling. "And trotting around after Missy Dopkin like a pathetic little puppy ... not a shred of self-respect ... when there's not a chance in hell she'd ever stoop to date you."

She paused to allow me time to experience the full impact of her attack. Wounded and frightened, I glanced over at the clock. I prayed that my father would soon be home to protect me, to bear witness to my mother's wrath. Rather than respond to her broadside, I chose to ignore it. "I think Helen was a good woman," I said, knowing that my continued defense would further infuriate her. "Pretty and smart and kind to a lot of people."

My mother pulled a shiny clip-on earring from her right ear. "Pretty? Smart? *Kind?*" she fumed.

"That's right," I replied. "Pretty, smart, *and* kind."

Lillian frowned. "More than me?"

"What do you mean?"

"Prettier, smarter, kinder than me?" She smiled—part threat, part twisted flirtation.

This challenge represented the inevitable point in the conflict where Lillian offered a graceful way out of the argument, a détente—the point at which my father and I would often capitulate. But rather than give her the answer she demanded, I dug deeper. "Yes, all that and more."

Lillian bit her lower lip. "Bastard," she said. She cupped her hand, raised it to her mouth, and allowed a stream of saliva to gather in her palm. She then extinguished the cigarette in her spit and flicked the wet cigarette butt to the carpet. "Bastard," she repeated and, diary in hand, stomped out of the room.

I sat in the chair for several minutes, my shoulders hunched, my spirit deflated. I could hear my mother making angry noise in the kitchen, no doubt preparing yet another strong cocktail. I looked around the room, at the wet cigarette butt on the floor. I yearned to be away from my home, away from the lake. I imagined the freedom that I'd have at college, how I'd wander the narrow streets of the Village and mix with people from places other than northern New Jersey. But mostly, I imagined my *escape*.

I soon heard Lillian's footsteps in the hallway. I quickly repositioned the baseball hat in front of the tape recorder, then turned to see her again standing in the doorframe, her menacing silhouette now augmented by the distinctive shape of a martini glass. I noticed that she had not returned with the diary.

"Can I ask you a question?" she asked in a manner not intended to solicit an answer. "What is it about you and Helen Lowenthal? What's your obsession with her? Why so defensive? Is it because you found her in the water? Is that what it is?" As if she were raising a ceremonial chalice, she held the martini glass up to her lips with both hands and took a long, measured sip. "Or did you have some twisted teenage crush on her?"

Horrified, I shook my head no.

"Or did your father put you up to this?" She took a sloppy gulp of her martini and swayed until her left shoulder pounded the doorframe. "You know, your father and Helen once had a thing."

I gripped the sides of my chair. "A *thing*?"

"A dalliance ... yes."

The likelihood of my father having an affair was improbable, bordering on impossible—and I knew from Lillian's prior bouts of jealousy that she was yet again manufacturing betrayals and abandonments where only love and commitment existed. "That's not true, Mom ... there's no way."

She snickered in a manner suggesting naivete on my part. After finishing off her drink and placing the glass on the carpet below, she dropped onto the mattress, her head on my pillow. The sight of my mother reclining on my bed—her hair wild, her arms outstretched, her legs slightly splayed—disturbed me. From her supine position, my mother lit yet another Pall Mall and blew the smoke upward. I glanced over at the tape recorder, at the glow of the red record light hidden behind my baseball cap—and I wondered what she might reveal if I could provoke her further.

I lifted the martini glass from the floor and placed it on my desk. "I was thinking that maybe a better question is, what is it about *you* and Helen Lowenthal?"

My mother pushed herself up from the bed. "Excuse me?" With lipstick smeared across her face, she reminded me of a fading, drunken starlet.

I leaned forward in her direction. "Yeah, what I'm beginning to think is that maybe *you* had an issue with Helen." I spoke with a confidence that I could have only inherited from my mother.

"What are you implying?"

"What I'm implying is that maybe you and Helen didn't get along so well ... maybe you didn't like her as much as you always said you did. And maybe, just maybe, you weren't too sad when she died."

My mother's confident air evaporated, replaced instead by a look of fury. "Bite your tongue!" she yelled. "Bite your tongue!" She picked at the chipped polish on her fingernails, then dropped back down on my bed and crossed her legs. "What is it with you, Ben? These crazy ideas. Are you drunk again ... drunk right now? Is that it? Tell me, what's going on in that sick alcoholic brain of yours?"

With Lillian's eyes locked on me, I dipped my finger into the bottom of the martini glass to pick up the few remaining drops of alcohol, and licked them off. "What's going on in this sick alcoholic brain of mine is that I'm wondering if there's some truth to what she said ... what she *wrote*."

Lillian propped herself up on the bed. "Truth to what *who* said? Some truth to *what*?"

I considered my response. I thought about those things we say that we can never take back—those things that permanently alter a relationship. "Some truth to the idea that you weren't just playing with Bernice," I said.

"You read it!" Lillian leapt up and smacked me hard across the face.

I rubbed my cheek. "You're damn right I read it."

She smacked me again, so hard that for a moment my vision blurred. "Well, so much for your lofty fucking morals and Helen's right to privacy," she said.

"I don't think my morals are the issue here."

"Your morals never seem to be the issue, do they? I think the rabbi would agree with that. Uncle Max, too, if he were alive. The damage you've caused." Lillian, ever observing the softest, most vulnerable spots of others, had tapped into a suppressed fear of mine—that, by humiliating Max, I had contributed to his decline, to his death. "Helen didn't see a damn thing. All she saw was me and your sister playing around. Then just a few minutes later, a half hour after Helen saw us... your sister was dead. And frankly, she lived longer than a lot of the doctors thought."

I recalled Helen's diary entry: *I saw Bernice's legs kicking. She was trying to push the pillow off with her hands.* "That's possible, I guess... but Helen saw something different, didn't she? She saw you kill Bernice... it's right there in her diary."

Lillian lifted the empty glass and held it above her mouth, her head up, her neck bent back like a fledgling bird awaiting food. I watched as one small drop of alcohol slid along the glass and dropped into her open mouth. "And why would I do that?" she asked. "Kill my daughter... my sweet Bernice."

I eyed the tape recorder. "The kindest explanation is that you couldn't stand to see her suffer anymore. You did it out of compassion, love... a mother saving her child from pain and a terrible death. *Euthanasia.*"

Lillian flattened her skirt with her palms. "It's not easy, you know... having a sick child... brutal in ways you can't imagine. I hope you never have to go through something like that. Bernice? Do you have any idea how many times I curled up next to her, stroked her hair until she cried herself to sleep? How many doctor's appointments I took her to? How many ER visits? How I made her up, lipstick and rouge and rollers in her hair, when she felt so ugly and wanted to be like the other girls, pretty and popular. Can you imagine how agonizing it is to see your child in such pain, with no hope for a better life? There are no words, Ben. None." My mother's lower lip trembled, and at that moment I felt deep sympathy for her. "It's a mother's right, you know, to spare a child from that kind of agony... a responsibility, an obligation... some would even say a sin if you don't."

I thought about the pain that my sister lived with—her spindly legs, her weak immune system, the deep psychic and physical pain that tormented her without relief. I understood why a parent might want to spare her child this kind of incomprehensible misery.

I thought about the change in our family's financial fortunes after Bernice died, how we were soon able to buy our house at the lake. As if requiring one more dose of fuel to sustain my battle with Lillian, I leaned over and, from the bed, grabbed her pack of Pall Malls. I tapped the pack against the heel of my palm until a cigarette slid out. I reached for the lighter and, with a flick of my thumb, lit up. As I watched my shocked mother, I took a drag and allowed myself to enjoy the chemical change—not unlike the one produced by alcohol—that washed through my body.

I looked out the window and saw my mother's yellow Fiat in the driveway. "Or another explanation... not as kind... is that Bernice was costing you a fortune. We couldn't get a house here, like everyone else. Couldn't get a new kitchen. You had to sell schmattas to make ends meet." I pointed toward the Fiat. "No money for a sports car. All the things you wanted, all the things that are so important to you, we couldn't afford. Bernice dies... and, *poof*, look at us now."

"How dare you!" Lillian screamed. She stood and took

an unsteady step toward me, but her right ankle buck-
led and her high heel snapped. She leaned close to me
and pulled the cigarette from my mouth. She placed the
cigarette to her lips and, as with the wine bottle shared
with Becca Gold, I could think only of some disturbing
intimacy between me and my mother. Wincing in pain,
she stumbled back to the bed and dropped with such force
that she bounced twice before settling onto the mattress.

Lillian forced a laugh—the same false laugh that she
often released after one of Uncle Max's stale jokes. She
wiped her mouth with the back of her hand, red lipstick
smeared now even more chaotically across her tense face.
She removed her shoes and tossed them to the floor. "You
and your stupid theories."

"Facts aren't theories," I said. I feared that the tape
was near the end, that it would stop at any moment, alert-
ing Lillian with a loud click.

"Facts aren't theories," she repeated. "A real Einstein
here. A real fucking Einstein." Her voice shook with such
rage and piousness that the filter governing a rational
person was for her inoperable. "You actually think I killed
Bernice because I wanted more money? Because I wanted
this house?"

"I think you wanted to end her pain, but I also think
this house means a lot to you ... and how you feel about
yourself."

"How I feel about myself, *really?*"

My father's arrival, heralded by the growl of his car's
rusted muffler, caused me to jump up. "Dad's here," I said
with great relief. We listened to the opening and closing
of his car door and the tap of his shoes on the slate path,
but then instead of the door chimes that would normally

announce his entry, we again heard his shoes on the path, the slamming of the car door, and the throaty exhaust.

"Your dippy father must have forgotten something," she said. "Maybe left his head at the hospital." Lillian sat up and reached behind her back, under her shirt. I watched as she unbuckled her bra. She exhaled deeply. "Aaahh, now that's better," she said, falling back onto the bed.

My mother and I sat in silence for a minute or so until she pointed to my trophy shelf. "That debate trophy. State finals, right?" She sat up, lifted the trophy from the bookshelf, and examined it.

"That's right, our team trophy."

"*Team* trophy," she said, "not individual. Well, I think we both know there's no way you'd win without Missy."

I thought about Missy's brilliant closing argument. Lillian was right: I wasn't good enough to win an individual award, and our team wasn't good enough to win without Missy.

My mother returned the trophy to the bookshelf. "So, you think I need this place to feel good about myself?"

"What I think is that you got a lot of your needs met when Bernice died."

"A lot of *my* needs?"

"Yes, your needs."

"And what about you ... you and your father? You know, I couldn't go to college because Papa lost everything. Lost it all because of that crooked piece of shit partner of his. But you? You get to go off to NYU ... everything paid for, full freight. That's something I never got, a fancy college degree. And not because I wasn't smart enough. I'm *plenty* smart. Smarter than your father, that's for sure. And to see you without even a *thank you?* Spoiled rotten!"

I had thanked both my parents many times for paying my tuition, my room and board; I fully appreciated my good fortune. "So you did it for all of us?" I asked, choosing not to respond to her attack.

Lillian reached for the empty glass, looked into it, and slammed it back on the desk. I thought about my own complicated relationship with alcohol and how I must have inherited it from my mother. "Had enough to drink?" I said, further provoking her. "Maybe you belong in the church basement too."

My mother threw the glass over my head: it cracked against the wall and exploded. "Watch yourself! I'm still your mother."

I looked up to the divot in the wall, down to the broken glass, and then over to my luggage, which was packed for my move to NYU the next day. "Not much longer you're not," I countered with the knowledge that this threat would evoke in her the most exquisite pain of abandonment.

"Perhaps you're right," she said. "Perhaps my mothering days are over." Lillian picked at the cuticle on her right thumb and tore at a tiny piece of flesh. She sucked her thumb for a few seconds and then calmly looked up at me. "So, you think I'm responsible? You think I killed my daughter, the child I gave birth to . . . and you think I did it for *this*?" She squeezed her thumb so that a tiny ball of blood rose and, like an engorged tick, rested on her skin. As she licked the blood with her tongue, I sensed in her a hint of resignation, the suggestion of some fundamental flaw in her psyche that she knew she could not escape.

"You think I did all that for *this*?"

I looked over at the machine, at the tape that was speeding to its conclusion. "On second thought, I don't think you did it. I don't think you have the guts," I said, hoping to provoke her.

"You don't think I have the guts?"

"The guts *or* the brains."

Lillian placed her head in her hands and tugged at her hair. When she looked up, I noticed a throbbing vein on her right temple. "Weak and stupid?"

I nodded. "Weak and stupid."

"So that's what you think of me?" she slurred. The distinctive growl of my father's car announced his arrival. Lillian gazed out the window, sighed, and returned to me. "You think a weak person could put a pillow over her child's face, strangle the last breaths from her in order to spare her the agony of an awful life? A miserable death? You think a weak person could stand up on that bimah two days later and eulogize the child she just killed? You think a weak person would stop Helen from destroying our lives? Everything we worked so hard for? You think a weak person would have the guts to push that bitch into the water ... into the rocks? Then hold her head down under the water while she was struggling to get back up on the dock? No, Ben, no! Only a strong person could do all that for the people she loves. Only *I* could do it."

I stared at my mother in disbelief, in horror: she had killed them both. I heard the tap-tap of my father's shoes on the slate outside my window. Lillian rose from the bed and moved toward my door. She glared at me with malevolence and with a certain misty vacancy, then placed her right index finger to her lips. "Our little secret," she said.

With a flick of her hand Lillian sashayed barefoot out of the room, and I heard her greet my father in the foyer. "Darling!" she said with the excitement of a giddy schoolgirl, her mood—or at least the presentation of her mood—transformed in a matter of seconds. "How's the world's best doctor? Busy at the hospital? Come, darling, come. I'll make you a cocktail. Moscow mule in a copper cup ... a cold one."

I lifted the baseball cap from the desk and placed it on my head—and as I reached for the tape player, the record button snapped upward and the cassette, marking its end, clicked to a violent stop.

Chapter 30

~~~~~~~~~

That evening I was so tormented by the weight of Lillian's horrifying confession that I experienced a numbness, an existential confusion that left me incapable of clear, rational thought. I vacillated erratically. One moment, I was resolute about telling my father; but mere minutes later, out of fear that the news would destroy him, I rejected that idea in favor of silence. And then, after two shots of vodka, I considered bicycling over to the Rockaway police and delivering the cassette to the officer who'd investigated Helen's death. I imagined that moment, when I would walk into the station and, with tape in hand, tell them that Lillian was a murderer—that she had killed two of the most beloved residents of Red Meadow Lake. That thought, though, was quickly replaced by fear—and the idea of being a moser, the cause of her downfall, and the ruin of our family became too much for me to bear.

The last thing I wanted to do that evening was share a meal with my mother, but Abe was insistent. "Come on, son, it's our last night together . . . just one more meal. It'll make your mother so happy." To placate him, to offer him the continued delusion that our lives were normal, I conceded—and, with an uncomfortable energy, the three of us ate dinner on the picnic table. The lake was quiet, except for two men who floated by on a motorless raft and dropped testing equipment into the toxic water. The fading sun illuminated the reflecting scales of a small-mouth bass, a lifeless fish that bobbed with the cadence of the water, its milky eyes and blood-red lips a gruesome reminder of the damage done. On the bank of the lake, a box turtle lay dead, its leathery carcass hanging from the shell.

"Monsters," my incensed father snapped in reference to the operators of Hope Quarry.

"I agree with you on this one," Lillian replied—a rare show of support for his generalized contempt for mercenary businesses. "Greedy bastards."

That night, on the eve of my departure for college, Abe regaled us with stories of his own undergraduate days—including the fraternity initiation in which he, blindfolded, swallowed what he was told was a cow's eye, only to find out later that it was nothing more than a ball of gelatin.

"Gelatin's more disgusting than a cow's eye," I said. "It's made of hoof . . . spine, too, I think."

"Maybe, but either way it showed I was committed to the group."

My mother didn't say much that evening. She fawned over my father, laughing at his jokes and making sure that his copper mug was filled and chilled. And she eyed me with a cool distance, the result of what had transpired between us just hours earlier. As I tried to avoid her gaze, I was overcome by the purest, most suffocating terror, for the thought that a monster had created me, nursed me, nurtured and loved me, now threatened to destroy me.

Eager to be away from Lillian, I finished my meal and excused myself with nothing more than a gruff mumble.

"What's gotten into him?" I heard my father say as I trudged up the lawn with my plate.

"No idea," Lillian replied.

I went to my room and locked the door behind me. My packed bag—the most jolting reminder of my emancipation—eyed me with bulging assurance. I sat down and put my feet up on the desk. As I looked around the room, my thoughts turned from Lillian and her sickening crimes and toward the things I would soon leave behind. There were the markers of my success, the trophies lined up on the shelf: baseball, basketball, debate (*team*, not individual), the Red Meadow fishing derby, even a grade school attendance award. On the wall, I'd hung a poster of Raquel Welch in her tattered, prehistoric bikini from *One Million Years B.C.* With some shame, I recalled Missy's reaction when she first saw the sexist poster. "You're a pig," she'd said, disgusted yet mildly amused.

And then there was the wooden desk on which I had over the years written so many papers, essays, homework assignments—all of which had brought me to this moment. I rubbed a rough patch of wood on the desk, a reminder of an impulsive adolescent urge when I carved *M + B* into the wood and then scraped it away out of fear that Missy—or my mother—would see it. I looked over to the tape recorder and hit the eject button. The cartridge shot up, and I pulled the cassette from the machine. I eyed the garbage can and tapped the cassette against my palm: I thought about destroying the recording.

Without my mother's confession, and without Helen's diary, there would be no proof of Lillian's guilt. I could continue my life as if that awful conversation had never occurred; I could pretend it was just my mother's dark humor, a dream, or a moment of alcohol-fueled delirium on her part; and my parents—and my grandparents, too—could go about their lives, pushing our sins further and further into the past with each cocktail party, with each summer musical, each shiva and seder. I could pretend it never happened. All I had to do was destroy the tape, and we could move on in some deeply flawed and agonizing way.

But I was not yet ready to make that decision—and I instead slipped the cassette into my suitcase.

Chapter 31

That night, I was tortured by a flurry of vivid and disturbing dreams, including one with a school of sickly fish caught in some fiery and haunting purgatory, one in which the regal egret that stood guard atop Split Rock was strutting about with Max's sequined turban on its head, and an erotic dream featuring Becca Gold that started out with a pleasing embrace, but ended with her impregnated and our futures ruined. My sleep was fitful as a result, and I awoke early the next morning to the sound of my father knocking on my bedroom door.

"Wake up, Ben, it's your big day!"

I rose from the bed and opened the door. Abe gave me a bear hug that made me gasp for air. His love for me was—unlike my mother's—so pure, so accepting, and so consistent, and his character so admirable, that I ached at the adversity he had faced in his life: my sister's death, a career that had fallen short of his potential, my mother's mistreatment of him. I feared that my absence would be difficult for him, for not only did he love me and enjoy my companionship, but he relied on me to act as a buffer when Lillian devolved into one of her ugly moods. He relied on me for a compassionate smile; he relied on me to put the sheets and pillows on the living room couch. And as he squeezed me with an intensity that conveyed every bit of his love for me—and, I believe, the pain of my departure—I wondered if his life would be better or worse without Lillian around.

He released me from his grip and pulled a twenty-dollar bill from his pocket. "Some spending money," he said, handing me the cash. "Don't tell your mother."

I looked over at the suitcase, at the pocket that held the cassette, and as I did so I heard Lillian preparing breakfast in the kitchen.

"How's Mom this morning?" I asked.

"She's fine, I guess. Upset that you're leaving...happy and sad. Happy for you, I mean. I think she'll be fine after a few days. And it helps that you're not too far away."

"Abe!" my mother screamed from the kitchen, a nasty bark that caused us to flinch. "What did I say about the milk from Shop-Rite? It's been terrible lately, bitter and thick. How many times do I have to tell you to get it from O'Dowd's? You can't go wrong with O'Dowd's." I heard the sound of a knife slamming into the chopping board. "Schmuck!"

With that one word, Lillian had announced that her idealization of her husband had ended—a rapid cycle that had run its course in under one day. For the foreseeable future, there would be no Moscow mules and no lavish praise of his medical skills, no rapt looks as he retold childhood stories. My father and I looked at each other, and we both understood that he would pay a steep price for my departure.

"Schmuck," he murmured to me, to himself. He shrugged in a self-conscious manner, one that suggested an acceptance that he would never be appreciated for his talents, for his kindness, for an unwavering loyalty that subordinated his own needs to the needs of those he loved, regardless of how they treated him. He reached for my heavy suitcase. "I'll get this in the car."

Seeing him so diminished infuriated me. I was angry not only at Lillian but at my father too. I was furious that he didn't defend himself and his principles. Can there be a point in a person's life, I asked myself, when kindness can bleed into weakness? When a person can be lauded for goodness one moment and then vilified for passivity the next? And can such a transformation occur without the awareness, without the consent, of the very person who is being diminished?

Sweaty and pale, Abe soon returned from the car. Like a pitcher warming up before the start of the first inning, he swung his right arm in broad circles, wincing with each rotation. "Heavy bag," he said. "How about we all have some breakfast and then hit the road?"

The thought of sharing another meal with my mother sickened me. "Sure," I said.

When we entered the kitchen, the table was already set. Lillian had prepared one of my favorite breakfasts: a one-eyed jack. Without looking up at her, I sat down at the table and drove my fork violently into the center of the yolk. I watched as the yellow liquid flowed like blood over the surrounding toast, and then I took a bite.

Lillian smiled—a discordant gesture in light of what

she had admitted to me. "I've been making those for you since you're two years old. And now look at you ... going off to college." She tossed a dishrag into the sink. She wiped her eyes, and a low moan emanated from her—from a place deep within. As if she were fatigued, she placed her palms on the countertop, leaned over at the waist, and dropped her head. She began to cry—first restrained whimpers and then painful wails, and finally a primal howl that caused my father to leap up from his chair and place his arm around her shoulders. "I can't do it," she said between heavy breaths. "I can't take my baby off to college. You take him, Abe, and I'll say goodbye here."

My father nodded at me, an indication that I should stand and hug my mother. The thought so disgusted me that I considered saying no. I had often seen her feign whichever emotion most suited her needs at the moment, and this display, even more so in light of the unforgivable harm she had done, did not move me in the least. My father nodded again. "Please," he mouthed with an innocence that I would never again possess—and I felt that I could not disappoint him.

I stood and approached my mother, who wiped the tears from her eyes with the dirty dishrag. She opened her arms and drew me into her—into her deathly embrace. The smell of cigarette smoke, perfume, and hair spray combined to form a sickening bouquet that caused me to gag. As I watched my father over her shoulder, I held my breath and tried to endure her vile touch—and each passing second, each breathless, agonizing second, brought me closer to calling her out for what she was: a murderer. But just as I was about to tear myself from her clutch and reach for the phone, just as I was prepared to call the police and tell them—and my father—what Lillian had done, she released me. I sensed that she somehow knew that she'd pushed the limits of my loyalty, that she could tell from the twitch of my muscles, from the cadence of my breath, that her life would be over if she held on to me for one more second.

Lillian stepped back. "I'm so proud of you, honey. Now you go knock 'em dead." Her choice of words made me shiver, and as Abe looked on with pride, she gave me a peck on the forehead and dashed off to her bedroom.

My father and I spoke little during the ride into the city. He focused on the road, while I worked the radio and replayed in my mind the conversation between my mother and me. As we turned a bend on Route 46 and the city's jagged skyline appeared before us, I began to day-dream about my new life. I thought about the romance of the dark Irish bars, the crooked streets of the Village, the pretty girls I would soon meet. I recalled my failed kiss on the steps of the poet's home, and I thought about Missy's new life at Cambridge.

"Holland or Lincoln?" Abe asked as we neared the city.

Missy always preferred the Lincoln Tunnel, even if we were going downtown. "Lincoln," I said.

After emerging from the tunnel, we cut through Times Square, with its dilapidated arcades and beckon-ing pornography and the most colorful collection of bums and junkies, gangsters and cops, pimps and prostitutes—a motley group, an ecosystem of sorts, that appeared to be enjoying their familiarity with each other. When we passed a woman in a tiny miniskirt and platform heels, I recalled my grandparents' party, when the butcher dressed up in a shiny blue suit with patent leather loafers and his wife wore a sheer blouse, a silver skirt, and knee-high boots. I felt ashamed of my family and my community, for how would we have felt if someone from outside our community had thrown a party in which the theme was middle-class Jews? We made our way down Seventh Avenue and then, encountering little traffic, over to the dormitory on the southern edge of Washington Square Park. There, Abe double-parked and opened the trunk. When I reached inside for the suitcase, he smacked my hands away.

"I'll do the honors," he said. "A father only gets to take his son to freshman year one time, you know." With extreme exertion, Abe lifted the suitcase out of the trunk and dropped it to the curb. He again rotated his right arm, stretching out his shoulder. "Want me to go with you up to the room?"

I looked up at the dormitory, at a little sliver of blue sky between the tall buildings. "I've got it from here, Dad."

My father shielded his moist eyes from the sun—from me. "Okay, Ben, you be good. Call as soon as you can. And we'll come visit as much as you want ... me and your mom. It's only an hour ... hour and a half ... that's all." He approached and wrapped his arms around me, hugging me not with the abandon of that morning but with tenderness, longing, sadness—and with a premonition, perhaps, of things to come. "I better get back and deal with your mother," he said. "Who knows what kind of shape she's in."

My father's reference to Lillian and her mood evoked in me a terrifying image: I pictured my kind, trusting father sleeping next to Lillian, next to a murderer. As I watched Abe close the trunk, I wondered if she was capable of hurting others, or if her violence toward Bernice and Helen was an aberration, a reaction to specific situations that would never be repeated. I wasn't sure, and I feared for my father's safety.

Abe walked over to the door and prepared to step into the car. Before he sat down, he turned and waved to me. "Love you, son."

I wondered what would become of him. "I love you too."

He sat behind the wheel and turned the ignition, which prompted the roar of his rusted muffler. I looked over to my suitcase, to the pocket in which I'd hidden the cassette, then looked back to see the car begin to roll down the street. On the sidewalk, a street vendor hawked soft pretzels from his cart; a toothless man joyfully tapped the bridge of his stringless guitar; an overwhelmed father tried to soothe his crying toddler. I lifted my suitcase and made my way to the dormitory. As I passed the distraught child, I made a silly face—one that, to my surprise, stopped the boy's tears and caused him to smile. The father nodded at me in appreciation: it was a simple gesture, evocative in ways that I did not understand, that had the unexpected effect of inspiring me to take the action that I had been resisting.

I dropped the valise to the sidewalk and turned back toward the street. "Wait, Dad, wait!" I ran after the accelerating car, but with each stride I lost more ground. I was on the verge of giving up when a jaywalker darted across the street and caused Abe to hit the brakes. Now within feet of the stopped car, I lunged forward and slapped the trunk. Surprised, my father poked his head from the window. "You forget something?"

"I did ... hold on." I ran to my suitcase, removed the tape, and jogged back to the car. As I looked down to my father, I thought of the many times my family debated the laws of the mesira, and whether one should ever be a moser, an informer. I thought of Papa's desire to report his thieving partner to the police and then Nana's contrary position that the protection of our community was paramount. From the driver's seat, my father looked up to me. I noticed that his eyes were wet, that he had been crying—and I passed the cassette through the open window.

"What's this?" he asked. He took the tape and, as if he had never seen one before, examined both sides.

"You need to listen to this, but make sure Mom's not there when you do ... or anyone else. Maybe listen in the garage when no one's around, maybe in your office ... but it has to be alone."

What my father thought at that moment, I did not know, but he appeared apprehensive, as if he feared the tape's contents.

"Sure thing," he said. "Anything else?"

"Nope, that's it. Do with it what you want ... up to you."

"All right then." He did a pit-a-pat drumbeat on the steering wheel, then put the car in drive—back to Red Meadow Lake and back to my mother.

Chapter 32

~~~~~~~~

One week after my father dropped me off at NYU, he called me on the dormitory pay phone. "Muriel's passed," he said in a rush, as if I were the first in a long list of people he had to call. "Heart attack... it was quick, God bless. The funeral's tomorrow. Can you come back for the service? And the first night of shiva?"

I had no desire to go back to the lake, to sit through another of the rabbi's sermons, *to see my mother*. But I had adored Muriel, a devoted woman who was an important and much-loved member of our family, and I knew that my failure to honor her life, her death, would be shameful. On the bus ride out to the lake later that day, I thought of my aunt and her love for Max, how she encouraged him to perform the roll dance despite his shame, how she watched his on-stage meltdown at my grandparents' golden anniversary with the disorientation and the pain of one who no longer recognizes her partner—and how she found him dangling from a microphone cord wearing his sequined turban.

As the bus moved through the musky swamps of Secaucus and then west through Clifton, Wayne, Parsippany, and beyond, I felt as though I were returning to the lake after a long journey abroad. For after only a week in the city, the tendon that had long tethered me to my community was already stretched so thin that I felt it might snap at any moment. Gone were Missy and the Denville Shack, gone were Split Rock, the clubhouse and First Beach—replaced now by the Cedar Tavern, Chumley's and McSorley's, Gerde's Folk City and the Bitter End. My assimilation with the city was so rapid—owing to both the city's irresistible forces and my own urge to belong—that my suburban life had become, if not a distant memory, one that was far enough away that I could resist its beckoning call.

When the bus pulled into Denville, feet from my mother's shop, Abe was waiting for me on the sidewalk. I looked out the window and saw him shifting side to side, his hand over his eyes to block the sun. His expression and his attire were both somber, a reflection of his sadness over Muriel's death. I tapped the glass to catch his attention, and he beamed when he saw me.

"There's my boy!" he called out as I stepped off the bus. He gave me a strong hug that had the effect of drawing me closer not just to him but to the lake as well. And for the first time, I found myself resisting his embrace, for to go backward, to return to the life of my upbringing—to return to my mother—was too painful for me to bear.

As we made the short drive to our house, I opened the car window and breathed in the last remnants of the Jersey summer air: thick and moist, with a distinctive density that to this day I believe is particular to northern New Jersey and that moves me with its profound weight.

"You ever listen to that tape?" I asked.

He turned and looked at me, and I could tell that he feared he'd disappointed me. "Not yet, but I will tonight. After dinner ... I promise."

We made the left on Upper Mountain, just yards from Tom & Mary's—the store where Missy and I had purchased our Wacky Packs and candy and Yoo-hoos, where Mrs. Lipsky gave me the rare nickel. I felt the pull of the lake, but was determined to resist it.

"How's Mom?"

My father paused to consider his response. "Not good since you left. She keeps talking about how things aren't the same at the lake anymore. Too many people gone. Even the butcher and his wife put their house on the market ... selling their shops and moving down to Coral Gables. They're finished with Jersey. Your mother ... your mother's gotten very nostalgic ... always talking about how much she misses Helen and the way things used to be."

"She misses *Helen*?" I asked.

Abe tapped the brakes and turned to me. "Why wouldn't she? We all do." As if to convey his commitment to Lillian, he punched the gas and powered up a small hill that always caused a fluttering in my stomach—a hill that we used to call a "tickle belly bump." When we pulled up to the house, my mother was standing on the front steps. She wore a floral sundress with a big straw hat. In one hand was a Pall Mall and in the other a cocktail. Her appearance, so colorful and festive, was inconsistent with the sadness of the occasion, violative even.

"Benjamin," she said. With her hands occupied by the

cocktail and cigarette, she offered me not a hug but a tentative kiss on the cheek—and the sensation of her lips on my skin caused me to shudder.

I struggled to reply to her, but all I could say was, "Mom." Uncomfortable in her presence, I went to my bedroom and closed the door. As I assessed the room, I became aware of a dated quality that I had not previously noticed. The carpeting seemed matted and nappy; a corner of the wallpaper curled like a dead winter leaf; cobwebs stretched between two upraised arms on a trophy; the Raquel Welch poster, with one corner torn, had faded from the glare of the sun. My room had been transported to a different era. Or, I asked myself, was it I who had been transported?

There was a knock on the door, and my father entered without awaiting my response. "Your mother's going over to the rabbi's to help with the arrangements for tomorrow. The funeral home, cemetery, food for shiva. And I'm heading to the hospital for a couple of hours ... check on a few patients ... some paperwork too." From his pocket, he pulled out the cassette. "And I'll listen to this while I'm there."

My father's intention to play the tape caused me alarm, as I feared what he might do—or not do—after hearing Lillian's confession. I considered snatching the cassette from his hand and making some excuse for my change of heart, but what instead governed was my desire to clear my own conscience by delegating a monumental decision to him.

Left alone, I walked down to the boathouse and pulled out a rod. I lifted up the floorboard and found a bottle of blackberry brandy from my old stash. After taking a few swigs, I sat on the dock and prepared to cast a line into the water, but I then smelled the chemicals in the water and remembered that the toxic, combustible lake was off-limits, that the fish had been killed. Instead, I got drunk on brandy and awaited my father's return.

I drank so much in such a short period of time that I passed out on the dock, and was awakened only by the nudge of my father's shoe against my ribs. When I looked up, he held in his shaking hand the cassette tape.

"What is this?" he said, his skin now an ashen gray. "The tape. What *is* this?" As I struggled to rise to my feet, my father grabbed me by the elbow and pulled me up. "What *is* this!" he yelled.

"It's me and Mom ... from the other day. She didn't know I was recording it."

"And she's saying what I think she's saying?"

I observed his pained face. "I'm afraid so."

He put the tape in his pocket and sat down on the dock, legs crossed. He shook his head. "Impossible," he said. "It's just not possible. Bernice and Helen? *Both* of them?"

My father looked out over the lake, and his subordinated position and his broken spirit elicited in me feelings of the deepest compassion for him. As I stared down at him, he seemed vulnerable, childlike.

"What are you going to do?" I asked. "With the tape?"

It was my father who now struggled to stand. "I don't know." He tried to push himself up off the dock. "Does anyone else know about this?"

I reached down, held his elbow, and lifted him up with care. "Just us," I assured him.

"Boys!" my mother called out from the lawn. We looked up to see her waving her straw hat. "It's all set, all the funeral arrangements. I got a lovely spread from Eppes Essen. I just love their novie," she said, referring to the Nova Scotia lox she preferred.

Abe pinched my arm. "Go to your room ... and stay there until I say so."

My father had taken an authoritative tone with me so infrequently that I obeyed without objection. I trudged up the lawn, brushed past Lillian, and then trotted to my room. From my window, I looked out to the grass and watched as Abe approached her. He at first appeared to be speaking calmly, but then he began to gesticulate and raise his voice in a confrontational manner. My mother shook her head in denial, pleading with him. It was at this point, when Lillian stomped her feet in fury, that my father pulled the cassette from his pocket and waved it above his head. He said something to her that caused her to turn back to the house, to the window in which I stood. I could see on her face a look of both the greatest contempt and mystification at my betrayal. After scowling at me from a distance, she turned back to my father, begging I assumed for him to hand over the tape. He refused, and she lunged in vain for the cassette.

Abe then said one more thing to my mother—a few words that caused her to break into tears, to pound her chest with her right fist. After watching her with pity, after resting his hand on her shoulder for a feather of a second, he marched up the lawn and—tape in hand—into the house. I ran over to my door and pressed my ear against the wood, hoping to hear what he was doing. The sounds were muffled, but I could hear that my father was making a phone call.

My father, the moser, was calling the Rockaway police.

Chapter 33

~~~~~~~~

Lillian was standing at the end of the dock when the police arrived, and I watched from my window as my father gathered with two officers on the lawn. He handed the cassette over and explained the chain of events, pointing to our house, to the Lowenthal place across the lake, to my grandparents' home as well. At one point, Abe pointed to my window and the two officers turned to look at me. Frightened, I ducked behind the drapes.

The wind was blowing in from the west, carrying with it noxious fumes from the lake—an acrid cocktail of chemical solvents and explosive fuel oils. In the distance, I could see the white-suited workers on their raft, their testing equipment dipping into the water. Only a few days had passed since the spill, and we were forbidden from operating motorboats on the lake, from doing anything that might trigger a blaze and further damage our beloved body of water. Despite assurances from the authorities that the lake would one day be restored to its pristine state, that they would restock the water with bluegills and catfish and largemouth bass, that the mussels would replenish and that the egrets would return to their lofty perches, we—like the family of the patient on life support—feared the worst.

A police radio squawked, its sharp clap echoing off the water. Leaving my father behind, the officers began their slow walk down the grassy slope, toward the dock. Lillian, alerted by the radio's call, watched as the officers approached her. She looked at my father and smiled, as if she had finally come to respect him. She then turned to me, my face now pressed against the window screen. She made a motion with her hands, one that called me to her—a mother beckoning her child. I thought of my life with her—not her terrible moments, but the moments when her goodness prevailed over her illness, her evil. I thought of the times she taught me to sail a boat, to worm a hook, to open a door for a lady. I recalled the look of terror on her face when she learned that my sister had gotten pneumonia, how she stayed with Bernice every night at the hospital, reading my sister books until they both fell asleep. Overwhelmed with feelings of love for my mother, I ran out of my room, past my father, past the officers, and into her arms.

She squeezed me with the love of a mother who would sacrifice everything for her child. She pressed her face into my neck, her tears wet against my skin. Instead of being repulsed by her intimacy, repulsed by *her*, I experienced a closeness so deep that I could not remember any of her darkest moments, but only the purest, most beautiful memories.

My mother gripped tight—a final spasm—and then released me, and when she did so I was pulled back into the grim reality of the moment. We turned to see the officers approaching, and as they stepped onto the dock, she gave me a tender kiss on the forehead.

Lillian walked with a humble gait down the length of the dock and, in an act of surrender, dropped her Pall Malls and lighter to the grass. I watched as the officers— each with a hand on her elbow—guided her back up the lawn and toward the waiting car, my father trailing closely behind. I heard the crackle of the radio and then the slamming of car doors. And as the cruiser drove away, up Lake Shore Drive, I caught only the quickest glimpse of my parents in the back seat and the flashing lights above.

Alone, shaken to the point of numbness, I retrieved my bottle of blackberry brandy and Lillian's discarded cigarettes. I sat on the dock, careful not to let my feet touch the poisoned water. I looked down to our wooden dinghy, which was tied to the dock. On the bench of the cedar boat were a few paper bags—even a half-eaten fried shrimp—from the Shack, along with a couple of oily rags; and at the bottom of the boat was a small puddle of the lake's combustible water.

I looked around the lake. What had once lived in the water was now gone—but above, life continued. A constellation of fireflies—tiny flickering furnaces—still danced and glowed in the late summer dusk; a white egret, all legs and neck, glided over the lake, then elevated in search of fresher water elsewhere; a long-eared bat carved wicked arcs through the sky before devouring a plump imperial moth. And I recalled the moment I saw Helen Lowenthal's bloated body slide up through a carpet of emerald water lilies and bob on the water's surface like a ghostly musk turtle.

I raised the bottle to my mouth and downed the remaining brandy. When I finished, a strand of sticky sweetness ran down my chin. The booze, coupled with what I'd earlier ingested, brought me past that pleasurable drunk I so enjoyed and instead to a dumb stupor, one that caused the dock to wobble and the sky to spin wildly around me. I reached for the pack of cigarettes. After breaking two Pall Malls, I extracted one intact and rested it on my lower lip; it took me three or four flicks of the lighter to get a flame, to light the cigarette. I lay down on the dock, the cigarette in my left hand. I looked up to the sky and wondered what would happen to my mother, my family, our community. I dropped my right hand into the flammable water, flicking the water with my fingertips. I waved my wet fingers under my nose, inhaling the lake's toxicity. I took a drag of the cigarette and held it in for as long as I could. I felt light-headed, stoned, blissfully disconnected from the world around me. When I exhaled, the lit cigarette fell from my hand, into the wooden dinghy, into the pile of oily rags. Dazed, I looked down to the boat. The rags began to hiss and smoke. A tiny flame spurted upward—and before I could move, I blacked out.

Chapter 34

~~~~~~~~~

Disabled by unconsciousness, by brandy, fatigue, and devastation, I saw on the blackest canvas of my mind an image of transcendent beauty. I imagined Helen, again floating up from the water—but this time not through a bed of lilies, not in her pink tennis outfit, her face blemished, tainted by the lake's slime. Instead I saw her rise up through the water's crisp surface, head first, launching upward, as if propelled by some subaquatic force. She was draped in a flowing white gown, her arms set back, raised like the Winged Victory. Free, unfettered, defiant, she rose up through a forest of flames, glorious bursts of light that infused her with the glow of some merciful god.

Beside her, standing strong and proud, was my sister. Bernice lifted her left hand above her head and, with her right, grasped the cloth of Helen's gown. I watched them elevate above the twitching tips of the flames and hover for a moment, kicking gently like leisurely swimmers. They appeared to smile at me—and beneath a pulsating halo, they waved. They touched their hands to their hearts and ascended farther, in the direction of Split Rock, in the direction of the egret's old post. As they crossed the ridgeline, Helen and Bernice reached their apex, where they burst into a flurry of opalescent shards, then co-alesced into a tight ball of white light that—like my sister's perfectly hit tennis ball—arced through the sky and disappeared into the dark vacuum of my soul.

In this vision, in this drunken dream, Helen and my sister had transmitted to me a powerful energy, and I found myself overcome with a feeling of exultation, of redemption. Soon, though, I was expelled from this trance—not by the sounds of the neighbors screaming from the shore and not by the howling sirens, but by an intense heat. As I came out of my blackout, I looked around to see that the lake, our beloved Red Meadow Lake, was—as in my dream—*on fire*. A devilish blaze, one that seemed to pour up from the muck of the mussel beds, rolled across the surface of the toxic water and spread outward, deliberate and methodical.

I watched as the inferno migrated north, toward the clubhouse, consuming a rowboat as it went, turning the craft into something resembling an eerie funeral pyre. I looked over to the shore and saw that our neighbors—the rabbi and his wife—were wailing with such grief that they fell to the ground and pounded the earth. I watched as their nervous terrier scampered back and forth across the shoreline, barking at the fire, trying to repel the blazing threat. And I watched as the constellation of fireflies fled the superheated air above the scorching waters.

I looked down to the charred remains of the dinghy, the small craft that I'd torched with my lit cigarette. I kicked the empty bottle of blackberry brandy—the last drop of alcohol I would ever drink—and wept, for I understood what I had done. In a haze of alcohol and horror, I stumbled across the smoldering planks, to the safety of land, and collapsed on the grass. As I watched the lake, as I felt its throbbing heat, I understood that in my drunkenness, in my sorrow, I had triggered a conflagration, the inadvertent annihilation of what we loved so dearly. And by doing so, by cremating the very symbol of our prosperity, I had ensured that our happiest memories would remain in the past, that the lake could offer us nothing in the future—and that the bittersweet ghosts of Red Meadow Lake would continue to delight us, to haunt us, for as long as we chose to remember.